THE WEIRD WORLD OF WES BEATTIE

ᒪᒪᒪᒪᒪᒪᒪᒪᒪᒪᒪᒪᒪᒪᒪᒪᒪᒪ

THE WEIRD WORLD
OF WES BEATTIE

John Norman Harris

FELONY & MAYHEM PRESS • NEW YORK

ᕫᕫᕫᕫᕫᕫᕫᕫᕫᕫᕫᕫᕫᕫᕫᕫᕫᕫ

All the characters and events portrayed in this work are fictitious.

THE WEIRD WORLD OF WES BEATTIE

A Felony & Mayhem mystery

PRINTING HISTORY
First Canadian edition (Macmillan of Canada): 1963
First US edition (Harper & Row): 1963
First Felony & Mayhem edition: 2006
Second Felony & Mayhem edition: 2018

ISBN: 978-1-63194-135-1

Manufactured in the United States of America

Library of Congress Cataloging-in-Publication Data

Names: Harris, John Norman, 1915-1964, author.
Title: The weird world of Wes Beattie / John Norman Harris.
Description: New York : Felony & Mayhem Press, 2018. | "First Canadian
  edition (Macmillan of Canada): 1963; First US edition (Harper & Row):
  1963; First Felony & Mayhem edition: 2006; Second Felony & Mayhem:
  edition 2018" -- Verso title page. | A reissue of an edition published first in
  1963 and reissued in 2006.
Identifiers: LCCN 2017060955| ISBN 9781631941351 (trade pbk.) | ISBN
  9781631941368 (ebook)
Subjects: LCSH: Sons--Fiction. | Murder--Fiction. | Belief and
  doubt--Fiction. | Trials (Murder)--Fiction. | Truth--Fiction. | Toronto
  (Ont.)--Fiction. | GSAFD: Mystery fiction. | Legal stories g
Classification: LCC PR9199.3.H345965 W45 2018 | DDC 813/.54--dc23
LC record available at https://lccn.loc.gov/2017060955

To E W.D. and L H.D.,
in whom Aunthood reached its finest flower

John Norman Harris is widely credited with having written the first genuinely Canadian mystery novel; in *The Weird World of Wes Beattie* (and its sister-novel, *Hair of the Dog*) he not only set his story in Toronto, but also crafted a plot that relied specifically on various Canadian preoccupations and concerns.

"First true Canadian mystery writer" would be sufficient accolade for most people, but Harris was also a gold-plated war hero: After graduating from university, and with Europe on the brink of war, he traveled to England to train as a pilot, eventually joining the RAF. In 1942 his plane was shot down over Germany, and he spent the rest of the war in a POW camp known as Stalag Luft III. While there, he was instrumental in planning the largest prison-break in the history of WWII. The story of the breakout was eventually turned into several novels and films, including "The Great Escape," starring Steve McQueen.

After the war, Harris returned to Canada, and built a thriving career in public relations and as a short-story writer. He died suddenly, in his late 40s, on a family vacation to Vermont. *The Weird World of West Beattie* was the only mystery he published during his lifetime.

The icon above says you're holding a copy of a book in the Felony & Mayhem "Traditional" category. We think of these books as classy cozies, with little gunplay or gore but often a fair amount of humor and, usually, an intrepid amateur sleuth. If you enjoy this book, you may well like other "Traditional" titles from Felony & Mayhem Press.

For more about these books, and other Felony & Mayhem titles, or to place an order, please visit our website at

www.FelonyAndMayhem.com

Other "Traditional" titles from

FELONY&MAYHEM

THE WEIRD WORLD OF WES BEATTIE

One

I T WAS A SMALL SEMINAR, attended by doctors, lawyers and social workers, for the discussion of medicolegal problems.

The discussion leader for the evening was Dr. Milton Heber, an eminent psychiatrist.

"I hope you will excuse the pulp-magazine title I have chosen for my little discourse," he said, "but I have been living in the weird world of Wes Beattie lately, and it is affecting my vocabulary. For the benefit of our distinguished visitors from the U.S.A., I will explain that Wes Beattie is a young man, age twenty-one, who is facing trial for murder in this city. The case is *sub judice*, so I must ask you to keep this information private.

I am using it simply because it is live and topical and illustrates the need for greater cooperation among our various professions.

"Now this weird world that Wes lives in is peopled by strange, sinister criminals, grown men and women who seem to have spent a lot of time conspiring against an obscure bank clerk. They are very real people to Wes, and their influence is everywhere. They are out to get him. If you play along with Wes, he will discuss this Mystery Gang quite rationally. If you express doubts or laugh at him, he gets shrill and hysterical; then he withdraws, and won't speak to anyone for days.

"A lot of people have been wondering what made Wes Beattie kill. A timid, shy, immature boy, not strong, commits a brutal murder. The Crown Attorney will present a credible motive. For our American friends, the Crown Attorney is your old friend the D.A. under a different name. Mr. Massingham, our genial Crown Attorney, will claim that Wes killed for money. He was due to inherit a substantial sum from his uncle, Edgar Beattie. Edgar was about to change his will and cut Wes out. So Wes killed him. All very simple. And all, in my opinion, completely false.

"Wes Beattie wouldn't have had the guts to kill for money. He wouldn't have killed for a free pass to Fort Knox. Then what was the motive?"

He smiled and looked at the small audience seated round the hotel salon.

"I will tell you, very briefly, why Wes Beattie killed. First of all, I will touch on the significant factors in his background. Wes's father came from what is called a fine old family, living in a stately home in Rosedale, one of the pleasantest residential districts in Toronto. His father, Rupert Beattie, married a girl his mother didn't approve of, and was kicked out of the home. There were two children—an older sister and Wes. The father went overseas and was killed in Italy. The mother neglected the children. So old Mrs. Beattie, full of contrition, took them away from the mother and raised them in Rosedale. The mother, I may say, had no objections that a little money wouldn't overcome.

"Family pride, more than love of the children, prompted the move. Young Wes was spoiled in a way, but he was, I feel, starved of real affection. The one relation he really loved and admired was his Uncle Edgar, a big, rather earthy man with what old Mrs. Beattie would call 'low tastes.' Uncle Edgar took Wes to ball games and circuses and gave him good birthday presents. I think he made Wes a little ashamed of liking flowers and music and paintings. Wes put on a lowbrow front to win Uncle Edgar's approval, but secretly he had less rugged tastes.

"Well, it all came out in the post-adolescent wash. Wes grew up a dreamer, a lazy boy, a chronic liar who would tell tall tales about having explored the Upper Amazon during his summer holidays and all that sort of thing. His school grades weren't good enough to get him into university, so they got him a job in a bank. He was careless and didn't progress very fast. He had a girl who encouraged him to spend a lot of money. He got into debt. He cadged and borrowed until his family was fed up with him. And at last he reached the fatal day when he couldn't beg or borrow a dollar from anyone at home or at the office, and that day came at a time when he desperately needed thirty bucks or so to take his girl to the Art Gallery Ball— she was on the junior committee.

"If Wes had been a teller, he probably would have borrowed the money from the till. But he wasn't, so what he did was the stupidest thing you could think of. He sneaked away early from the office one Thursday last May, and went to the car park behind a place called the Midtown Motel, over Spadina way, which is really just a hotel and restaurant with some motel units behind it as a gimmick. It is sometimes jocularly referred to as the Mothel, short for motor brothel.

"Wes went to the car park, looked through the cars, saw a woman's handbag in one and stole it. He stuffed the bag under his raincoat and was making off when the car park attendant caught him. He tried to lie out of it. He said the car was his girlfriend's car and the purse was hers too. She was in the bar, and he had come back to get her purse for her. But then the real owner of the handbag came along and claimed it. Wes tried to break away and run. But they took him to the police station, where he told more lies. He gave a false name and address. He said that the girl he had been with was a nice girl, who had obviously run away when the trouble started, because her parents would have been horrified to learn that she had been drinking at a motel; then he decided he had been with a married woman who had a jealous husband, and that *she* had been forced to run away.

"The upshot of all this was that Wes was dragged into police court next day, convicted and sentenced to two months for theft."

"Next day?" a voice said. "And he got two months for a first offense?"

Everyone turned to look at the questioner. He was a short, slender man whose enormous head was surmounted by a mop of wiry black hair. He wore outsize horn-rim specs, behind which he frowned in ferocious concentration.

"Shut up, Gargoyle," somebody said. "Don't interrupt."

Dr. Heber laughed. "Discussion is most important in our little project," he said. "Please don't hesitate to interrupt. Yes sir, Wes *did* get two months for a first offense, and he *was* tried the next day. Perhaps we could go back to that aspect later."

"I certainly think we should," the little man with the large head said.

"Very well. Now everything that Wes said and did at that time indicated an emotional disturbance requiring skilled therapy. What he got was two months in Guelph, where he was a bad prisoner, and when he came home he was moody, surly and withdrawn. He had already made up a story of having been framed by a mystery gang of crooks, and he plagued all his relations with the story until they were sick of it.

"Nevertheless, they handled Wes with considerable intelligence and sympathy. They humored him. An uncle got him a job with an ad agency. They tried to rehabilitate him. But another uncle—Uncle Edgar—behaved with a notable lack of sympathy. He took the attitude that Wes was a rotten little sneak thief who had turned to crime the moment he couldn't get what he wanted honestly. He wanted no part of him.

"Now Uncle Edgar's approval was all-important to Wes. He bugged the man. He phoned him and wrote letters. He said that the theft charge was a frame-up. He went to the police and demanded the address of the woman witness whose handbag had been stolen. They naturally wouldn't give it to him. They don't want released convicts to go persecuting witnesses. This was fuel for Wes's imagination. The woman was a member of the gang, he said. But Uncle Edgar was obdurate, and he had a new will drafted, cutting Wes out. I honestly do not believe that the will had anything to do with what happened.

"For the benefit of our international guests, I will quickly run through the details of the actual murder. Edgar Beattie lived in an old-fashioned apartment where he was looked after by an elderly housekeeper, who was also a distant relative.

"The old lady is arthritic and goes to bed very early. One Friday evening she had gone to bed, leaving Edgar sitting on a sofa watching the television and drinking a few bottles of beer. At about ten-thirty something woke her up and she lay awake listening. All she could hear was the television, but after several minutes she heard the sound of a telephone being dialed—her hearing is quite acute. She called out 'Ed-gar!' but, getting no reply, she shuffled into the living room and found Edgar lying dead on the sofa. Beside him was a heavy blackthorn stick, which normally resided in an umbrella stand in the vestibule. It had been used to crush Edgar's skull with a single blow, delivered with maniacal force.

"The police conducted the normal routine investigations, in the course of which they found some fingerprints on the telephone which were neither the housekeeper's nor Edgar's. They checked them against the prints of known criminals in the files and found they belonged to one Wesley M. Beattie, who had served two months for theft.

"At the time it didn't seem important. After all, he was a relative. But a police inspector called on Wes and questioned him. Where had he been on the night of the murder? Drinking beer with a couple of guys, he said, and he had also gone to a show. The guys were called Pete and Al, and he couldn't remember the name of the film. But, most significant of all, he insisted that he had not been in or near his uncle's apartment for over six months. The housekeeper later corroborated this.

"So he was taken to headquarters, where he changed his story. He had spent the evening of the murder with a girl at her house. He wouldn't name her—note the pattern—because she was a nice girl and her parents would be horrified to know she had been keeping company with an 'ex con.' Wes likes tough words like 'ex con' and 'stir.' Police told him that a nice girl wouldn't let him hang, so he changed once more—and again we see the pattern—into a married woman with a jealous husband.

"Then after a few hours of that, he abandoned all efforts at realism and produced his conspiracy story, which goes like this: This gang that had framed him was still after him. But he was after them, too. And so was Uncle Edgar. Uncle Edgar had only been pretending to think that Wes was guilty of the theft. In reality, he was ruthlessly tracking them down. The woman witness was the key to the whole thing. She was one of the gang. Uncle Edgar was on her trail, and eventually he would have laid the whole pack of them by the heels.

"However, the brain that runs this gang is pretty crafty. He got one of the gang to call Edgar and warn him to lay off—or else. But you couldn't frighten old Edgar like that. No sir.

"So they worked this frame-up. One of the dolls in this mob picked Wes up and lured him to her apartment, and that's where he spent the evening of the murder. The cunning witch got hold of Wes's key container and slipped in a key to Edgar's apartment, as part of the frame-up. Meanwhile, other members of the gang went to Edgar's place and finished him off. Very well, you say, who was the girl? Where is the apartment?

"But Wes says he was driven to the apartment at night by a roundabout route. He went in by a rear entrance. He can't even guess what *district* it's in. Far from getting the license number of the girl's car, he isn't even sure of the make. The girl's name was Gail—she never told him her last name. Confronted with the evidence of the fingerprints, Wes stumbled a bit, then decided that this gang had invented some subtle photographic process for transferring prints. And so, Wes was charged with murder.

"And now I'll tell you my theory of how it happened. Wes tried every device to win back Edgar's approval, but Edgar, being a blunt fellow, simply rejected him. That rejection so disturbed his emotional balance that he was led to kill his great hero. He probably toyed with the idea for some time. We don't know, for instance, exactly when he obtained a key to the uncle's apartment, or how. On that fatal Friday, everything came to the boil. He went to the apartment and let himself in, and the uncle, watching TV, with his back to the door, did not hear him. Wes may have planned new entreaties; he may have stood there quivering for several minutes before frustration rose in him and nerved him to pick up the blackthorn stick, take two strides and deliver one smashing blow.

"Then, I think, he stood there, reeling with horror at what he had done. It was, of course, an insane act, and I do not think he took the consequences of the act into account at all. As the climax approached, he wasn't even thinking about getting away with it, or possible punishment. It was a blind impulse.

"He knew, of course, that the elderly housekeeper was there. He probably knew that her hearing and eyesight were good for a woman of her age. But he *certainly* knew that she was extremely immobile and very feeble. It takes her a good five minutes to collect her two sticks, pull herself painfully out of bed and make her way to the living room—and longer if she pauses to put her teeth in and find her spectacles, slippers and dressing gown. As I said, he probably took none of this into account; but if he had, if she had appeared to be at all dangerous—if, for instance, the uncle had called out his name—then, I fear, the old lady would have been dealt with quickly and in panic. The same thing would apply if she had succeeded in getting to the living room before he had left the premises. But the fact is that she didn't.

"And, in the circumstances, I believe that Wes's first impulse, when he began to realize what he had done, was to give himself up. I think he went to the telephone, peeled off his gloves—the absence of fingerprints on the murder weapon itself could indicate a degree of premeditation—and, barehanded, started to telephone the police. But then the housekeeper called out, and Wes panicked and departed.

"There is something rather wonderful about what took place after that. The horror of the deed was so great that it was completely blotted out of his memory. He couldn't face it. His mind rejected it, and wove the whole thing into the fantasy which he was already partly living in. This became the work of the gang. The gang had killed his uncle, and Wes and his uncle, shoulder-to-shoulder, had been fighting their villainies. This fantasy allows him to live with himself. He has retired into his dream world, probably forever, and there we plan to leave him. But gentlemen, if proper therapy had been applied at the time of his first arrest, all of this would have been avoided. Now then, the gentleman who had some questions. Let's hear from him."

All of the lawyers present were acquainted with Sidney Grant, who was known to his classmates as the "Gargoyle." He looked, they claimed, like some evil figure leering down from a Gothic cathedral. They remembered him best in a characteristic attitude, sitting on the dressing table in the large attic bedroom which he had occupied for years, and frowning down on his guests like some Mephistophelian judge, while he argued endlessly.

The Gargoyle had been called to the bar only a few months before, but, unlike most other young lawyers, he had not gone into an established firm. He had hung up his shingle and commenced the practice of criminal law in the lower courts, where he was already establishing a reputation as a tough battler.

"Okay, Gargoyle, fire away," someone said, and Dr. Heber smiled.

"Question one," Sidney Grant said. "Why such a stiff sentence for a first offense—on the theft charge?"

"Answer one," Dr. Heber said. "The magistrate was like some Fielding character. Wes Beattie broke down in court and made a rather sorry exhibition of himself. He was still trying to lie his way out of it, and he got this old Colonel Blimp magistrate pretty angry, so he threw the book at him."

"Question two," Sidney said. "Why was he tried next day? Why wasn't the case remanded for two weeks so that Beattie could get himself a bit organized? I mean, if he'd pleaded guilty he would simply have got a suspended sentence. If the case had been remanded..."

A beautifully groomed young lawyer stood up at the back of the room. "Dr. Heber," he said, "there is no use trying to protect me any longer. Gargoyle Grant is going to find out all about it, so I will confess. Sidney, I was Wes Beattie's counsel in the magistrate's court, and I have to take a share of the blame."

"James Bellwood!" Sidney said. "What were you doing in the police court anyway? Not your class of client at all."

"Mr. Grant," Bellwood said, "you may go jump in the lake. Our clients get into the magistrates' courts every now and then, usually by mixing alcohol with gasoline. But this case was different. For the visitors I must explain that I am a junior in a very high-class corporation law firm, the sort of firm that my learned and belligerent friend treats with amused contempt. And I will state that if ever one of our clients gets into an action in which Mr. Grant represents the opposition, we will advise him to settle right away, because Mr. Grant is going to be one of our great courtroom lawyers."

"Flattery will get you nowhere, Bellwood," Sidney Grant said with a satanic grin. "Tell us about the Beattie bit."

"Very well. I will have to stick my neck out a bit, but I trust you will regard this confession as being under the seal. My firm has a client called the Superior Trust Company. The secretary of the company is one Ralph L. Paget, who comes out strongly on the side of dignity, propriety and other engaging virtues. One morning at four A.M. Mr. Paget phoned the senior partner of my firm, Mr. Claude Potter, and told him that his nephew, Wes Beattie, was in the cells charged with theft. There was a tremendous flap. Mr. Potter phoned me—I live hell and gone out in Port Credit—and said to come in and bail this kid out and try to hush up the scandal as much as possible. It seems that the kid lived with his granny, old Mrs. Charles Beattie, who had recently lost her husband and was in delicate health. The shock was likely to kill her, because Wes was, quote, the apple of her eye.

"I found the kid in a frightful state. The police had been questioning him—no duress, force, violence or threats, of course. They said he got the bruise on his cheek when he fell downstairs. He'd been caught with the goods on him, so I said there were two things he could do. He could go in and plead guilty, or he could ask for a remand. But meanwhile Mr. Paget had joined me, and he said that a remand would give the papers a chance to get the story and blow it up. I felt that his fears were exaggerated. Wes tearfully tried to tell us some weird story which did not in the least resemble the first statements he had made to the police.

"He said that some Englishman had called him at the bank where he worked, and had offered him a terrific job—as an executive trainee! The man said he represented an English company about to open up a Canadian subsidiary. He wanted Wes to come for an interview to his hotel and told him he would send his secretary to pick Wes up and drive him there. Wes got permission to leave the bank early; the secretary picked him up and drove him to the Midtown Motel, where she parked and walked with him to the rear entrance of the bar. Then she remembered she'd left her handbag in the car and sent Wes back to get it. He must have got confused and taken the wrong handbag from the wrong car, he said. And then, when they looked for the secretary in the bar, she wasn't there. She vanished, he said, into thin air. Mr. Paget got quite angry. He said, 'Wes, I'm sick of your silly lies. You simply get yourself all tangled up in them.'

"Anyway, I talked to the man from the Crown Attorney's office, and he said his witnesses would be in court, and one of them—the woman whose purse had been stolen—was from out of town—Sudbury, I believe. He would be only too happy to proceed, naturally. I met Mr. Potter and Mr. Paget and urged that we get a remand, in the hope that the witness wouldn't show up two weeks later. But Mr. Paget said no, it would be terrible to have this disgrace hanging over the old lady—his mother-in-law, Wes's grandmother. The papers might try to make something of a youth from a prominent family stealing from parked cars.

"So, much to everyone's surprise, the case was heard that morning. Wes pleaded Not Guilty, and tried to tell this silly story of his. The magistrate kept interrupting him, and then, on cross-examination, the prosecutor tore him to shreds. Why had Wes concealed the handbag under his coat? Because, Wes said, he felt silly carrying a woman's purse."

"Which makes good sense," Sidney said. "I dare *you* to carry a woman's purse in that district. You'd be accosted!"

There was much laughter.

"True enough," Bellwood said. "But the owner of the purse was there, she certainly identified her property, and she said that Wes had hung on to the bag even after she claimed it. Wes was asked why, if he was innocent, he had twice tried to break loose, and run away. He said he was frightened and confused. Under fire his features trembled and the tears flowed, and old Cartwright was disgusted. He said Wes was a disgrace to his entire background, et cetera, et cetera, and gave him two months."

"A very pretty mess," Sidney Grant said. "And just what you can expect when you try to hush things up. Damn it, the woman had recovered her property. I'll bet she never would have returned to give evidence if the thing had been remanded."

"I entirely agree with you, Gargoyle," Bellwood said. "Fine," Sidney Grant said. "But another thing occurs to me. Why, Dr. Heber, don't you simply look this woman witness up, bring her to see Wes Beattie and convince him that she is not a member of a sinister gang? You could show him that his Uncle Edgar wouldn't have had any trouble locating her and that there was no brain to warn his uncle to 'lay off—or else.'"

"My dear Mr.—er—Grant," Dr. Heber said. "We have no interest whatever in exploding this fantasy of Wes's. The moment we question his story he gets wildly hysterical and then withdraws, virtually into a catatonic trance. There is no communicating with him on any other terms than that his story is accepted. We are happy to let him live in this weird world of his."

"Well, how about his counsel in the murder trial—Baldwin Ogilvy? Isn't *he* interested in checking this thing out?"

"Well, no," Dr. Heber said, and smiled. "Please be discreet about this, but Wes's defense will simply be insanity. These delusions will save him from the gallows. The Crown will, I understand, accept the plea of insanity and that will be that."

"I would still like to talk to that woman witness," Sidney Grant said. "Women keep vanishing into thin air. This is one who could be found."

"Then, if it will give you any satisfaction, Mr. Grant, I suggest that you find her and talk to her. Meanwhile, Wes sits in the Psychiatric Hospital on an attorney general's remand warrant, living in his world of fantasy which he will probably never leave again. The reality is too horrible for his mind to contemplate."

"It's a funny thing," Sidney said. "Twice this man has gone through the same routine. 'I was with a nice girl—her parents mustn't know.' Then 'I was with a married woman who has a jealous husband.' Finally 'I was the victim of a vast conspiracy.'"

"That is the way Wes Beattie's mind works," Dr. Heber said. "He has a long history as a chronic liar."

"The boy who cried 'Wolf' too often," Sidney said. "Well, sir, I *am* going to find that woman witness, the one whose handbag was stolen."

"Good for you," the psychiatrist said. "And good luck."

Two

THE NAME AND ADDRESS of the woman witness were easy to find. The court office had the information, as well as the Crown Attorney's office, and a stenographer had been sent to the police court from Jim Bellwood's office to take down the proceedings against Wes verbatim, because the magistrates' courts were not themselves equipped with court stenographers.

All sources agreed that the woman whose handbag had been stolen was Mrs. Irene Leduc, of 428 Baylie Circle, Sudbury, Ontario.

So Sidney Grant summoned his secretary, Miss Georgina Semple, an elderly woman with incredible red hair piled high on her head, and dictated a registered letter to Mrs. Leduc, stating simply that he had legal matters of a confidential nature to discuss with her.

His letter was returned by the Sudbury post office, which stated that there was no such address.

"Ha!" he said gleefully, and wrote to a lawyer friend in Sudbury asking him to check on the whole business. Was there any address *like* the one given, or was there a Mrs. Irene Leduc who had been a witness in the Toronto case?

In due course a ribald reply came from the friend, saying that no such woman existed and advising Mr. Grant to be more careful in future when he picked up stray females in bars. Miss Semple, who had large brown eyes and a knowing air, could not suppress her amusement at the reply.

Tracing the woman witness was not, after all, going to be simple routine.

Sidney Grant took the first opportunity to visit the Midtown Motel and examine the register. According to Bellwood's transcript, the woman witness had been a guest at the motel. The manager was inclined to be hostile. He didn't like people, especially lawyers, nosing in his register—but the law was the law. And Sidney discovered that a Mr. and Mrs. G. Leduc, of Sudbury, Ontario, had booked in at the Midtown at 11 A.M. on Thursday, May 11, the day of the theft for which Wes Beattie had served two months in prison. He further learned that the Leducs had checked out at 8 P.M. on the same day.

No doubt all the fuss about the theft had driven them to change hotels, Sidney decided. But, most important, he took down the license number of the Leducs' car, which was noted on the registration card.

Back at the office, he asked Miss Semple to check the car license with the Parliament buildings. It proved to be a black Dodge sedan, belonging to a car rental agency on Dundas Street in Toronto.

"Now what do you make of that, Georgie dear?" Sidney asked Miss Semple.

Miss Semple had spent most of her life in a large law office, from which she had been superannuated. A pillar of virtue herself, she was nevertheless knowing in the ways of the world.

"What do I make of what?" she asked.

"A woman, claiming to be Mrs. Leduc, of Sudbury, rents a car in Toronto, books a motel room at eleven A.M. and gives it up early the same evening."

"The afternoon is a lovely time of day, they say!" Miss Semple said archly.

"This woman had her purse stolen in the motel car park. The thief was caught with the goods on him. *Next* day the woman, using this same name and address, went into court and gave evidence against the thief," Sidney said.

"Well, really!" Miss Semple said. "What some women won't do! I suppose she is a local woman who rented the car and went to this motel with her boy friend. She rented the car because she knows that motels take down license numbers, and she wanted to pretend she was from out of town. Her husband probably thought she was shopping at Simpson's."

"That's the way it looks," Sidney said. "But if this is a false name, why would she take a chance and appear in court if she didn't have to? She had recovered her property, after all."

"Immoral women can be terrible prudes," Miss Semple asserted. "I mean I knew a notoriously wanton female who was *shocked* if anybody used a bad word. A woman might take a high-and-mighty moral attitude to a sneak thief at the very moment she was being *flagrantly* unfaithful to her husband."

"I suppose so," Sidney said. "But I would certainly love to talk to this woman. In fact, I made a boast that I would. However, she seems to have made herself pretty scarce."

"Why don't you check with the car rental people?" Miss Semple said. "They might have a lead."

"By golly, I will," Sidney said. "First free minute I get." Sidney Grant did not have many free minutes. He spent a great deal of time in the lower courts, working for small fees, and office work filled the rest of his time. He could not even afford the modest luxury of an articled law student.

But nevertheless he managed to get around, being active and wiry, and in due course he got around to the car rental agency, where the manager was proud to show off his record system.

"When we rent a car," he told Sidney, "we open one of these dockets. See? A manila envelope. On the outside we write the details of the vehicle and the renter. Like time of rental, mileage out, mileage in, name, address and driver's license number of the renter. So you tell me the date and all, and maybe I can turn up this rental you're interested in."

"Mrs. Irene Leduc," Sidney said. "Sometime about May tenth or eleventh."

The man disappeared and returned after a short delay with one of the dockets.

"Got it right here," he said. "Now, this vehicle was a black Dodge, and we booked it out at ten A.M. Mrs. Irene Leduc, Sudbury, Ontario. She drove it—holy cow!—she only drove it six point four miles. Boy, it would be a lot cheaper to take taxis! And she brought it back seven P.M. Now here's her driver's license number. You want that? Not checkin' up on the little woman, I hope?"

"Eh?" Sidney said.

"Your wife isn't givin' you trouble, I hope," the man said.

"Definitely not," Sidney said. "She doesn't get the chance. I am a devout bachelor. What is there *inside* the envelope?"

"Well, there won't be anything," the man said. "See, like when the renter buys gas and oil, they pay cash and get a receipt, and we file the receipts in here. Like we refund the money they pay out. And parking tickets or speeding tickets that they hand in—we file them here too, although a lot of creeps just tear their parking tickets up and throw 'em away."

"So there's nothing in this envelope?"

"Well, she'd hardly buy any gas, see? Hold it, though—she did!"

He fished a flimsy receipted bill from the envelope.

"Nope. She had trouble. Fuel pump repairs, a buck fifty, which between you and I is highway robbery. Maybe that's why she brought the car back."

The bill said "Mac's Garage" and was receipted "R. Phelan."

Sidney Grant wrote the details in his notebook, thanked the man for his trouble and returned to the office. "I think we may have a line on the elusive Irma La Douce or Irene Leduc," he told Miss Semple. "Just check this driver's license number out with the Parliament buildings, will you?"

Miss Semple was back in the inner sanctum within three minutes, and she laid a slip of paper in front of her employer. It said: "Mrs. Irene Ledley, 28 Bayview Circle, Toronto."

"Well I'm blowed," Sidney said, and pulled his own driver's license out of his wallet. "Do you suppose she just flashed the license and gave a wrong address, or do you think she actually cooked the license?"

"Very easy to cook it," Miss Semple said. "Look—she could type a four in front of the twenty-eight to make fourtwo-eight, and she could alter 'Bayview' to Baylie by changing a couple of letters."

"I suppose," Sidney said, "you could erase Toronto and type in Sudbury—both seven letters."

"And you could sign Irene Leduc to make it look like Irene Ledley," she said. "I suppose Mrs. Ledley was having an affair, and she wanted to cover her tracks."

"And then appear in court under her false name," Sidney said. "Tomorrow I am going to visit Bayview Circle. I don't want to phone, but I'd like to catch her when her husband is at the office. Unless I'm wrong, she'll be so scared that she'll tell us anything we want to know."

"Blackmail!" Miss Semple said.

"Persuasion," Sidney corrected.

Bayview Circle was in a fashionable suburban area, and Number 28 proved to be a modern split-level house complete with car port, breezeway and Chinese elm hedge.

Mrs. Ledley, however, did not appear to be a typical suburban housewife. She was in her early forties, and there was charm as well as intelligence in her features. She was a little hesitant about admitting a stranger to the house, but Sidney insisted that his business was confidential and could not be conducted on the doorstep.

"Very well, do come in," she said, and led him to the living room.

"Mrs. Ledley," he said, when they were seated, "I have no desire to cause you any embarrassment. But last May somebody rented a car and then rented a unit at the Midtown Motel, using your driver's license as identification."

"*My* driver's license?" she said. "How could that *be?*"

"You were not the person who rented the car?" he asked.

"No! I've never rented a car in my life. What are you implying, Mr. —er—Grant? I don't think I like this."

"I'm implying nothing, Mrs. Ledley. Would you mind showing me your driver's license?"

"Not at all," she said. "Hold on, I'll get my handbag." After a brief search, she found the handbag hanging on a doorknob, and from it produced a small leather folder containing a long plastic envelope. In its compartments were various credit cards and insurance papers and the owner's paper for her car.

But no license.

"Well, that's the oddest thing," she said. "It *couldn't* have fallen out. I wonder what can have happened to it?"

"When did you last have occasion to look for it?" Sidney asked.

"Oh, I don't suppose I've looked at it since I put it in there last March," she said.

"And you wouldn't remember what you were doing in May—around the tenth and eleventh of May?" he asked.

"Heavens, no! We had a holiday in Tobago at Easter. Then in June we went to Ireland. My husband handles diamond drill equipment, and we went to Ireland where there's some drilling on mining properties, and we were there till September, and when that was finished we bought a Peugeot and toured Europe all through September. But May..."

"You have no idea how or when you lost your license?" he said. "I would suggest that you lost it early in May. Is that possible? Nobody stole your purse in May, did they?"

She looked at him in blank bewilderment. "Is this really important, Mr. Grant?" she said.

"Yes, it is. It may be a matter of life and death."

"Well, hold on then. I have a diary in which I write down social engagements. It may give me some clue. Wait a minute, will you?"

"Certainly," Sidney said, and he watched her closely as she left the room.

Was she stalling for time? Had she altered her license and then destroyed it? If so, she was a pretty cool operator. Sidney looked about the room. One split level was much like another to him, but the general arrangements of Mrs. Ledley's house showed quiet good taste, and her manner had a dignity which did not fit in with sordid affairs at motels.

She returned with a diary and a large brochure on coated stock. "We're in luck," she said. "Wednesday, tenth. Mining Awards Dinner. Royal York Hotel. There was a big mining convention on that week, and my husband and I attended several functions. And incidentally, I've just remembered a funny thing. Strange how things come back to you, isn't it?"

"Yes, the human memory is tricky," he agreed.

"Well, anyway, at these conventions a lot of big companies put in hospitality suites—snake rooms, they call them. You know, a big living room with a bar, and a couple of bedrooms opening off it. And people go pub crawling from room to room, having a good old freeload. Well, after this dinner, Ken and I went to several rooms, and I had quite a scare."

"Really?"

"Yes. We were in this suite, and I threw my coat and handbag on the bed in the adjoining bedroom—quite a few women left their coats there. Well, when I went to get my coat, I got a start, because there was my handbag lying on *top* of my coat, and I had left it *under* my coat, and there was over two hundred dollars in it. I felt such a damn fool! My husband would never let me hear the end of it if I lost all that money so stupidly. Well, I quickly pulled it out and counted it, and it was all there. But do you suppose some woman opened the bag and pinched my license, and I never missed it?"

Sidney looked at her with frank admiration. "That is quite possible," he said. "The timing is right. You said Wednesday, tenth?"

"That's right. Here's the program. Warm-up cocktail party Tuesday evening, and then, for some delegates, the cocktail party continued without interruption until Friday, May twelfth. This dinner was on the Wednesday."

"The night before your license was used to rent a car," Sidney said.

"How very strange!" she exclaimed.

"Now then, Mrs. Ledley," he said, "I'm going to be nasty, just to save time and trouble. The woman who used your license rented a motel room and a car. She appeared in police court as a witness against a young man who stole her handbag. She was seen by lawyers, parking attendants and others. If you are that woman, now is the time to say so, because there are plenty of people who can identify you. And if you *are* that woman, and if you now tell me so, it will go no further. I will promise you full protection."

"I am *not* that woman," she said, calmly, but with a note of anger. "I have told you I'm not. You may take me to all your witnesses and I will defy them to say I am. I have told you the truth, and nothing but the truth, and I resent your insinuations."

"Which I withdraw and apologize for. I wouldn't have bothered you at all if this were not a desperately serious matter. Would you mind letting me have a photograph of you, which I will return in tonight's mail?"

"So you can check up on me with your witnesses?"

"Yes. So that I can positively eliminate you. And I know that that will happen."

"All right," she said, and laughed. "You really don't think I'm the motel affair type, do you?"

"No," he said. "And I wonder if I could keep that convention program."

"Certainly," she said. "It's just junk. It has a complete list of the delegates and registered guests and their wives, broken down by occupations—you know, mining engineers, brokers and so on. Only one thing is missing."

"And what is that?" he asked.

She smiled mischievously. "There is no heading for Call Girls," she said. "And there seemed to be some of them about. Conventions! Heavens!"

Sidney left with the photograph and the convention program, but an hour later he mailed the photograph back. James Bellwood was prepared to state positively that Mrs. Ledley was not the witness who had claimed that Wes had stolen her handbag.

Which left Sidney Grant with a convention program—and a receipted bill for fuel pump repairs. He had spent sufficient time looking for Mrs. Leduc, and for no return at all. But what, he wondered, would Wes Beattie make of it, if he knew how very thoroughly Mrs. Leduc had vanished? There would be fuel for the imagination of a boy with schizophrenic delusions.

Sidney Grant thought about it. What possible explanation could there be for Mrs. Leduc's conduct? Miss Semple had a theory. "Either this woman was married to a very rich man, or her boy friend was a very rich man," she said. "It was very dangerous for them to meet, which made it all the more exciting. I mean that if her husband was rich and she got caught, he might divorce her with a very poor alimony settlement. So getting this fake driver's license will be a great help to her on other occasions."

"And why did she give evidence in the police court?" Sidney said. "Moral indignation?"

"No, I don't think so, Mr. Grant. The policeman had taken her address and had asked her to show up in court. She was afraid that if she didn't show up, there might be a hue and cry after the stolen driver's license or something like that."

"Uh huh," Sidney said. "Something like that. At any rate, she has covered her tracks with complete success."

Three

"**M**R. GRANT, WHAT ON EARTH are you doing with my handbag?" Miss Semple demanded with a note of outrage.

"What handbag?" Sidney asked innocently, tucking his secretary's purse under his coat.

"Why, my—*Mister* Grant, who steals my purse steals cash. I'd vastly prefer that you robbed me of my reputation."

"Look," Sidney said, "I'm caught with the goods on me. What story should I tell in order to lie out of it?"

"You could say you were a lawyer," Miss Semple said. "Just doing a little experiment to put yourself in a client's position."

"He isn't a client," Sidney said, "but otherwise the story is true, and anybody will believe it, especially in the absence of previous convictions for theft. In other words, I could really be stealing this purse, but get away with it. You caught me red-handed. I laughingly explain and hand the purse back. Now this boy Wes Beattie, who stole this purse..."

"Wes Beattie? Not the one who murdered his uncle? Will we be assisting Mr. Baldwin Ogilvy in his defense?" Miss Semple asked, lighting up like a switchboard.

"No, no, no," Sidney said. "I just got challenged to find a certain woman, the one we've been looking for, Mrs. Leduc, and it made me curious. Now suppose this Wes Beattie wanted to steal that purse. Suppose he opened the car door, airily took it out and carried it openly, swinging it. Would the parking lot attendant challenge him?"

"He might," Miss Semple said. "But the bluff could work."

"Well, suppose he *did* challenge him—'Hey, where are you going with the purse'—the thief could smile and say, 'Just taking it to its owner in the bar.' Martin Luther said 'Sin boldly.' Excellent advice for thieves. Poor young Beattie floundered around looking for some plausible explanation and just got himself all tied up. By the way, keep this all strictly under your hat with your gorgeous curls, Miss Semple," Sidney said.

"Is it necessary to tell *me* that?" Miss Semple said sniffily. "I've worked over forty years in law offices."

"Sorry," Sidney said. "Well, I've still got your purse and I'm walking off with it, sinning boldly. Challenge me."

"Here, you!" she said. "Where are you going with my purse?"

"*Your* purse," Sidney said, looking puzzled. "Oh, for goodness' sake, have I made a mistake?"

"You most certainly have, young man, and I've got a good mind to call the police."

"Oh dear," Sidney said. "It must look really awful. I'm sure you think I'm a crook. Would you please just check the contents and assure yourself that I haven't taken anything?"

"That would work, in all likelihood," Miss Semple said.

"Wes Beattie was just too stupid to change his ground at the instant when the owner of the handbag appeared," Sidney said. "He is what is technically called a crazy mixed-up kid. But I *still* want to talk to Mrs. Leduc and find out why she sent the boy up the river."

"And have you explored every avenue?" Miss Semple asked.

"Aye, and turned every stone," he said. "Except one. It can't possibly get me anything, but damn it, I shall turn it anyway."

All of which led to a futile visit to Mac's Garage, where various mechanics laughed coarsely and told Sidney that he needed to see a headshrinker.

"Listen, bud," one man said, "we might do fifty, sixty little jobs a day. So we should remember fixin' a fuel pump last May? You must be nuts."

"But how about R. Phelan? Is he around? He's the man who receipted this repair bill."

"Rick Phelan? Are you nuts? You expect to find him here during the hockey season?"

Sidney Grant asked for further enlightenment and learned that Rick Phelan was a hockey player who worked only in the summers at the garage. He was, in fact, the greatest prospective defenseman to come down the pike since the late Bill Barilko, and in order to see him Sidney had to catch him when his team was playing in Toronto. This he managed on a Sunday in February, when he found the hockey player in a hotel room not far from the Maple Leaf Gardens.

"Sorry to bug you on a Sunday morning," Sidney said. "And the question may sound exceedingly stupid, but…"

"Stupid questions? I answer dozens," Phelan said. "Fire away."

"Well, last May you did some repair work on a black Dodge," Sidney said. "It was a rented car, and you made out a receipt for a dollar fifty which you gave to the driver. The driver was probably a woman, and she may have had a man with her. The specific trouble was in the fuel pump. Now, is there any chance that you might remember anything at all about such a transaction?"

Phelan shook his head and looked at Sidney Grant sadly. "Boy, you are an optimist," he said. "Now what odds would you offer against me remembering anything about a deal like that?"

"Plenty," Sidney said.

"Sure. Wouldn't anyone? But I'm tellin' you chum, don't do it! You'd lose. The fact is I remember that black Dodge loud and clear, but I'm not sure I ought to tell you anything about it."

"Why not?" Sidney asked.

"Because," Phelan said, "you're not the first guy to come askin' me questions about that Dodge. And if you knew what happened to the first guy that come, maybe you wouldn't be so keen."

"What happened to the first guy?" Sidney asked, and he could feel an old prickling in his calves and a pounding in his temples as he said it, though he asked his question casually enough.

"What happened to him?" Phelan said. "He got murdered. That's what happened to him. No kidding, either."

"Murdered?"

"Yeah. You probably read it in the papers. This guy Edgar Beattie—his cousin or something bashed his skull in. That was the guy that come askin' about the Dodge."

"And you think there was some connection?" Sidney asked.

Phelan laughed. "Hell, no," he said. "Although for a few days it gave me a funny feeling, until they caught this nephew. It kind of made me wonder."

"Tell me about it," Sidney said. "Tell me every detail. This is very, very interesting indeed." He felt faint and giddy, and he had to help himself to a glass of water.

"You mean that? Every detail?" Phelan said. "I don't want to be called L.P. Phelan, but if you really want it I can give you the full treatment."

"I want the full treatment," Sidney said.

"Okay, okay, just like this Mr. Beattie," he said. "And then maybe you'll tell me what this is all about. Anyway, see, this Mr.

Beattie came along and just like you he wanted to know about the Dodge. That was early in September. So I told him sorry, you know, what routine job did *you* do last May? Well, he was a very pleasant guy. He said sure, he understood that it wasn't likely, but he asked me would I *think* about it. He also handed me ten bucks, which I didn't like to take. But he said, 'Go on, buy your wife a fur coat.' He said I should get a couple of jugs or a few cases of beer and just think about dames and Dodges and fuel pumps. He said something might come back to me, and he really wanted to get a line on this dame.

"Well, like I said, I hated to take his ten bucks, and I didn't take it very seriously. But then one night I was lying half asleep and something flickered. I remembered making out a receipt. An experienced man can always spot a rented car, so I just automatically made the receipt out. I tried to hand it to the fellow in the car, but he brushed it off and said, 'Just gimme my change.' The dame sort of gave me the eye and reached out and took the receipt and stuck it in her handbag. Well, I thought about that, and then it all started to come back, just like watching a television show. So I phoned this Edgar Beattie and he was tickled pink."

"What all did you tell him?" Sidney asked.

"Well he wanted every detail you could think of, so I told him the whole thing. Like I was servicing this Olds convertible, a very flashy car belonging to a very flashy guy. A guy called 'Bunny,' who used to come in quite a lot, and always wanted to gas about hockey. He was the sort of guy who tries to make out he was once a pretty hot-shot hockey player, and this was strictly from the horse. You can guess which end. For instance, he told me he was on New York Rangers trading list, and if it hadn't been for the war he'd have been in the N.H.L. All that jazz. Well, you know, I'd string him along and ask him did he play for Marlies or St. Mikes maybe, but all he ever played for was his high school team. This all leads up to it, so don't get impatient."

"I'm not," Sidney said. "Just keep right on going."

"Well, anyway, while I was putting new wiper blades on the Olds, this black Dodge pulled in, hopping like a bunny. So, just kidding like, I said, 'Go on, Bunny, see if you can hop like that,' and I offered to bet him five that it was fuel pump trouble. He wouldn't take me. Then this dame, very nicely upholstered, got out of the Dodge and came over, while the guy with her just sat there. She said please could I fix her car in a hurry, and I told her I knew what was wrong and it wouldn't take long. So she went and sat in the car, and I went over to the air pump to check the tires on the Olds, and then this guy from the Dodge came over, steaming mad, and wanted to know how goddamn long I expected him to wait. I told him just till I finished with the customer I was working on, and I told him to keep his shirt on. He was one of these handsome guys with a kind of ugly expression, and he was just turning around when Bunny jumped out of his car and yelled, 'Hi!' The other guy swung round, and Bunny went up to him holding out both hands and saying, 'Well, well, well, long time no see,' and all that stuff. But the guy from the Dodge gave him the fishy eye and said, 'Hi, Bunny,' and walked off. You know, cold as a Polar bear's nose.

"Well, you should have seen Bunny! He stood there with his mouth open, and he looked like a little boy that didn't hold his hand up soon enough in school. So he turned to me and said, 'How do you like that, Rick? My old pal! What would you do if some old teammate of *yours* gave you that stuff?' I told him in my business the first thing you had to learn was the difference between the rear end of a horse and the rear end of a truck, and that made him laugh, so away he went. So then I fixed the fuel pump and that was it.

"Anyway, Mr. Beattie had said to phone him if ever I remembered anything, so I did, and he was so pleased he slipped me a twenty. I told him to forget it, but he shoved it in the pocket of my dungarees. Only I couldn't remember the last name of this Bunny, although I serviced his Olds quite a bit. Mr. Beattie said would I find out the next time the guy came in, and phone him, but don't tell this Bunny that anyone was asking. He said he was trying to track down this dame, but she'd gone off to Europe or something, and maybe he could find out about her from the guy.

"So next time Bunny came in, I took down the name and address from his credit card and called Mr. Beattie, and I'm telling you, he was a great sport and a big spender. He came down and gave me fifty—which made eighty bucks in all—for nothin'!"

"And can you remember Bunny's name now?" Sidney asked anxiously.

"Sure. Now I can. Peter L. Mayhew. Lives out in Scarborough. Now, do you mind telling me what this is all about?"

"Do you mind very much if I don't?" Sidney said. "I mean, you've been very good, and I hate to give you the brush, but the thing may be dynamite."

"I get it," Phelan said. "Well, I'd sure like to know—I mean this Mr. Beattie was a real nice guy, but..."

"Well, one of these days, if I ever find out the whole story, I'll tell you," Sidney said. "Meantime all I can say is thanks a lot, Rick."

"That's okay, that's okay," Phelan said. "I get the message."

"Georgie dear," Sidney Grant greeted his secretary on Monday morning. "We've got hold of something very, very curious. And where it leads to I couldn't guess."

"Have you found Mrs. Leduc?" she asked.

"No ma'am. But this I have discovered. Wes Beattie, who is awaiting trial for murder, has a fantastic story about being the victim of a conspiracy. He claims that his Uncle Edgar, at the time he was murdered, was trying to find this Mrs. Leduc, who had once given evidence against him. And he claimed that Mrs. Leduc had vanished. Well, I have now discovered that Uncle Edgar *was* trying to find the lady and was spending cash on the search. He was really anxious to find her. Nobody believes a word Wes says—but I've proved that two of his claims are true.

"He also says that, when Uncle Edgar got close to the quarry, somebody called him up and warned him to lay off—or else. Maybe that was true as well."

"Will this have any bearing on the murder charge?" Miss Semple asked.

"That is another matter," Sidney said. "They have some pretty solid evidence that would require a lot of shaking. Fingerprints on a telephone. But the suggestion that there was some sort of conspiracy might stir things up a bit. Meanwhile, would you please look up one Peter L. Mayhew in the city directory and find out where his office is?"

Peter L. Mayhew proved to be one of the fifteen vice-presidents in a large advertising agency, and, before heading for the magistrate's court, Sidney ran him to earth behind a desk which consisted simply of a huge sheet of thick plate glass mounted on wrought-iron legs.

Mayhew was fair, with long blond lashes and a thin blond mustache. He wore an expression of amused disdain, and there was an irritating superiority in his speech. "Precisely how can I serve you, Mr. Grant?" he asked.

Sidney outlined the incident at Mac's Garage, as related by Rick Phelan and watched closely at the caution which crept into Mayhew's features as the tale proceeded. When Sidney had finished, Mayhew got up and poured himself a glass of water from a thermos jug on a table behind him.

"Well?" he said.

"Well," Sidney said, "all I want to know is who was this old pal who snubbed you so royally?"

Mayhew laughed lightly. "Nobody," he said. "There was no such incident. This mechanic fellow must have a vivid imagination. Send him around and I'll give him a job in our copy department. We *need* guys with creative imagination."

"You can't remember the incident?"

"No," Mayhew said, "and for the very good reason that it never took place. Look, old boy, if any old chum cut me dead, I'd remember, because under this tough, cynical exterior I am really a very sensitive guy. Was there anything else?"

"Yes," Sidney said. "Is that what you told Edgar Beattie when he came here to ask you about it?"

"Edgar Beattie? Who is Edgar Beattie?"

"A man who came here to ask you about that nonexistent incident," Sidney said.

"Nobody ever came here, I tell you," Mayhew said, the bantering tone yielding to a touch of asperity. "Who *is* this fellow?"

"Oh, come, you haven't heard of Edgar Beattie?" Sidney said. "Get with it."

"Oh, you mean the man who was murdered by his nephew?" Bunny Mayhew said. "Yes, of course I've heard about him, but I never had the ineffable pleasure of making his acquaintance. Now, if you don't mind, I have the odd spot of work to do..."

"Thank you so much for your trouble, Mr. Mayhew," Sidney said.

❁ ❁ ❁

Lunch that day for Sidney Grant consisted of a chicken salad sandwich and a cup of coffee, consumed at his desk, after a frantic morning in court defending various characters of the minor underworld.

"It's true, Miss Semple, it's true," he said between bites. "Someone *did* call Edgar Beattie and tell him to lay off. I'd be prepared to bet heavily on it. Our friend Mr. Mayhew called Mrs. Leduc's boy friend, and the boy friend called Edgar. And now, by golly, I am going to find the boy friend and see what he has to say about it."

"How can you find him?" Miss Semple asked.

"There is a magazine about ad agency people and such like," Sidney said. "I think it's called *Marketing.* I'll bet they have biography files about important people in the ad game, although I don't know if they'd go as low as agency vice-presidents. Anyway, call them up and find out if they've got a file on Mayhew. If so, find out what school he went to. What high school, that is. I've got an idea."

While Sidney finished his coffee, Miss Semple returned to her desk and made the call. She came back with the information neatly written on a slip of paper. "He went to Annette Street Public School and Humberside Collegiate Institute," she said. "Right here in the city."

"Good," he said. "Well, I've already spent a lot of time on this thing, and now I'm going to invest in a cab fare to Humberside for a little historical research. This is a luxury I'm going to allow myself, so, if you will just mind the shop, I'll be on my way."

The school authorities were polite and helpful. The secretary directed Sidney to the library, where the librarian armed him with half a dozen back copies of *Hermes*, the school year-book, covering the years 1938 to 1943.

Sidney sat down at a long table, where he worked with curious teen-agers trying to peer over his shoulder. Each year-book was crammed with group photographs of teams, and it did not take long to find a hockey-team picture with P. (Bunny) Mayhew in the rear row. Mayhew also appeared with the junior team of the previous year.

Sidney carefully listed the players on both teams. After all, according to Phelan, Mayhew had more or less described the man at the garage as an old teammate. "What would you do if an old teammate gave you that stuff?" or words to that effect. After duplications had been removed, there were fourteen names on the list. A list of war casualties in a later yearbook further reduced the number.

Sidney looked at the short list for several minutes, scratching the whiskers on his chin with his left hand as he did. All that was necessary really was to seize Mayhew, tie him to a polygraph lie detector and read the names to him, but there were obstacles in the way of such a bold scheme. As he stared at the names before him, an idea began to flicker in the back of his head, and the familiar satanic grin slowly spread over his face.

Sidney reached into the briefcase on the floor beside him and pulled out the mining convention program which Mrs. Ledley had given him. Patiently, painstakingly, he went down the columns of names, checking the high school hockey players against the mining people. And then, suddenly, he had it.

But although he had found a duplication, his lawyer's training forced him to continue with the job until he had checked out *all* the names, to make sure that there weren't *two* duplications.

But there was only one. Howie Gadwell had been a defenseman on the Humberside hockey team; Howard G. Gadwell, listed as a "broker-dealer," had been a registered guest at the mining convention.

It was just after five o'clock when a taxi delivered Sidney Grant in a high state of excitement at the building where Bunny Mayhew had his office.

"I thought we had finished our business," Mayhew said coldly.

"How wrong you were!" Sidney said. "*Mister* Mayhew, you told me a big, fat fib, and don't attempt to deny it. I've got a good mind to tell your mother."

"Look, before I get mad, I'd advise you to get the hell out of here," Mayhew said.

"Presently, presently," Sidney said. "But first, why didn't you want to tell me that it was Howard Gadwell who snubbed you at Mac's Garage?"

No polygraph was needed to chart Mayhew's reaction. "You're nuts!" he yelled.

"And after Edgar Beattie came to see you, you called Gadwell and warned him that a gent was looking for him, didn't you?"

"Get the hell out of here, you…"

"Easy boy! And did you call Gadwell again today and warn him that *I* was looking for him?"

"Look," Mayhew said, "I told you this morning that there was never any such incident as you described. Now if you want to barge in here and start calling me a liar, you'd better be prepared to take the consequences."

"I'm all prepared," Sidney said. "I'm on my way to see Gadwell to tell him that *you* gave me his name, and you can try to convince him that you didn't."

"Do what you damn well please, but get out of here," Mayhew almost screamed.

"As you say. I'm on my way to Gadwell," Sidney said.

He had his hand on the door when Mayhew called him back, and when Sidney turned around, he found that Mayhew had positively shrunk. "Okay, you win," Mayhew said. "I'd just as soon you didn't go to Gadwell. It was him, all right. Now tell me what it's all about."

"He was with a lady at the garage," Sidney said.

"Sure. Quite a dish," Mayhew said. "Then this burly character came in here, and naturally I took him for a jealous husband."

"Naturally," Sidney said, barely suppressing a smile.

"So I stalled him off. I said I couldn't remember meeting anyone at Mac's. Then I phoned Howie Gadwell and warned him. I said I didn't think much of the way he snubbed his old friends, but all the same, no matter how they act, you've got to stand by your old friends. But in the paper it said this Beattie had been divorced for years."

"What was Gadwell's attitude?" Sidney said.

"Damned rude, actually. He told me it was a good thing for me that I'd kept my mouth shut, and if I valued my health I'd better still keep it shut. Well, then I really let him have it. I said he could be damn well grateful and he'd better lay off that tough talk, so he took the other tack and got all old palsy. He said this dame was dynamite, so please keep quiet, and he'd give me some free shares of some Moose Pasture stock he was promoting.

"Well, when I saw in the paper that Beattie had been murdered, I was pretty scared—I want no part of that stuff. So when I saw that this nephew had murdered him, I was a pretty relieved boy."

"I guess you were," Sidney said. "And now, if you'll give me a rundown on Gadwell, I'll go away and leave you alone. But don't tell him I was asking, if you don't mind."

"Don't worry—I won't," Mayhew said. "What do you want to know?"

"All I can find out about Gadwell—business connections and all that. Love life, et cetera," Sidney said.

"Well, in business, Howie is a sort of minor wheel," Mayhew said. "He owns pieces of things. Radio stations, a commercial film company, a night club. He started out as a phony stock promoter. He operated a boiler room—you know, a room where about twenty salesmen sit phoning to suckers all over the continent, pushing these mining stocks. He's been in trouble with the SEC in the States, and with the Stock Exchange and the Ontario Government securities people here. I haven't met him for years—except that once —but I've sort of followed his career."

"What about women?" Sidney asked.

"Gosh, I haven't got all night," Mayhew said. "His women are innumerable. He's been married about four times, but after his last divorce I think he learned his lesson. He likes girls. And he has this approach, you know; with his studio making TV commercials and all, they say any girl can get a bit to play if she approaches High Grade Howie the right way—like without her clothes. One of his earlier wives was Sharon Willison, the TV singer."

"Did you recognize the girl he was with at Mac's Garage?"

"No, never saw her, but she was quite a dish," Mayhew said. He was a very different man from the superior being who had first welcomed Sidney Grant in the morning, and seemed only too pleased to appease his interrogator in any way he could.

During the days that followed, Sidney Grant did a lot more checking on Howard Gadwell, but he avoided the direct approach. He went back to Mrs. Ledley, who did not know Gadwell, but met her husband, who did. From Mr. Ledley he obtained the names of mining people who knew Gadwell and disliked him—it was a goodly list—and whenever he had a spare minute, he called on them and asked the same question: Who was Howard Gadwell keeping company with at the mining convention last May?

Some of the men were evasive, and some didn't know, but in due course Sidney came upon a mining engineer with an office on Bay Street who knew and was willing to tell. The engineer's name was Val Eckhardt, and he was a big man with a bald dome and a craglike jaw.

"Sure I know who High Grade Howie's girl friend was," Eckhardt said. "She was the wife of a fellow I know. A geologist from the Kansas School of Mines, and a very nice guy. He brought his wife down to Toronto from northern Quebec for the convention, and she promptly fell for Gadwell."

"And the name?" Sidney said.

"The guy's name is Wicklow, Tex Wicklow, he's called. I don't know the wife's name. Someone he met in Montreal, I believe."

"Do you know," Sidney asked, "if she was an old flame of Gadwell's, or if this was a sudden blooming of love?"

"I couldn't be sure, but I've got an idea they'd met before, and she just decided that Gadwell was the playmate she needed for this week in Toronto."

"Well, that would explain some things," Sidney said. "So Wicklow was busy around this convention, and his wife would be able to slip away to a motel for a few hours of bliss with Gadwell."

"Why slip away?" Eckhardt said. "She had a nice suite all to herself at the hotel."

"All to herself?"

"Sure. You see, the first night of this convention there was a warm-up cocktail party, and around eleven Brother Gadwell scooped up six or eight guests and took them for dinner to the Rathskeller, just across Front Street from the hotel. I wasn't in on the party, but I saw it—I was at a nearby table. Madame Wicklow was fairly high and throwing herself all over Gadwell, while poor Tex tried to ignore it and got quietly loaded. On the way back Tex fell behind the main party, and managed to stagger in front of a fastmoving cab. They rushed him to St. Michael's Hospital unconscious, with a suspected skull fracture, and he spent the next ten days being looked after by nuns, just as a contrast to his normal female companionship. Well, his good lady didn't even break stride. She just whooped it up for the rest of the week with High Grade Howie, who was looking pretty prosperous at the time."

"Then there was absolutely no need for them to slip away anywhere else?"

"No—they had a very cozy setup," Eckhardt said.

Eckhardt thought that Wicklow was working at a drill site in far northern Quebec and managed to confirm the fact by means of a telephone call. "They push the drills down into the hard rock, fifteen hundred, two thousand feet," Eckhardt said. "The shaft of the drill is made of hollow pipes, and when they drill a section, they pull up the pipe and take out the hard rock core. Wicklow's job is to examine the drill cores and figure the mineral content. He wouldn't have his wife with him up there—they stake their wives out in Rouyn or Amos, or even Montreal or Toronto."

Getting in touch with Wicklow proved to be difficult. His drill site had two-way radio connections with the air base at Senneterre, Quebec, but mails were slow and irregular. Ken Ledley, when the problem was put to him, suggested that Sidney fly up and interview Wicklow on the spot.

"A nice idea," Sidney said. "But this little investigation is my own. Nobody is paying me, and I just can't afford the time, let alone the money."

"Well, you seem to have some bug in your head about this," Ledley said. "And I'm kind of curious about why somebody would steal my wife's driver's license. I'll bet I can fix it to fly you up there at the company's expense—not my company, but the owner of the mining property."

"How could you work that?" Sidney asked.

"Oh, hell, there are always legal problems," Ledley said. "You aren't a member of the Quebec bar, but there are bound to be papers that have to be notarized or something of the sort. If you put your fee high enough, they'll jump at it. Just leave it to me."

A couple of days later Sidney was summoned to the office of the Capuchin Mining Company, where he was asked to take certain papers to the company's drill site near the shores of James Bay and make some arrangements with the boss of the site. Mr. Ledley had worked well. Sidney could leave on a Friday and return on Sunday, and he would receive a fee of five hundred dollars as well as his traveling expenses.

Miss Semple was terribly worried about his flying off into the wilds among a lot of tough mining men and wanted him to get a complete survival kit, a revolver and a battery-operated electric blanket. Sidney compromised by getting a fur hat with ear flaps and a pair of fleece-lined fur mitts.

He moved off from Malton in a TCA Viscount on the milk run to North Bay, Earlton, Rouyn-Noranda and Val d'Or-Bour-lamaque, where, on expert advice, he purchased half a dozen forty-ounce bottles from the Quebec Liquor Commission and went on by taxi over a well-swept road to Senneterre.

It was all very new and wonderful to the city-bred Sidney. The air terminal at Senneterre was set beside a snow-covered frozen lake. It was crowded with all sorts of bush types—prospectors, drillmen, Indians, geologists and engineers—and bush planes of many types were loading up with strange cargoes and winging off into the wilderness.

Sidney embarked in a DeHavilland Beaver, flown by a veteran pilot about nineteen years old, and loaded with machine parts, sleigh dogs and mining men. He was lucky enough to sit beside the pilot and get a superb view of the countryside, which consisted of spruce forest and small lakes stretching off to a far horizon. Fights broke out among the dogs in the rear, and some of the men were airsick.

"Don't worry," the pilot said. "When the men fight and the dogs get airsick, you've got *real* trouble."

They landed on an airstrip bulldozed out of the solid spruce forest, and Sidney finished his strange journey in a caterpillar snowmobile.

He was accommodated, along with the young pilot, in the camp's executive suite, a prefabricated hut with eight bunks, a fat Quebec heater, a two-way radio and a large collection of pinups, records, paperbacks, playing cards, chessmen and cribbage boards. He was given a royal welcome, partly because of the refreshments he had brought.

He had his meals in a cook shack where the drillmen, who spoke a French that was incomprehensible to Sidney, wolfed vast quantities of food amid an obbligato of weird ingestion noises. He had pie for breakfast and heard learned arguments about the specific gravity of the crust. He heard many tall tales of the north, including one about a sample of the cook's pie crust being sent to the assay office by mistake and causing the Capuchin stock to shoot up forty cents a share. The rumor got out that a natural substitute for Vinyl floor covering had been discovered. He heard about a diamond drill head breaking off far underground and being drawn fifteen hundred feet to the surface by means of a poultice which contained over two hundred pounds of mustard. He sang songs and drank whisky far into the night with the engineers, in a flimsy shack in the remote bush, with no other human habitation between him and the North Pole.

He completed his legal business with considerable efficiency, and he met Tex Wicklow, a somewhat disenchanted geologist. At first Wicklow got the idea that Sidney was representing his erring wife, and the geologist swore that he wouldn't pay her a cent, not even on a court order, but Sidney convinced him that all he wanted was to locate the lady.

"Well, good luck to you, boy," Wicklow said. "And when you find her, keep her. She left me last September and took everything I owned that wasn't screwed to the walls. All she left really was bills, and plenty of them."

Her maiden name, Wicklow said, was Swann, and she had come originally from Saskatoon. Her mother, a widow who had remarried, still lived in Saskatoon, but Janice Wicklow had not communicated with her for years. Wicklow had met her during a wild furlough in Montreal and had married her on impulse.

"I was bushed," he admitted. "All marriages of guys coming out of the bush ought to be purely provisional for six months. I keep marrying the damnedest women every time I get back to civilization."

Janice had indeed known Gadwell before her marriage and had welcomed him as a long-lost lover when they met in Toronto. "High Grade Howie was in the chips," Wicklow explained. "Money has a fatal attraction for that gal, and this guy Gadwell is quite a hand with the wenches."

Wicklow had not heard a word from his wife since her departure. He suspected that she had gone to join Gadwell. "But that guy won't be nearly as keen on her when it comes to supporting her," he said.

Sidney asked for a picture of Janice Wicklow, and the geologist was able to produce a large selection from the Gladstone bag under his bunk. Janice had been a model in Montreal, and there were shots of her modeling furs, dresses and lingerie. There were even some of her modeling something invisible, like perfume.

"Mrs. Wicklow doesn't appear to have been a prude," Sidney said.

"No, that was never her problem," Wicklow agreed. "Don't let these hyenas see those artistic poses, or they'll want to pin them up."

Sidney picked out half a dozen shots which Wicklow was happy to let him take, and then the two men rejoined the other inhabitants of the executive suite, who were singing to the accompaniment of a five-string banjo.

On Monday morning, somewhat bemused, but back in Toronto, Sidney laid a selection of model photographs, obtained for the purpose, in front of James Bellwood, the lawyer who had defended Wes Beattie on his theft charge. "Identification parade?" Bellwood said, looking the pictures over carefully. "Well, here you are."

He put his finger on a photograph of Janice Swann Wicklow. "That," he said, "is Mrs. Leduc, the witness who said that Wes Beattie stole her purse."

"Well, I'm blowed," Sidney said. "I lightheartedly agreed with Dr. Milton Heber that I would track her down, but I had no idea how elusive she was going to be."

"And now you've done it. Nice work, Gargoyle," Bellwood said.

"No, I haven't found her. But at least I know who she is," Sidney said. "And I can put Missing Persons on the trail, as well as the Canadian Association of Credit Bureaus, so we should be able to interview her soon. If anybody can find her, the credit boys will. She's as addicted to shopping as Lorelei Lee."

Four

FOR A COUPLE OF DAYS after his northern expedition, Sidney Grant was in a quandary as to how to proceed. He arranged to have a discreet look at Howard Gadwell in a bar and caught another glimpse of him in a restaurant. The direct approach to him promised only a brush-off. Until Mrs. Wicklow could be found there was little point in further investigation of the alleged conspiracy.

However, Wes Beattie's hour of trial was approaching. Shortly he would be brought before an assize court and charged with murder. His counsel would—as things were—enter a plea of insanity, and if the Crown were prepared to accept it, Wes

Beattie would be locked away quietly to inhabit his weird world for the rest of his life.

At length Sidney decided that Wes Beattie's counsel, Mr. Baldwin Ogilvy, Q.C., ought to know about Gadwell and Mrs. Wicklow, so he called him. But Ogilvy was a Member of Parliament and was away in Ottawa, so the next best thing was to inform Wes Beattie's relatives.

By a strange fluke of real estate values, Sidney Grant lived only a block and a half away from the old Beattie house. Rosedale, a charming quarter of the city, had been mainly built up with large, late-Victorian houses. Some of them, in the modern era, had proved too expensive for private ownership, and they had been converted into rooming houses. As a student, Sidney Grant had shared the large attic of such a house with two of his fellows, and when marriage claimed them he stayed on. It was the sort of house that could have been designed by John Betjeman or Mary Petty, and Sidney loved it.

The old Beattie house, a block and a half away, was much the same type of building, but when Sidney, one evening, yanked on the old-fashioned bell pull, he was amazed to see another touch of authenticity: a maid in cap and apron answered the door—a dear little old bird of a woman who could well have peeped from the garret of a Mary Petty house.

She had a large pink angular nose and she talked as one whose adenoids have never been attended to. "Yes sir?" she said nervously.

"Is Mrs. Beattie at home?" Sidney said.

"Oh, no sir, Mrs. Beattie is never A Tome in the evenings," the maid said. "P'raps you might like to write to her and state your business, sir."

"Oh. What time are you expecting her?" Sidney asked.

"Oh, she's here, but she's not A Tome, if you understand what I mean. I mean she never sees visitors that call except in the morning."

"Oh. Well, would you mind giving her my card and telling her it's an urgent matter concerning her grandson?"

"Not a *tall* sir. A *nurgent* matter you said, sir? Concerning Mr. Wes?" She looked most anxious.

"That is correct," Sidney said.

"Oh, well, that's different, sir. Will you come and wait in the hall, please, sir, and I'll just hurry and tell Mrs. Beattie." She scampered away, bearing Sidney's card on a little silver plate.

Sidney stood on the Persian rug in the large entrance hall and examined the glorious curve of a stairway designed to be descended by beautiful women in evening dresses, and silence gathered about him like a fur robe. Presently he heard a quick step on the parquet floor behind him, and he turned to see a man approaching in a somewhat agitated manner.

The man was stoutish but firm, and although evidently in his mid-fifties, there was no gray hair among his neat brown waves. His collar was noticeable for its starched whiteness, and his blue pin-striped suit was a beautiful thing.

"Ah, Mr. Grant?" he said. "Is this anything that can't wait till morning? Couldn't you come and see me at my office?"

"Certainly," Sidney said. "Do you mind telling me who you are?"

"Not at all. Paget is the name. Ralph Paget. You'll find me at Superior Trust. Mrs. Beattie doesn't like to be disturbed in the evening."

"It was actually Mrs. Beattie that I asked to see," Sidney said. "And since I'm downtown all day, I took the liberty of calling in the evening. But in fact I probably ought to give my information to Baldwin Ogilvy, so I'll wait till he gets back from Ottawa."

"This is something concerning the murder charge against Wes?" Paget said. "The whole subject is very painful to Mrs. Beattie, who is rather old. I'll be glad to see you in the morning and pass along anything that Mr. Ogilvy ought to hear."

"Fine. I'll give you a call," Sidney said, and turned toward the door.

But the little maid came fluttering into the hall at that moment and spoke to Paget in a deferential way. "Oh, Mr. Paget," she said, "Mrs. Beattie said she would see Mr. Grant."

Paget looked irritated. "I don't think there's any need, really," he said.

"Oh, but I think she wants…" the maid began.

Paget shook his head and exhaled in a resigned manner. "Very well. Won't you come in, Mr. Grant?" he said.

Sidney was ushered into a drawing room which astonished him. Every piece of furniture or fitting in it was either modern or Georgian, yet the sum total conveyed the idea of late Victorianism, and the three women sitting in upright chairs and sipping coffee heightened the effect.

"Ah, Mrs. Beattie, this is Mr. Grant," Paget said. "Mrs. Beattie, Miss Claudia Beattie and my wife. Would you care for a glass of brandy?"

When Sidney had found a chair, and had been furnished with a fine, ancient brandy, Mrs. Beattie turned her long, thin, aristocratic face toward him. She appeared to be past eighty, but sat up very straight in her chair and talked in a high, well-bred voice.

"You have, I believe, some information concerning my grandson?" she said.

"Uh, yes," Sidney said. "You see, I heard that your grandson suffers from delusions. He has a story about being persecuted by a mysterious gang of criminals."

"That is true," the old lady said. "I'm afraid that poor Wes was always something of a romancer, but this tendency increased greatly following —well, as a result of some trouble he had in the spring."

"To be specific," Sidney said, "he claimed that last spring he was framed by these crooks and sent to jail on a theft charge. He claimed that the woman witness who said he stole her handbag had—in a valuable phrase of his own coining— vanished into thin air."

"Yes, he did," Mrs. Beattie said. "He tried to get her name and address from the police, but they refused to furnish the information, because they did not wish her to be persecuted. We quite understood, and we were no more desirous than she of having any further embarrassment over the business."

"He also claimed that his Uncle Edgar was searching for this woman witness at the time he was killed, and that, when he got on her trail, a man phoned him and told him to lay off."

"I didn't know that," Mrs. Beattie said. "But it would be typical of Wes."

"Well, Mrs. Beattie, I became curious about it and did a little investigation. I discovered very definitely that Edgar *was* trying to locate the woman, that she *has* vanished into thin air, that she gave a false name in court and that it is extremely probable that a man *did* call and warn Edgar to lay off."

"*Really!*" Mrs. Beattie said.

"In other words, there are points in this fanciful tale of your grandson's which aren't so fanciful after all."

"That is most interesting," Mrs. Beattie said. "But, Mr. Grant, does this in any way affect the main issue? I mean, does it alter the fact that poor Wes murdered my poor son Edgar? Or, for that matter, does it *really* indicate that he did not steal this woman's purse?"

"Well, to take the second point first," Sidney said, "this woman used a stolen driver's license to rent a car and a motel unit. Both the car and the unit were given up on the same day. She was with a man who was not her husband. I can find no logical reason why they should do what they did. I mean they took elaborate precautions for concealing an illicit affair, when in fact it was unnecessary. That suggests that perhaps there is something in Wes's frame-up story."

"What possible motive could they have for framing a wretched bank clerk?" Paget demanded testily.

"I don't know," Sidney said. "But it seems possible that they did. Now, if Mr. Ogilvy can show that there *was* some sort of conspiracy on foot, he might cast real doubt on Wes's guilt in the murder."

"Absolute nonsense!" Paget said. "The boy's fingerprints were found on the telephone in Edgar's apartment. By his own admission, corroborated by the housekeeper, he had never visited that apartment since his trouble in the spring. And, in

case there is any doubt about the telephone, the housekeeper
has absolutely identified it as the instrument which has been in
the apartment for twenty-five years at least."

"She can identify it?" Sidney said.

"Yes. Edgar painted the hall three times during that
period, and there are paint splotches from each operation
on the telephone. Furthermore, someone once scratched a
telephone number on the Bakelite with some sharp instrument—the point of a pair of compasses, I believe. The Crown
has gone into it very thoroughly because of Wes's ridiculous
claim that his fingerprints were transplanted. Now, in the
light of all that, do you really think there is reasonable doubt
of his guilt?"

"I'm not the jury," Sidney said. "But I felt that this information might suggest some line of action to Mr. Ogilvy."

Sidney was aware of the close scrutiny of the three women,
and he shifted uneasily and looked at them in turn.

Claudia Beattie was fiftyish, with large feet and a large,
porous nose, which had been powdered with extreme care-
lessness. All of her attempts at make-up seemed amateurish,
like secret experiments with cosmetics by a teen-age girl in a
convent school. Her hands were large and coarse, and her face
was long and sad, but there were hints of character about it.

Her sister, Mrs. Paget, was smaller, and smart. There was
nothing amateurish about her dress or make-up. As she scruti-
nized the visitor, her lips were pressed into a thin line.

"So you don't take much stock in the conspiracy theory?"
Sidney said.

"None at all," Paget said. "Of course, I was perfectly aware
that Edgar was looking for this woman, and I knew about the
man calling."

"You *were?*" Claudia said, turning her equine features
toward him.

"Certainly he was," Mrs. Paget said. "Edgar told him all
about it."

"*Really?*" Mrs. Beattie said. "He never said anything to *me.*"

Everyone stared at Ralph Paget, and he began to look a trifle flustered. "There was no need," he said. "I told Marcia at the time, and we debated whether we should say anything, but we came to the conclusion that it would only stir up a lot of unnecessary scandal."

"I really don't know what you mean, Ralph," Mrs.Beattie said.

"Well, damn it, it was all very simple," he replied. "I mean to say, Edgar asked me to have a new will drafted for him. We held his will at the company, you know. Under the old will, the bulk of his estate went into a trust to provide for Florence Churcher, the housekeeper. She had a life interest in it, and then the trust fund was to be divided between Wes and June, who also inherited the small residue of the estate. June, Mr. Grant, is Wes's sister.

"Well, of course, during the past few years Edgar has had tremendous luck gambling in the mining market, and that altered the whole picture. Instead of being a few thousand dollars, the residue of the estate became worth close to two hundred thousand, after the trust for the housekeeper had been set up. Edgar had no intention of putting so much money in the hands of young Wes, after the theft business. Instead, he wanted to set up life trusts for Claudia and the housekeeper, with everything reverting to June eventually. And June would get an immediate bequest of nearly one hundred thousand."

"And nothing, of course, for his beloved sister Marcia," Mrs. Paget said with an acid smile. "Not even his second-best bed."

The glance of disapproval which her mother turned on her was all but imperceptible.

"But Ralph, stop beating about the bush," Claudia said. "What has all this got to do with Edgar looking for that woman?"

"I'm *coming* to that, for heaven's sake," Paget said. "At any rate, Edgar was a blunt fellow and forthright by nature. He wanted Wes to know what he was doing, and why. So last August, when you were all at the lake, Edgar came around here one evening by arrangement and read both wills—the one in force and the draft of the new one—to Wes, in my presence.

"He said, 'Wes, you knew about this other will, and I don't want to change it without telling you. I don't want you to retain any false hopes, in fact.' Well, Wes listened calmly enough, but then he put on a sort of tantrum. He said he didn't care *what* Edgar did with his money; he could leave it all to a home for sick cats, for all he cared, but he added that he was glad his sister would get something. Then he got tearful and said he wouldn't object to anything at all that Edgar did, if only he would do one last thing for him—namely, search out this woman witness and talk to her. He said that would soon prove whether he was a sneak thief or not. It was a very good stall, if you know Edgar. It appealed to his sporting instincts. So he said all right, he would hunt up the witness and talk to her, and if Wes was right he wouldn't change his will. So he left the whole matter in abeyance."

"And do you mean he couldn't find the witness?" Claudia said.

"No. He wisely refrained from telling Wes anything about this search. But he came to me. He said this was a damn funny thing—the woman couldn't be found in Sudbury at all. She had obviously given a false name in court. It *did* seem a bit suspicious, until you remembered that she had been staying at this motel. Obviously she was under a false name at the motel and used the same name in court."

"Possibly committing perjury and certainly risking exposure," Sidney said.

"Quite. It did seem odd. Then Edgar thought he had found the woman. There had been some jiggery-pokery with her driver's license, but she was off on a motor tour of Europe with her husband, so Edgar said he would wait until she came back and would question her privately. He refused to tell me who she was. But you know what a bull Edgar was when he went after anything. Instead of simply waiting, he started trying to track down this woman's lover, and the lover got to hear of it. Edgar *told* me that the man called him."

"And warned him to lay off?" Sidney suggested.

"No, of course not. He simply called Edgar and said he'd heard Edgar was looking for him. He asked what Edgar was after. And Edgar told him. Well, the man said he had gone to the Midtown Motel with a woman who was not his wife. They had booked in under another name. This man claimed he was looking out of the motel window and saw Wes in the very act of stealing the handbag, and he saw the parking lot attendant seize him. So he sent the woman out to identify her bag and get it back. Unfortunately, the motel people insisted on having Wes arrested and charged. He and his lady friend cleared out right away because all the stir had frightened them. *He* had thought that was the end of it, but next day he learned that this stupid woman had actually gone into court and given evidence. She was a little upset, and she thought she *had* to. She hadn't realized that she could simply vanish. But the man was insistent that he, personally, had witnessed the actual theft, and dragging the whole matter up again and causing all sorts of marital discord wasn't going to do Wes any good at all. So, he suggested that Edgar should..."

"Lay off," Sidney said.

"Well, yes, if you want to put it that way."

"And did Edgar appear to be satisfied with that answer? Did the man give his name?" Sidney asked.

"No, the man refused to give his name, but Edgar was perfectly satisfied," Paget said. "After all, the explanation made complete sense."

"Not quite," Sidney said. "The lady who was touring Europe with her husband is back. I have talked to her. She was not the woman witness. Her driver's license had been stolen and doctored to provide false identification for the woman witness—who has vanished without a trace."

"I find it odd," Mrs. Beattie said, "that you did not disclose these facts before."

"I thought about it very carefully," Paget said. "But it was so patently obvious that Wes was guilty that I couldn't see dragging in this sordid little intrigue for the papers to make a sensation of. And since the police had handed Wes over to the psychiatrists, and the psychiatrists assured us that Wes had a perfect insanity defense, it would simply become an irrelevant red herring."

"Is a red herring ever relevant, I wonder?" Sidney said. "This one might be."

Claudia had been sitting staring at Paget, and suddenly she burst forth emotionally. "Do you think Edgar would have given up before he *met* that man, *and* the woman, face to face?" she said. "If you do, you didn't know Edgar! He was the most pig-headed man that ever walked. He wouldn't let *anyone* stall him off."

"Well, Claudia, my dear, you are entitled to your opinion, but on this occasion he talked very reasonably, and I think he planned to let the matter drop."

"And did he alter his will?" she said. "Did he do *that?* He promised Wes he would find the woman first."

"Well, no, he hadn't actually altered his will at the time of his death," Paget said.

"Too bad, eh, Claudia?" Marcia Paget said, quietly enough that Mrs. Beattie did not hear.

"Then what becomes of Wes's portion that he can't inherit?" Sidney asked.

"That," Paget said with great asperity, "would scarcely classify as being any of your business, Mr. Grant. I really do not see why we have discussed all these private family matters in your presence. And now, unless there is something else?"

"I'll answer your question, Mr. Grant," Claudia said. "If either June or Wes predeceased Edgar, or were unable for any other reason to inherit, his or her share was to be divided equally between Edgar's sisters—Marcia and me. So if you want to make Marcia the murderer, there's your motive. She'll get fifty or seventy-five thousand dollars because the will wasn't changed." Claudia Beattie giggled horsily and rather affectedly.

"Your little joke is not in the best of taste, Claudia," Mrs. Beattie said. "Actually, since you have heard so much of our private business, Mr. Grant, you may as well know that Edgar and Marcia were not always on the best of terms. He felt that Marcia was well provided for, and therefore he wished to give Claudia a little additional security. Now, specifically, what have you to suggest?"

Sidney opened his mouth to speak, meaning to divulge the names of Howard Gadwell and Janice Swann Wicklow as the Midtown Motel lovers. But as he glanced at the four faces in the room, another thought struck him, and for a moment he stammered ineffectually.

"Well, just this," he said at last. "I believe that, with a little research, I could find the names of those two people—the man who called Edgar and the woman who was with him. I think we might show that there was something fishy about the motel business. Then Mr. Ogilvy might check through the other statements made by Wes and see if *they* could be substantiated. It might alter the whole line of his defense."

"I think it unlikely, Mr. Grant," Mrs. Beattie said. "Unless poor Wes pleads insanity, the Crown will concentrate, with ruthless logic, on the presence of those fingerprints and will get a verdict of guilty. All we would achieve would be the introduction of a scandalous element which would please the evening papers immensely. However, my son-in-law will convey this information to Mr. Baldwin Ogilvy, and any decision will be made by him. And we are all very grateful for your kind thought. Betty will let you out."

To Sidney's sensitive ear, this sounded like a hint that he should leave, so he arose and went to the hall, where he had left his coat and hat on a high-backed chair. But there was no Betty to let him out, and Ralph Paget appeared and saw him off the premises. His manner was chilly.

As Sidney proceeded along the street, a little dejected at the outcome of his visit, a strange feeling came over him, and he glanced nervously over his shoulder. Then he stalked on again angrily. The delusion that one is being followed, he decided, is the first step toward the full-scale heebie-jeebies. However, the feeling persisted, and he turned around and had a good look.

There was, indeed, a female figure some distance behind him, but she did not look at all sinister.

However, when he reached his own house, he stepped inside the iron gate and waited in the shadows, and presently he recognized his pursuer as Betty, the maid. She was hurrying along and looking up anxiously at each house. At Sidney's house she paused and peered into the darkness, but did not see him.

"Are you, by any chance, looking for me?" Sidney said quietly.

The maid jumped back and screamed at the shock of finding her quarry only four feet away, and then suddenly she ran back in the direction from which she had come. Sidney called after her, but she kept on going. He stood thinking for a moment, then shrugged and went up to bed.

On the Friday following he received a letter on the letterhead of the Superior Trust Company (office of the vice-president and secretary). It said:

> Dear Sir:
>
> Your interesting suggestions with reference to the defense of my wife's nephew have been given due consideration, but the decision is not to alter the plan already adopted.
>
> Mr. Baldwin Ogilvy, Q.C., states that it is a prime objective of the defense to exclude any reference to the previous criminal record of an accused person except as it may come out in the expert evidence of psychiatrists in establishing the history of delusions.
>
> An attempt to prove that there were suspicious circumstances in the matter of the theft conviction would actually weaken the delusion theory, which is the mainstay of the present defense plan.
>
> We, the family of the accused, are most grateful for your unsolicited interest in the case, and we feel that you are entitled to some compensation for any

expenses you have incurred. We therefore enclose
a check for five hundred dollars ($500.00) on the
understanding that you will take no further action
in the case and will regard what has taken place as
completely confidential.

Yours faithfully

The signature was that of the pin-striped uncle, but the
style suggested the influence of the grandmother.

"Miss Semple," Sidney called out, "is this office badly in
need of five hundred smackers?"

"I should say it is," Miss Semple replied, appearing in the
doorway of the private office.

"That's what I was afraid of," he said. "Well, quickly, before
I weaken, grab your notebook and take a letter. To Ralph L.
Fuss-Paget at the Sacred Trust Company or something; get it off
the letterhead. Here goes. Dear Sir, I am most grateful to you
for sending me an unsolicited check for five hundred dollars,
bracket, repeat sum in figures, close bracket, period. Paragraph.
I had no intention of intruding in matters which were not my
concern, but having by chance—that's a lie for you—having
by chance come across information concerning Mr. Wesley M.
Beattie, I felt it my duty as an officer of the court to place the
information in the hands of Mr. Beattie's counsel. Paragraph.
Owing to Mr. Ogilvy's absence in Ottawa, and to the fact that
the case will come up shortly, I took the information direct to
the family of the accused. There is, of course, no charge for this
service, and I shall feel free to disclose the information I have
obtained in any manner I may see fit. Yours faithfully. How's
that, Georgie?"

"Splendid," she said. "I didn't like the tone of Mr. Paget's
letter at all. And I feel sure you are right to tell him what to do
with his money—badly as we need it."

Which brought the case of Wes Beattie and his weird
world to an end, Sidney decided, and he thereupon put the
whole thing out of his mind and went off to Lake Simcoe

for the weekend to fish through the ice with some suitable companions.

But he still couldn't entirely kill the desire to interview Mrs. Janice Swann Wicklow and find out what had impelled her to give evidence in the police court under a false name.

Five

IN THE YEAR 1908, or some fifty-odd years before Wes
Beattie was caught with the goods on him, a crocodile of
wretched girls in hideous skirts and middies filed out of an
orphanage at Southsea, on the south coast of England, each
girl carrying a large hamper, and proceeded to a line of horse-
drawn four-wheelers which awaited them. Some hours later a
tender fed the girls into the maw of the Cunard liner *Lobelia*,
where they were herded to bunks in the steerage for nine days
of misery and seasickness.

From this traumatic experience Betty Martin, one of the
orphan band, emerged at a wharf in Montreal, frightened,

weeping and homesick for the orphanage which was the only home she had ever known. Ahead of her lay she knew not what. Red Indians, perhaps, with scalping knives. Grizzly bears and timber wolves.

Betty Martin was somehow conducted to Bonaventure Station and deposited in a colonist car which, ten hours later, debouched her on the platform of the old Union Station in Toronto, where the matron in charge of the little group handed her over to a heavy-set man with impressive whiskers.

The heavy-set man collected her box and led her to a carriage, trying to reassure her that all would be well, but poor Betty cried and cried until the man helped her up to sit beside him on the driver's seat. Shortly afterward they were proceeding at a spanking trot up Jarvis Street with its great, shady horse-chestnut trees and its fine mansions, and Betty began to feel a little happier about coming to the wilds of Canada.

At last she was deposited at the rear entrance to the residence of young Mrs. Charles Beattie, where she curtsied to the cook and was conducted to a garret room all of her own.

At first Betty could not believe her good fortune, being barely fourteen at the time and unskilled in the ways of the world, and she was so happy to have found a good situation that she buckled right down to work in order to give satisfaction to her new mistress, who was a regular queen of a lady, with a cook, a parlormaid, two housemaids and a man who doubled as gardener and coachman.

Betty was the junior among the servants, but with the years her status rose, owing to the departure, one by one, of all the others. In later years a Latvian cook joined the establishment, but she was a daily woman, which, in Betty's opinion, did not count.

But in all those years Betty never lost her awe of Mrs. Beattie, who was so clever and beautiful and seemed to know even what a body was thinking; and, just as she had been instructed at the orphanage, Betty never put her own opinion against that of her superiors.

For that reason Betty was in a frightful dither on the Sunday morning following Sidney Grant's visit to the Beattie house, because she had told Mrs. Beattie a lie, and she was planning to break the Rules. She had told Mrs. Beattie that she felt a head cold coming on and didn't feel she should go to church for fear she might give it to others. Mrs. Beattie accepted the story with her customary calm—secretly suspecting that there was some scrumptious television program which Betty intended to watch, and she let Betty help her with her dressing, regardless of possible microbes or viruses. Mrs. Beattie, someone had once said, didn't really believe that microbes would move from a servant to a member of the upper class.

And then, as soon as Mr. and Mrs. Paget and Miss Claudia and Mrs. Beattie had been bundled into the Jag and were on their way to the cathedral, Betty embarked on a very bold course indeed. She hurried back to her mistress's bedroom, seized the pearl-gray telephone with trembling hands and dialed a number. Then she stood waiting, anxiously, shaking her free right hand impatiently. Finally a great relief came over her features and she spoke.

"Oh, Miss June, Miss June," she said, "I'm so glad I got you before you went out, Miss June. I've been trying to get you for ages—in bed? You weren't up, Miss June? Oh, dear me, I *am* sorry, Miss June. Oh dear, you just take some aspirins and a nice cup of tea and you'll soon be right as rain. Miss June, they've been having terrible rows, oh, awful—no, not shouting at each other, that's not their way, Miss June, and you know it. Just speaking sharp and all upset, and it's about Mr. Wes. Miss June, you were always a one for rows with your aunties. I really said Miss June should be here....Well, this young lawyer came, Mr. Sidney Grant his name is, and he knows something about Mr. Wes. He thinks maybe Mr. Wes didn't steal that lady's purse after all, and he thought that might help with the murder charge. He wanted to tell Mr. Ogilvy, Mr. Wes's lawyer, but Mr. Paget knew about all these things only he never told anyone except Miss Marcia, and your grandmother was ever so

cross with him, and Miss Marcia took his side and of course
Miss Claudia took the other side, and they told Mr. Grant that
they would tell Mr. Ogilvy all about these things but they never
did. Your grandmother said it would serve no useful purpose,
so Mr. Paget wrote a letter to Mr. Grant that said one thing
and meant another. He made it look as if he'd told Mr. Ogilvy,
but he didn't really though he didn't actually tell a fib. Very
proud of himself he was, and your grandmother said it would
do nicely, but Miss Claudia said it was the worst kind of lying
because it was so sneaky and Miss Marcia called her a silly
old B., right in front of your grandmother. She used the word
for lady dog, Miss June. Well, they said that Mr. Wes is safe—
they will put him in a lunatic asylum and they won't hang
him—so why stir up a lot of trouble in the newspapers, and
Miss Claudia said really who cared what became of poor Mr.
Wes so long as the B. family name wasn't dragged through the
mud? And then they *really* set about her, Miss June. Oh, Miss
June, did you ever see those bullfighting pictures at the cinema
where gentlemen on horses stick things in the poor bull and at
the end the battledore comes along and kills it? Yes, Miss June,
mattledore, that's the word…oh, pardon, matador. Anyway, Mr.
Paget and Miss Marcia went at her and *at* her, and finally your
grandmother came in like the—like that head bullfighter and
she said: 'Claudia, your remark was both unkind and uncalled
for and was prompted solely by a desire to create trouble, of
which we have already had more than enough. The welfare of
Wes is the only thought in any of our minds.' And Miss Claudia
started to sniffle the way she does, and she burst out sobbing
'Boo hoo hoo hoo hoo' and dashed up to her room and spent the
entire evening taking her Girl Guide medals out of their frame
and cleaning them.…Miss June, it's naughty of you to laugh
like that.…Well, Miss June, I thought they shouldn't ought
to have sent poor Mr. Grant away like that, so I followed him
home, but he took me for a cutpurse and leapt out at me— it
gave me such a start. Miss June, he really *did* jump out, and I
ran as if the Old Gentleman himself were after me, and then I

didn't know what to do. Well, I said, Miss *June* should be here, *she* would know what to do. Oh, Miss June, I always said you were just like a *man,* the way you can do things....Oh, no, no, no, Miss June. I did *not* mean that. It isn't the fishing season yet, Miss June, but you know very well you're very pretty and *romantic.* Just you wait, and Mr. Right will come along one of these days....Oh, Miss June, you must *not* say that—it's naughty. Mr. Wrong is *not* more fun than Mr. Right...Well, Miss June, if Mr. Grant can help my Mr. Wes, and he's your own baby brother, well, I think we ought to find out everything, and the only way is for you to go and see him. See Mr. Grant. Oh, please, *please* go and see him, Miss June. Mr. Sidney Grant...what's he like? Well, very handsome. Not like movie actors, but handsome in a nice, *wholesome* way. No, he is *not* ugly...Well, quite tall, taller than me...oh, Miss June, he is *so* over five feet, a lot more. Five foot six at *least.* Please, please, Miss June, promise me you'll go and see him? Oh, Miss June, Miss June, I *knew* you would, I knew it, I knew it! I'm so happy, Miss June, but now I must fairly dash and get the beds made."

Whereupon Betty Martin drew breath and hung up the telephone.

❀ ❀ ❀

Miss Semple's office was divided in two by a mahogany railing, a relic of a bygone era. Beyond the railing, next to the outer door, stood a row of plain chairs, which were often occupied by a sorry collection of prospective clients who sat shifting uneasily and watching in wonder as Miss Semple's fingers flew over the typewriter keys.

Miss Semple ruled the waiting clients with the authority of a headmistress, and often, when a client had departed, she seized a spray gun and sweetened the air with pine tar scent. Some of Sidney Grant's clients went without bathing except at such times as they were herded into showers at the Don Jail or the Mercer Reformatory. Some of the female clients were so drenched with

California Poppy or Soir de Paris that their presence was felt long after their departure. Usually there was, among the waiting ones, a worried parent with a truculent teenage boy.

When Sidney Grant arrived at his office on Monday morning, he let himself in by the private entrance and peeped out nervously at the waiting ones on the row of chairs. Instantly his eyebrows shot up, and he pressed the buzzer for Miss Semple. "Things are looking up," he said. "Beaver coats, yet! Don't tell me she's up for dope pushing or hustling?"

"No sir," Miss Semple said, a trifle stuffily. "The young woman who has so *obviously* aroused your interest is Miss June Beattie, who wishes to see you about a matter which she doesn't care to discuss with *me*."

"The hoyden!" Sidney said. "Georgie, do you realize who she is?"

"Certainly," Miss Semple said. "Shall I send her in?"

Sidney grinned wickedly and nodded, and a moment later June Beattie entered his private office with casual grace, glanced about her in calm appraisal and said, "Hi!"

"Hi," Sidney replied politely. "Won't you sit down?"

She sat down, pulled a package of cigarettes from her pocket and lit up.

"So you are Mr. Grant," she said.

"I am. And what can I do for you?"

"Blowed if I know quite," she said. "I have this grand-mother, and she has a slave. She found some loophole in the Emancipation Act of 1832 which allows you to keep any slave you catch coming out of an orphanage on the first bounce. This Betty—the slave—managed to smuggle a message out of Granny's moated castle in Rosedale in a bundle of laundry. The message, when decoded, said to go and see a tall, dark, hand-some lawyer called Sidney Grant. Betty followed you home herself, but you leapt out at her, knocked the knife out of her hand and beat her to within an inch of her life. She only just escaped by feigning madness."

"That is substantially correct," Sidney said solemnly.

"Betty also tells me you know something to the advantage of my poor idiot of a brother. No one in the family has told me anything about the case. Will you please explain just what this is all about?"

"Very well," Sidney said. "You probably know that your brother has a pretty good insanity defense, based on certain delusions he suffers from. You've heard about the mystery gang that framed him on a theft charge?"

"Yes, I've heard bits and pieces. I'm afraid it sounds like a typical Wes story."

"Fine. Now amongst all the feverish nonsense, Wes kept insisting on one concrete point, namely, that the woman who claimed he stole her purse had disappeared. He further claimed that Uncle Edgar had been trying to locate the woman, and that a man called Edgar up and warned him to lay off. Nobody has been taking any stock in this yarn. But then I found that your Uncle Ralph *knew* that Edgar had been searching for the woman and also knew that a man *did* call Edgar, but didn't think it was worth while telling anyone."

"That would be my Uncle Ralph," the girl said. "Uncle Ralph always knows best."

"Does he indeed? Well, he and your aunts and grandmother were so hostile when I went to see them that I decided, rightly or wrongly, not to tell them everything I know. The fact is I know the names of the two people who were at the Midtown Motel when Wes was arrested. And when you consider their behavior, it just doesn't add up. If that deal wasn't fishy, neither is the Restigouche River."

"And where does this lead us?" she asked.

"It establishes the fact that there are two people who *could* be conspirators. It points out that several statements of your brother's which were regarded—by psychiatrists and others— as sheer fantasy, are in fact true. So it struck me that before Baldwin Ogilvy agrees to locking his client away in the funny farm, he might like to investigate the whole bang shoot and see if there is a better line of defense."

"Look, Mr. Grant," she said. "Let's face it. Wes is a poor fish. It isn't his fault. That awful old woman, my grandmother, has dominated him to the point where he is a spineless dreamer. Last spring I inherited a little money from my grandfather's estate and immediately pushed off on a world tour. I was in France when I learned that that poor sweet idiot Wes had been sent to jail. I phoned home and offered to catch the next plane, but it was all over. So I carried on with my tour, and when I was in New Guinea I got this *awful* news about Uncle Edgar.

"Now, so far as I'm concerned, Wes is finished. The kindest thing to do would be to put him quietly to sleep. What's the point of living on and on without freedom? And he'd never be really free even if they turned him loose. So what is the point, really, in worrying about his defense?"

"Miss Beattie," Sidney said, "you are not the judge nor the jury. It isn't for you to decide the guilt or pass the sentence. Everyone charged with a crime is entitled to the best defense. It's up to the Crown to prove him guilty beyond reasonable doubt, and until that moment he is presumed to be innocent. My feeling is that the damning evidence of those fingerprints should be ignored for the time being—because it tends to hypnotize everyone— and every statement Wes made should be checked out and proved false, *if possible*—or true. I think that the activities of these people who sent Wes up for theft should be investigated to see if they had any motive for framing him. The kid is entitled to the full treatment before he's locked away.

"Look what happened before. Mr. Paget insisted on the case being rushed through in order to hush it up and save your grandmother embarrassment. So Wes was convicted and given two months. With a proper defense, there isn't a chance in this world that he would have been convicted. The case would have been remanded, and two weeks later there would have been no witness. Do you want that to happen again?"

"No," she said. "You mean that that officious old woman Ralph Paget caused all this trouble by taking charge?"

"Don't quote me, but he did," Sidney said. "But he won't push Baldwin Ogilvy around. Ogilvy will take the best line of defense he can see, regardless of consequences. So obviously he feels he's on the best thing with the insanity defense."

"Wait a minute," she said. "This dear old Betty was yattering at me on Sunday morning when I was hung over to the eyeballs, but she said something..."

"Yes?"

"I can't remember exactly what. But something like this: Uncle Ralph and Gran decided not to pass along to Ogilvy what you told them, but Uncle Ralph wrote you a weasel-wordy letter intimating that he had. Does that make sense?"

Sidney pressed the buzzer. "Miss Semple," he said, when his secretary appeared, "get the story from those prospective clients and make appointments for them, will you? And will you bring me the letter from Ralph Paget, please?"

A cursory glance at Paget's letter showed that nowhere had he stated that he had told Baldwin Ogilvy anything at all.

"You are quite right, or Betty is quite right," Sidney said. "Well, I am going to keep things straight by writing to Ogilvy and giving him the facts. Then there isn't much more I can do. I can't interfere in Ogilvy's case. Of course..."

"Yes?" she said.

"If the theft case was a put-up job, then Wes's family might want to have it investigated so that Wes's name could be cleared—on that score. Small potatoes alongside the murder, but..."

"But you could do it without poking your nose into Ogilvy's business?"

"Possibly. Anyway, let me buy you a coffee. Miss Semple will get the dope from those unfortunates on the penitents' bench."

"Wonderful idea," she said.

They walked to the Honey Dew on Bay Street and settled in a remote corner with two large mugs of coffee.

"Tell me how you found this information about the theft charge," June Beattie said.

Sidney laughed. "It will sound a bit wild and fictional," he said, "but the way it started was this. I suggested to a certain gent that your brother's fantastic story of a conspiracy could be punctured very simply. Find the woman whose purse was stolen, investigate her *bona fides* and *prove* to Wes that he was full of wet hay. This gent challenged me to do it. So first I found that the woman had given a false name and address in court. Then, at the motel, I found that she'd registered under the same false name—but that they'd noted down the license number of her car. The car proved to be rented, and to rent it she'd used a driver's license. I got the number, and it turned out that the license had been stolen and altered!

"Now then—suppose you and I wanted to cuddle together for warmth at the Midtown Motel. We wouldn't require a car. We could take a cab or walk and merely pay a deposit. So it struck me that the car was not rented for the purpose of flim-flamming the motel. Why *was* it rented then, and driven for six or seven miles only? One possible explanation—to work the frame-up described by your brother.

"Well, the woman who rented the car had some minor repairs done, for which she paid cash and got a receipt. She recovered the cash from the rental agency and gave them the garage receipt. That led me to the garage and the mechanic who did the job.

"By an unholy slice of luck, he remembered the car— and the man and woman in it. While they were at the garage, one of the mechanic's regular customers greeted this stranger—the man—as an old school chum and got snubbed. But the thing I learned there which drove me further along the trail was this: your Uncle Edgar had been to the garage too!

"Well, I went to see this regular customer—an ad man called Mayhew—and he said he couldn't remember anyone snubbing him. He also denied that your Uncle Edgar had called on him, which was a patent lie. So I put on my deducin' suit, smoked an ounce of shag and got Watson to lend me his needle. I went to the school where these two old chums were supposed to have been educated and got a list of names from the school yearbook. Mayhew, by the way, had referred to the stranger as 'a former teammate.' Hockey, in all probability. Am I boring you?"

"No, my dear man, you are fascinating me with your colossal acumen."

Sidney blushed, but continued. "Remember that the woman had used a stolen driver's license? Well, the owner of the license thought it might have been stolen at a mining convention. And she had given me a list of delegates to this convention. So I found a name on the convention list which was duplicated on the teammate list!"

"Extraordinary!" she said.

"Elementary," he said modestly.

They both laughed.

"Anyway, I went back at Mayhew, and forced him to admit that this man—his name is Howard Gadwell, and keep *that* under your hat —was, in fact, the man who had snubbed him at the garage. Further patient research into Gadwell's rich and varied love life turned up the fact that the woman was probably the wife of a geologist off in the bush in northern Quebec. So I flew to this mining camp in a ski plane, found the geologist and got a picture of the wife, who had by this time deserted her husband. Well, one James Bellwood positively identified the geologist's wife as the woman who had accused your brother Wes of pinching her handbag."

"Good heavens!" she said. "You're not making this up?"

"No ma'am," he said. "Now this man and woman— Gadwell and Janice Wicklow—had absolutely no reason I can see to go to the Midtown Motel. They had a more convenient love nest. Is that fishy enough for you?"

"Very, very suspish," she said. "Good lord, it ought to be investigated right down the line. Where is this dame now?"

"She has vanished," Sidney said. "Several department stores would like to talk to her, but she can't be located."

"Mr. Grant," she said, "or may I call you Sidney? Sidney, would you be able to go on investigating if *I* retained you to look into the theft charge angle?"

"I would," he said. "I'd have to let Ogilvy know what I was up to as a matter of courtesy, I suppose. But I can't see anything wrong with it."

"All right," she said. "This is a business deal. I have several hundred dollars in the bank, and my friendly banker will probably let me have another thousand. I'm going to send you a check as a retainer and you carry right on. I owe this to poor old Betty, who is all the mother Wes ever knew."

Back at the office, Sidney Grant wrote a letter to the eminent Mr. Baldwin Ogilvy, Q.C. He drafted it carefully in longhand and corrected it meticulously before handing it over to Miss Semple for typing. It read:

Dear Sir:

I have been retained by Miss June Beattie to investigate the circumstances under which her brother, Wesley M. Beattie, was convicted of theft on May 12 last, with a view to clearing his name of this charge. The investigation is, of course, to be discreet in order not to prejudice the case at present before the courts.

It appears to me very likely that Mr. Beattie's claim—namely, that he was the innocent victim of a conspiracy in the matter of the theft charge—is well founded.

I had earlier obtained certain information leading to this conclusion, and I called you with a view to telling you about it, as it might have had some bearing on the charge of murder which Mr. Beattie now faces. Unfortunately you were in Ottawa, so to save time I called on Mrs. Charles Beattie and Mr. Ralph Paget and gave them the information. Mr. Paget told me that he would convey it to you and that you would decide whether it was of any use in the defense of your client.

Mr. Paget wrote to me last week and said that your decision was to let the matter drop. Miss June Beattie, however, wishes these suspicious circumstances to be fully investigated, and, unless you have serious objections, it is my intention to act on her instructions.

Any matters arising from the investigation which may have a bearing on the murder charge will of course be communicated to you at once.

Yours faithfully,
Sidney Grant

"And that," Sidney said with a wicked grin, as he signed the typed copy, "may give Mr. Ralph Paget something to think about."

Six

THE MIDTOWN MOTEL was situated on a busy street in the west-central part of the city. Facing the street was a main section, containing various bars and restaurants, plus several stories of conventional hotel bedrooms. Running off to the rear was an extension of one story, which contained motel units with private entrances. In one angle of the T thus formed there was a swimming pool, which was empty in winter. In the other angle was the car park, which could be reached by driving through an archway from the street.

Sidney Grant, however, reached it by walking through the archway, and then he stood in the middle of the car park in order to survey the scene of Wes Beattie's first battle with the law.

As he stood there, a short, stocky man with gray hair marched toward him with a military stride. He was wearing a maroon greatcoat with golden frogs, and a ceremonial hat with enough scrambled egg on it for a full admiral.

"All right, now, move along," the man said. "You can't stand around 'ere all day. Might catch cold."

Sidney looked the man full in the face, a face like old mahogany with a road map of red veins on it, and stared at the little piggy blue eyes which peered out at him. On an impulse he reached into his pocket and pulled out a bill. He had actually reached for a dollar, but, owing to a ghastly error, what came out was a ten. On impulse, Sidney extended it toward the man.

"Can't I have just a little look?" he said plaintively.

The ten-spot acted like a magnet, and the man's fingers began twitching and creeping toward it, even as he glanced nervously over his shoulder to see if anyone was watching. Temptation won, and the ten-spot was whipped with great rapidity into the pocket of the maroon greatcoat.

"We 'ave to be a bit careful," the man said in a mollified tone. "We get all kinds of snoopers around 'ere. Private dicks lookin' for license numbers, peepin' Toms, that sort of thing."

"Peeping Toms?" Sidney said.

"Blinkin' right! Look, them motel units. Some people get careless about droring the curtains, and the things you see! Gord Almighty, these dames! If my missis knew the things I seen around 'ere, she wouldn't 'alf 'ave kittens!"

"When I'm cleaning windows!" Sidney sang.

"Window cleaning ain't in it," the man said. "Blimey! Sometimes the bloke gets up and goes to the office, eight o'clock like, and leaves the dame in bed. Nine-thirty, maybe, she rings for black coffee and orange juice. Well, I 'andle room service orders to the motel units along with keepin' an eye on the car park. I go in with the tray, and blimey O'Reilly! Talk about sights."

"And do they pay you money as well?" Sidney said, leering conspiratorially.

The man chuckled wickedly.

"You do the room service, eh?" Sidney said. "Ice and mixers and all that stuff?"

"That's right. I work odd hours. Like Friday and Satday I might go on till two or three A.M. and take time off through the week."

Sidney inhaled deeply, and caught a whiff of the man's breath. It would have flunked on any breathalyzer test known. There was no mistaking how the man had achieved such a rich and costly complexion.

"Well, friend, wot's your business 'ere?" the man asked with the friendly curiosity of a well-bribed petty official.

Sidney Grant had a sudden inspiration. "Well, some people are coming to town," he said. "There's these girls— what I mean is, there's these friends, and my—my wife and I wanted to have a party with them. Some place quiet and private, and I wondered..."

"When they coming?" the man asked sharply. Sidney gulped and looked nervous.

"Tonight," he murmured with a sheepish grin.

"Well, friend, you come to the right place," the attendant said. "Now you just nip in there to the office and tell 'em you want Unit Six. That's a suite, like. Two bedrooms, two bathrooms, showers, nice living room, wide-screen TV, kitchenette with stove and fridge, air-conditioned, all the rest of it. Just book it in your own name and pay in advance, thirty-six bucks. No questions asked."

"Gee, that's great," Sidney said, looking pleased and relieved.

"You can bring your own mixers if you like—save a bit of money. But I can fetch you anything you like—them nice clear ice cubes, mixers, bottle of liquor..."

"Well, gee, we'll bring our own liquor, but you can bring us mixers," Sidney said. "I guess I'd better hurry in and book the suite. What's your name, by the way?"

"Sam," the man said. "Just ask for Sam Black. Call room service and ask for anythink you want."

"That's swell," Sidney said, and hurried off to the front office.

It was early, not yet nine o'clock, when a smart new Oldsmobile pulled into the car park of the Midtown Motel and backed up to the door of Unit Six.

Sam Black hurried over to offer a hand with the luggage, but the luggage consisted merely of two feminine overnight bags, two office briefcases and a large brown paper bag which any connoisseur would recognize as coming from one of the retail outlets of the Ontario Liquor Control Board.

The two young women who emerged from the car kept looking at each other and giggling nervously.

The driver of the car, a tall, handsome youth, started for the door of the unit but turned back.

"Gosh, Sid, maybe I better not park right here," he said.

"Yeah, that's right," Sidney Grant said.

Sam Black chuckled and said, "Pull over there into that line. You'll be okay there."

He took the key from Sidney's hand, opened the unit and ushered Sidney and the two girls in. "One bedroom there, one this side, bathrooms attached," he said. "'Ere's your air-condi-tionin' knob, switch the TV on there, kitchenette in be'ind."

The girls shed their coats and started to take off their gloves, but then one of them giggled and pulled her left glove on again, and the other followed suit. Black saw the gesture and grinned.

"Nothing to worry about 'ere, miss," he said ingratiatingly. "Now then, need any mixers?"

"Soda, ginger ale and ice," Sidney said.

"Oh, and I like Seven-Up. Bring some Seven-Up," June Beattie said. "And have you got those salted peanuts? Can you bring a can of salted peanuts?"

"Surely, miss. Won't be 'alf a tick," Black said, and went out, standing aside at the door to let the other man enter.

"Well, how did we do?" June asked when the door had closed.

"Very nicely. To the manner born," Sidney said. "You may have laid it on a bit too thick, but Sam Black doesn't seem to be a subtle fellow. He, by the way, is the man who caught your brother with the purse on him, and he was one of the witnesses against him in the police court."

"A charming specimen," June said. "Now then, Kay, darling, Sidney says this man is so far gone in voyeurism that he gets his kicks from watching other voyeurs voying. Live it up, kid. Start an affair on that sofa with your husband, but try to act as if he isn't your husband."

"That's the ticket," Bob Duffy said. "Come on, Kay darling. Enough of this holy matrimony bit."

"And as for you, young Gargoyle," June said, "get your coat off, loosen your tie and sit in this armchair. I will sit on the arm and smother you with burning kisses."

"This is the nicest piece of research I ever dreamed up," Sidney said.

June made sure that the door was unlocked and then proceeded with the scenario.

Black, running right with the form book, entered without knocking and apologized profusely as the two couples flew apart in wild confusion.

"I say, old man, won't you join us for a quick one?" Bob Duffy asked, grinning guiltily.

"Well, I don't like to be a spare part at a wedding," Black said, "but I don't mind a quick one. Scotch and soda, if that's all right."

Sidney poured three ounces of Scotch into a glass with some ice cubes and a splash of soda, passed it to Black, then began to fix drinks for the others.

"Here, sit in this armchair," June said. "Kay, get some music going, dear. Gee, Mr. Black, it sort of gives a girl confidence to have a man like you around as chaperon. I'll bet you have to do some chaperoning around here. Do they have many wild parties? Oh!"

She put her hand over her mouth and giggled shrilly. Bob Duffy, out of sight of Black, held his nose and turned his thumb down to indicate that the act was going too far. But Black's gaze was fastened on Miss Beattie's décolletage, and he was having far too much fun to worry about minor details.

"Hah!" he said, drinking deep of the Scotch. "I see some parties around 'ere. You girls are too young to know the goings-on, believe me."

"I'm over twenty-one," June said coyly, brushing her hand over his forehead.

"Well, 'ere's luck," Black said. "But just remember to lock that door and keep the curtains pulled. *I'm* not twenty-one yet, and I 'ave to keep walkin' back and forth."

He chuckled throatily and downed the balance of his drink in two gulps.

"No, no more, thanks," he said, as Sidney reached for his glass. "Got a couple of chores to do—got to run. But…"

"Can you come back later and have one? We'd *love* to have you. You're *cute,*" June said.

Black blushed prettily.

"Well, about 'alf an hour there'll be a quiet spell, like as not. If you wouldn't mind?"

"Oh, of course not! Do *come!*" June said. *"You'd* like to have him, *wouldn't* you, Kay?"

"Oh, yes indeed," Kay said, stretching her mouth wide and articulating carefully. Her manner suggested that she wanted nothing more than to be alone with her lover, but that she didn't dare say so.

"Sure, come on in, first chance you get," Sidney said. "But this time, knock, you naughty man," June said archly.

"And you see you lock your door, miss," Black said, and thereupon departed into the night.

When he had gone, Sidney Grant made sure the door was locked and then all four shook helplessly with laughter.

"June," Bob Duffy said, "you were corny as hell. Frightful."

"Ay'm over twenty-one, you cute old rascal," Kay Duffy mimicked mincingly. "Oh, that cute baby speech of yours. Why, you'll never see twenty-four again, you saucy baggage!"

"Shut up," Sidney said. "No dissension in the cast, please. Everyone was dandy, and we've established the right rapport. Now the idea is to get him talking, bragging, until we can pump him without seeming to. Peeping into bedrooms seems to be the exploit he is proudest of, so that may be the start. We'll work round as painlessly as possi ble to his great exploit of arresting Wes Beattie, the notorious murderer."

"What do you expect to gain from this, Gargoyle?" Bob Duffy asked.

"I want to ask him about Janice Wicklow, who gave her name as Mrs. Leduc, and about the boy friend who was with her here. They must have paid him a reward for recovering that purse. He can probably tell us something about them. *If* there was actually a conspiracy, though, he may have been a paid hireling. Now if we seem interested in that business, he may clam up. But get him bragging and we may have something."

"Well, that makes sense," Duffy said. "Now how do we all fit into this little plan?"

"You two are gaga about each other, and you'd like to be alone," June said. "But you won't come out and say so. I'm a naughty little tease, trying to make Sidney jealous and frustrated and keep the party going. Sidney is too much of a country boy to belt me one and tell Black to go peddle his peanuts. But Sidney is so thrilled by this mad adventure that he's enjoying it all and being nice to Black so as not to make a fool of himself. Is that psychologically sound?"

Bob Duffy roared with laughter. "Don't get analytical," he said. "Just carry on. I hope your brother will appreciate our efforts, making such disgusting exhibitions of ourselves to help him out."

"He'll never know," Sidney said. "But this is our prime chance to find out if these people *were* actually working some flimflam on Wes, or if they had some other nefarious scheme on foot here that was interrupted by the purse bit." For half an hour the four people sat up chastely and watched a TV show, until they were interrupted by a discreet knock on the door.

"Take your positions for Act Two," June Beattie said, and the Duffys got up and went into a bedroom.

Sidney, his tie off, and a stiff drink in his hand, answered the door.

"Oh, maybe you changed your minds," Black said, grinning. "I just thought…"

"Oh, heck, come on in," Sidney said. "Glad to see you. Have the other half."

As Black entered, Bob and Kay Duffy were emerging from the bedroom. He blushed guiltily, but she held his arm and looked up at him with admiring sheep's eyes. June was straightening her blouse and skirt, but she looked up roguishly and called "Hi" in that little-girl voice.

Black was pushed into an armchair and furnished with another strong drink.

"Got a bit of a quiet spell," he announced. "The boss has gone in to dinner with some TV people."

Conversation began slowly this time. Bob Duffy said it was easy to see that Black had been in the army. Black said yes, he'd been in India, Hong Kong, Eye-rack, Egypt and Gib. Infantry for a start, then in the military police.

This led quite naturally to his favorite subject, namely, the things he had seen in Sister Street in Alexandria, and while inspecting certain establishments in Baghdad, and presently they were back at the Midtown Motel and June, looking like a naughty boarding-school girl telling stories in the dormitory, wanted to know about the local goings on.

The whisky was taking effect. Sidney quietly recharged the glass, and Sam Black, unable to resist stardom, threw discretion to the winds. "Well, now, I'll tell you," he said. "P'raps I shouldn't…"

"Oh, go on," June said.

"Well, like one afternoon 'ere—some people *like* the afternoon—there was this couple. Just like you, this bloke asked me to come in and 'ave one. Well, I did, and 'e said to come back later, maybe 'alf-past three, and 'ave another. Well, I did. I come back, and 'is wife—well, she was supposed to be 'is wife—she said she was going to take a shower while we 'ad our drink, so we sat down over 'ere like, 'im and me. So she goes in the bedroom and gets undressed. But there was this cupboard door with a full-length mirror, see? And it was opened just so, and from where I sat I could watch her, in the mirror. Stripped right down to the buff she did, and me sitting there drinking and trying to listen to this bloke telling me about some deal— didn't 'ardly 'ear a word of it, I didn't. Right down to the buff. Then she 'ops into the shower and I sat back sort of gahspin', and tryin' to pick up the thread of this story the bloke was feedin' me, when out she comes with a towel and *dries* 'erself, right in the same spot! Gord, I'm tellin' you, I was weak! Then she starts gettin' dressed, and me watchin' every move, you may believe it! And then the bloke drops 'is glass and it 'it the edge of the little table and broke. Well, she looked up and caught my eye in the mirror, and was my face red! But wot do you know? She just give 'erself a little shake and winked at me!"

"Oh, the brazen hussy!" June said.

"Tellin' me!" Black said. "*She* wasn't no better than she ought to be! Well then, you may believe it or not, just as you choose, but of all the things to 'appen! This bloke 'ad got up, and 'e's lookin' out the window into the car park, and suddenly he sings out."

Sidney, who was walking behind Black's chair, stopped still and froze.

"Yes sir," Black said. "'E sings out, 'Look! There's a kid going through the parked cars. He's taking something out of *our* car. Nip out there and grab 'im.' Blimey, I gave myself a shake and out I went, and 'ere's this kid, lad of about eighteen or twenty, comin' 'ind end foremost out of the car and shovin' something under his raincoat. I grabbed 'im quick, and 'ere it was this dame's 'andbag. She must have finished dressin' awful quick, because she come out while I was strugglin' with 'im and claimed 'er bag."

He drained his glass and looked expectantly at Sidney, who jumped forward and seized the glass at once. Black paused irritatingly while Sidney refilled it, then leaned forward to gain impressiveness for his next remark.

"And you'd never guess who that kid was," he said.

"No, who?" June said.

"It was none other than this 'ere Wes Beattie, that's now up on a murder charge. I'm not kidding you, either."

Black could not have been more pleased with the effect of the story on his listeners. They gasped.

"Now, can you beat that?" Black asked, and took a pull at his drink.

"No sir, I can't even come close to it," Bob Duffy said.

Sidney, whose manner had suddenly changed, strolled over to his briefcase and removed some photographs from it. He walked behind Black's chair and extended a photograph of Janice Wicklow before the attendant's eyes.

"Was this the woman, by any chance?" he asked tonelessly.

Black suddenly froze. The evil grin disappeared from his face, and anger slowly replaced it. He turned and glowered at Sidney.

"Say, what is this?" he demanded.

"Do you know this woman? Is this the woman?" Sidney said.

"Never seen 'er in my life," Black said. "Say, what the 'ell are you tryin' to pull off?"

"And is this the man?" Sidney went on. "Did he pay you well?"

Black started visibly as he looked at Howard Gadwell's picture, obtained from the files of a newspaper office.

"Never seen 'im either. 'Oo is 'e? Wot's your game, mister?"

"He is a rich stockbroker named Howard Gadwell," Sidney said. "He must have known you. He must have known the kind of show you would fall for. How much did he pay you?"

Black leapt to his feet, and his face was blazing. "I tell you I never seen this bloke in my life," he snarled. "'Oward Gadwell? Never 'eard of 'im. Why should 'e pay me?"

"To shut up," Sidney said. "Not to tell the whole story in court. Mr. Gadwell wanted to stay right out of the business, didn't he? He disappeared and let the woman carry the can back."

"Listen, mister," Black said. "We don't like no snoopers around 'ere. What are you after, anyway? Took *me* for a bleedin' mug, didn't you, you and your dames..."

"Easy, fellow!" Bob Duffy said. "You might make us cross."

"Pack of snoopin' bloody Nosy Parkers," Black said, but as Duffy moved toward him he dashed out and slammed the door.

"Well," Sidney said, "we now know all we need to know and all we're likely to find out here. But it is past all doubting that those people worked out a frame-up for Wes Beattie, and a very neat one too."

"Just how was it done?" Duffy asked.

"They rented a car and booked a suite here," Sidney said. "Gadwell called Wes and made him a juicy job offer. Wes swallowed the bait. Knowing Black's tendencies, Gadwell was able to get him out of the way while some girl—posing as his secretary—drove the car out of the car park and went to pick Wes up. Then Gadwell, with the aid of a striptease by Janice Wicklow, kept Black rooted to the spot long enough for the girl to drive Wes back here and park. The girl led Wes across to the bar entrance, leaving a handbag in the car. Then, at the entrance, she missed her purse and asked Wes to go back and fetch it. As soon as he turned, she walked through a corridor, which I have explored, and out to the street. She just disappeared. When Wes turned back to the car, Gadwell smashed his glass as a signal to Janice to hurry up and dress. Then he sent the well-bribed Black out to catch the boy. Black didn't *know* he had been bribed. He only knew that Gadwell tipped well. Then Janice finished dressing quickly and dashed out to claim the purse. Neat, eh?"

"Good lord!" Duffy said. "It could happen to anyone."

"But to a chronic liar it was fatal. Realizing how weak the truth would sound, Wes tried to think of a better story. Well, June, your classmate and her good man have done a noble service. Hope you don't feel too dirty after amusing Black. But let's keep all this strictly beneath the headgear." It was so agreed, and the party adjourned to a spaghetti house for a late supper.

Seven

"**M**R. BALDWIN OGILVY CALLED," Miss Semple said. "He seemed very anxious to get in touch with you. He said would you either call him or go to see him at his office this morning."

"Yipe," Sidney said. "Storm warnings. I'd better get it over with right away. I think I'll walk around there right now."

After the partying of the night before, Sidney did not feel in first-class shape to face an angry Baldwin Ogilvy, so he decided to dive right in before he had time to think about it. On arrival he was ushered straight in to the great man's presence, and he found a very angry Ogilvy indeed. "Just what is the meaning of all this, Mr. Grant?" Ogilvy demanded. "What is this mysterious information that Paget was supposed to give me?"

"We're going to save time, sir, if I start right at the beginning," Sidney said. "But first let me make one observation. When I was a law student at Osgoode Hall, we had some lectures on criminal law from an eminent counsel, who said—I remember the words well: 'When you defend a man on a criminal charge, remember that, no matter how worthless, despicable or vile he may seem, you are right there in the dock with him. The whole world may regard him with loathing or contempt, but you have to stand right by his side and defend him as if he were your own brother.'"

"Do you recall the name of this lecturer, by any chance?" Ogilvy said.

"Yes sir. It was Mr. Baldwin Ogilvy," Sidney replied.

Ogilvy grinned. "This not-too-subtle flattery won't get you very far, Grant," he said. "Nevertheless it's nice to know that one's words are remembered."

"Well sir," Sidney went on, "everybody—even his loving sister —seems to regard Wes Beattie as a poor fish, so nobody paid much attention to his statements. Conclusions were jumped at, and everything was decided on the basis that Beattie's story was a tissue of lies from start to finish. And now I can virtually prove that there was a conspiracy against him in the matter of the theft."

"Paget never even discussed the matter with me," Ogilvy said. "I don't like being kept in the dark. Let's hear your story."

Speaking very quickly, Sidney led him through the whole course, from Mrs. Ledley to Sam Black, and Ogilvy listened with close attention.

"Now then," he said when Sidney had finished, "this has very serious implications for the defense. Two psychiatrists—one retained by us and one by the Crown—have developed a theory of insanity based on the premise that all this conspiracy business was a figment of Wes's imagination. In the light of your discoveries, it might be claimed that Wes worked a very cunning trick. In short, that he murdered his uncle and made up the same sort of yarn that he had used before. In other words, that he deliberately planted this pattern of insanity. If he can't explain his fingerprints on that telephone, no jury is ever going to believe that he didn't kill his uncle. So there are just two courses open."

"Yes?" Sidney said.

"One is to forget all about your discoveries and go ahead with the insanity defense. The other is to investigate Gadwell, find out what his motive was and see if he can somehow be tied in with the murder. For instance, if there were some way of showing that Edgar had persisted in his desire to meet Gadwell, and that Gadwell had agreed to a meeting on that Friday night, one might create a reasonable doubt. But in any case, either your investigation should be buried and forgotten, or it should be pursued to the end."

"Which do *you* favor, sir?" Sidney asked.

"You probably know me well enough not to ask," Ogilvy said. "Look—this blasted family of Beattie's retained me to defend him, but they've done just a shade more coaching than I am willing to accept. Paget, in his God-given wisdom, is deciding what I should be told and what I shouldn't. Grant, I am going to withdraw from the case. My position is too embarrassing. Now then, Wes is over twenty-one, and he has not been declared incompetent. If he were, then his nearest relative is the sister—also over twenty-one. Is she capable of being discreet?"

"Yes sir," Sidney said. "She's a bit of a mad hoyden, but essentially she is a responsible person."

Ogilvy looked at him closely. "Careful, Grant!" he said. "Now I am going to write to Paget, who seems to act for the family, and explain to him that I am withdrawing. I shall also call the sister—have you got her number? And I will privately recommend to her that she should persuade her brother to retain *you*. Grant, I feel that you have already proved your competence to handle the matter."

"Thank you, sir," Sidney said, with some confusion.

"And on Monday, when Wes comes up for remand, I will go into the magistrate's court and make a statement about my withdrawal just to keep the record straight. Now you understand, Grant, that I have a duty to defend this man, and I would not withdraw if I did not feel that under the circumstances you can defend him better than I could."

Sidney suddenly felt a queasy sensation in the pit of his stomach. Taking over a murder case from the great Baldwin Ogilvy was a fairly hefty responsibility.

"By the way," Ogilvy said, "you will want to talk to Heber. Heber claims that Wes's alibi for the evening of the murder is patently phony. He had Wes make a tape recording under sedation, and he says the discrepancies in the story stick out like a sore thumb."

"That's nice," Sidney said. "I'll go and see him—if and when I am retained to defend Wes."

"You will be, Grant," Ogilvy said. "I want to see you do it. All right, you're young, but you've got a brain. When I think of all the stupid lawyers I know with white hair, I'm not at all concerned about a bright young fellow having a crack at something."

Sidney went back to his office with spasms of elation alternating with qualms of uneasiness in his emotional make-up.

But there was no time to sit around and think. The case was due to come before the assizes in two weeks, and it was absolutely necessary to find out just why Howard Gadwell and Mrs. Wicklow had wished to frame Wes Beattie.

Sidney Grant had a profound conviction that money would be the motive if it were ever discovered, but it was impossible to see how Gadwell could profit from the downfall of Wes Beattie.

Unless—and a dark suspicion was already beginning to crystallize—unless Gadwell had been acting for someone else.

The position of Ralph Paget was going to require a certain scrutiny. Someone who knew Wes's nature had organized the plot against him. Someone who knew that, in May, he was desperately short of funds. Someone who knew his tendency to lie. Paget had known these things.

Paget, too, had been primarily responsible for railroading the case through the magistrate's court and sending Wes to jail. Paget had known that Edgar was looking for Mrs. Leduc—and had kept his mouth shut about it. Could Paget have engineered the telephone call to Edgar, trying to persuade him to lay off? Edgar, according to Paget, had accepted the story told by his anonymous caller. Had Edgar suspected his brother-in-law and pretended to believe the story in order to lull Paget's fears?

Paget had briefed Baldwin Ogilvy, had encouraged the insanity defense and had withheld vital information from Ogilvy. Any connection that might be established between Paget and Gadwell would put the lid on it. After all, Mrs. Paget stood to gain by the murder of Edgar Beattie before the will was changed—but *only if Wes were convicted of it.*

On Friday evening Sidney Grant invited June Beattie out for a quiet dinner at La Chaumière, a French restaurant where it was possible to get a quiet corner and talk.

❀ ❀ ❀

"What I want from you, Miss Beattie," Sidney said, when they had loaded their plates with hors d'oeuvres, "is a rundown on the family relationships. I want to know where everyone fits in."

"Do you want the full story," she said, "or the abridged version, which only takes a couple of days?"

"The abridged abridged version," he said.

"All right then. We start with Gran. You've met her. Reared in opulence in Rosedale, educated in Toronto, England, Switzerland, France and Germany. All the accomplishments of a lady. Rich. Inherited money. Disappointed in love, I suspect, and married young Charley Beattie, an up-and-coming, as a man who could manage her inheritance. Charley did very well because he brought in the money faster than Gran could spend it. Gran *despises* money and gets rid of it as fast as it comes into her possession. Charley and Gran had issue as follows.

"One: Edgar. A low-lifer. Charley liked horses, fights, and so on, in secret, but Edgar loved them openly. A disappointment to Gran. He was persuaded to stand still at the altar of a fashionable church for long enough to get married to a gal of Gran's choosing—also a friend of Marcia's. It didn't take. No offspring. Divorce. Since then, Edgar has lived as a reconstructed bachelor. At least, up to the time he ceased living.

"Two: Claudia. Went to school in England and never recovered. Flat feet, horse face, decent stick generally. As a Red Cross girl she was exposed to the entire Canadian Army during World War II, but failed to achieve even a flaming affair.

"Three: Marcia. Married Ralph Paget, English bank clerk bent on improving his social status. Marcia is hotly tipped as next chapter regent of the Imperial Order, Daughters of the Empire. She is still trying to extirpate faint traces of her husband's lower-middle-class origins—like calling Gran 'Mother B.' They have two grown-up kids—a girl married to a doctor in Montreal, a boy who is some sort of economist in the Department of Trade and Commerce at Ottawa.

"Which brings us to Number Four: Gran's pet, Rupert, a poet and philosopher in whom she found her highest hopes realized. Unhappily, Rupert, when a sophomore at Trinity, went to a stag banquet, where the main entertainment was a girl called Darleen, a smashing creature dressed in a small square of black velvet. She played the piano-accordion and tap danced. The boys whistled and howled, and Darleen—a genuine beauty queen at sixteen—loved it. Just for the hell of it, the boys pushed poor Rupert into dating Darleen. Rupert, who had never met any girls except the suitable ones—you know, the ones destined to be given in marriage at the fashionable churches— fell head over heels. The girl tortured him, I'm told. He tried to orient to her milieu. She, on the other hand, was aware of the Beattie opulence.

"There came a black day when Mr. Maggs, Darleen's father, called at the old family home. Mr. Maggs was a well-known conductor. Street car, not symphony. He had grievous news. There was a family crisis. Money was to be handed over. But Rupert, the impractical romantic, stole away and married the girl. Five months later their union was blessed with a sweet little baby girl. Me."

"A charming story," Sidney said.

"Ah, but there's more! Gran was inconsolable. She insisted that Rupert be hurled forth into outer darkness. He had made his bed, let him lie in it. He and Darleen got an apartment just off Dupont Street. Rupert sold encyclopedias. There was a depression on. His father secretly subsidized him—so did his sister Claudia. But Darleen was one of the great spenders and had a weakness for gin. When World War II broke out, Rupert rushed happily from his wife's arms to the King's. He went overseas and was naturally commissioned, being a former Trinity man. After he had left, Wes was born. He never saw his father. I can just remember poor, suffering Rupert.

"Us kids were picked up every Sunday by the chauffeur and taken to see Gran, a traumatic experience for any Dupont Street kiddy. Gran bought us proper clothes and heaped expensive presents on us. Darleen converted many of the clothes and presents into cash for the purchase of gin.

"And little June became very smart at parrying Gran's questions about where that nice reefer coat had gone. She also knew enough not to talk about all the nice men who came to the apartment—army, navy, air force, Yanks, Australians, Norwegians. It was a ball, it really was.

"And then Rupert was killed in an armored car in Italy, and Gran was stricken with remorse. She offered to take us kids and raise us. Darleen accepted, at a price. We were whisked away, with Mummy weeping ginnily. She wasn't a bad sort. It was just the circumstances that were so utterly bloody.

"I adjusted with no trouble at all. I simply commenced a twelve-year battle with Gran and Marcia, who wanted to make a lady of me after the Marcia fashion. They never got to first base. But little Wes missed his Mummy, and cried. They bought him Teddy bears and kiddy cars and bribed him in various other ways, but Mummy hung on. He got to know that it was slightly naughty talking about Mummy, but he clung to me a good deal, as I was the one thing from the old environment.

"Gran wanted to change his name. 'Wesley' had the most frightful Methodist connotations—although Darleen named him after a cowboy singing star, not after that renegade Anglican priest. She named me after her favorite female film star. But Wes was Wes, and he wouldn't *have* any other name.

"He won his point, but apart from that Gran dominated him as only she can. She was utterly unscrupulous. Tears, ridicule, bribes—any weapon that came to hand was used. She was a goddess to Wes, a goddess who had to be appeased. On the face of it he was Gran's pet, but I think he knew even then that there was no real love in it. He was a bit delicate, and she kept him around home a lot instead of letting him go out and get his hair mussed. But she also—the unscrupulous old woman— destroyed his confidence in his ability to do *anything*. Anything she didn't *want* him to do, that is.

"Well, Grampa, old Charley, was *my* pet. He was my secret lover. He made life bearable for me. He was a bit strict with Wes, but quite fair on the whole. However, Wes's great hero was Uncle Edgar, who took a shine to the boy, or felt sorry for him. So if you think Wes ever had a chance, you're wrong. I think that basically he was artistic, but Gran and Marcia would give art a bad name with *anyone* who had artistic leanings. They are literally vultures for culture. I mean they like *dead* art.

"They dress up and go to art gallery openings and condescend to the artists. They dress up and go to symphonies and applaud just the right amount. They like everything that is correct and approved by the top aesthetic authorities, but they never love anything *madly*. Wild enthusiasm ain't in 'em. It's this godawful *pallor* that is so frightful. Beethoven doesn't need to be dead, but they *make* him dead, and they make the French

Impressionists dead, and the Old Masters and Shakespeare and everything they touch with their clawlike hands.

"There is the tragedy of Wes—that he was never able to develop his real enthusiasms. And me, I've never had anything *but* enthusiasms, pro or con.

"So that's the historical background. Coming to modem times, Grampa got sick a year ago last fall. He had a stroke, but he recovered, and Gran took him off to Arizona to convalesce. But the minute they got back, he had another stroke and he was laid up over Christmas, and then he had a worse one and was paralyzed right down one side and speechless. Well, it dragged on till February, when he died.

"Well, Marcia, bless her charitable soul, she said it was just too much for Gran with only Claudia and Betty and the cook, so what did she do but sell her house and move back to the old home to help with the nursing. That was just before Christmas. Mind you, Marcia had practically haunted the place before that anyway, but there she was, back and trying to run the joint. I had moved out to my own apartment as soon as I was twenty-one, so it didn't affect me, but Claudia was highly incensed at Gran for letting her get away with it.

"This was all very cozy for Marcia, if not Ralph. They had always been up to their ears, what with Marcia's clothes and entertaining, and this move got rid of their mortgage and all that, and they made a nice profit on the house, so all of a sudden they were in the chips.

"Naturally they were on Wes's neck. He was supposed to pay board, but he was always months behind and always biting Gran's ear for something, and she would nag and complain but give it to him. Marcia and Ralph started this bit about the boy needing discipline to straighten him up, and *he* got pretty fed up.

"I told him the only thing to do was get out on his own, and he said he would, but Gran talked him out of it. I don't know why. Well, Grampa died, and he left Wes and me some money. Five thousand dollars each. Wes's money was tied up till he was twenty-five, because Grampa knew he'd just squander it. I got my share in April and immediately proceeded to squander it on this trip to all the places I ever wanted to see. And then Wes got arrested, and you know all the rest."

Dinner was far advanced by the time she had finished her recital.

"Why," Sidney asked, "would Marcia want to come home?"

"Heirlooms and such," she said. "Protecting her interests. She figured that if she got well established there, Gran would get feebler and feebler and gradually Marcia could take over and maybe push Claudia out. She likes all that antique furniture and the old family mansion bit."

"Tell me exactly what Baldwin Ogilvy said to you," Sidney said, changing the subject.

"He said he was calling me as Wes's nearest relation. He said he felt that he had been put in an impossible position and had to withdraw from the case. He understood that I had retained a Mr. Grant to work on other aspects of Wes's criminal career, and he said he wanted to offer a friendly suggestion which I could do what I liked about. The suggestion was that I get into the Psychiatric and talk to Wes and perhaps persuade him to retain you. And that was it. Oh, he delicately suggested that I didn't need to discuss his call with any other relatives."

"And you're going to see Wes tomorrow?"

"Though Hell should bar the way. Oh, *by* the way, how come you spilled the name Gadwell to our little friend Black? I thought you wanted to keep Gadwell in the dark. Won't Black tell him about you?"

"Maybe he will. I wanted to get Black's reaction to the name. What I wanted to know is just how much Black *did* know about the frame-up. If Black calls him, he won't have *my* name. I signed in as George Leduc. He might have taken the Duffys' license number, which would give him *their* name. We'd better warn them that they might get a phone call. I have no objection to Gadwell being made a bit uneasy—provided he doesn't know too much too soon."

They bought a bottle of Marsala, and drank it slowly by candlelight, and the conversation drifted away to other matters. If Miss Semple could have observed them leaning over the table and talking cozily, she might have clicked her tongue disapprovingly. But Miss Semple was with the girls at her Friday-night bridge club.

Eight

DURING HIS DISCREET RESEARCH into the character and habits of High Grade Howie Gadwell, Sidney Grant had tried several times to get in touch with Sharon Willison, a TV songstress of some renown, who had once been Gadwell's wife. But Miss Willison traveled a lot. Sometimes she was in New York, holding a can of toilet-bowl cleanser in front of a videotape camera, sometimes she was in Hollywood, singing a number in a show, and once she had been at Las Vegas in a night club performance.

The information which Sidney had gathered on the subject of Gadwell was nebulous. He owned pieces of things, he promoted things, he skated on thin ice. But he managed to protect the image of a great spender. He did all the fashionable things, like going to the big fights, the World Series and the Kentucky Derby. He went to Palm Beach and Nassau. Head waiters called him by name and showered him with attention.

Financially, it didn't quite add up.

On the Saturday morning following his dinner with June, Sidney Grant once again dialed the number of Miss Willison's apartment on Jarvis Street (at the north, or more respectable, end) and was delighted to get an answer. It was necessary to bear down in his investigations in the few remaining days before he would be publicly proclaimed as Wes Beattie's counsel.

Miss Willison was not too happy about being disturbed, but she graciously consented to an interview at eleven, and she had all her charm turned on as, wearing a stunning housecoat, she welcomed Sidney to the apartment.

"Are you bringing your own photographer?" she asked. "Or do you want us to supply some shots?"

Miss Willison showed an understandable irritation when she learned that by "interview" Sidney had not meant an interview for a magazine article, but, to do her credit, she remained polite. She had arranged a splendid pose, curled up on the end of a sofa, with a coffee tray beside her on a low table, and it was all wasted. Nevertheless, she poured Sidney a cup of coffee and looked at him inquiringly.

"Miss Willison," he said, "I wanted to ask you a few questions about one Howard Gadwell."

"If I had known that," she said, "you wouldn't be here."

"I'm sure it's a painful subject," he said, "but I urgently need to know something about the man. It is literally a matter of life and death, and anything you say will be kept in complete confidence."

"I'm a lousy chooser when it comes to husbands," she said. "But Howie was the bottom. He makes the others look good. What did you want to know?"

"What makes Howie tick?" he said. "Where does his money come from? The way I figure it he should have been broke years ago. Most of the things he's interested in are sick."

"That's the old Gadwell touch," she said. "Big, big talk, sad performance. But I don't see why I should talk to you about Howard. I want to forget him."

"I guess he didn't treat you very well," Sidney said. "But I am representing a young guy whose life has been ruined by Gadwell, and I can't find out why. And unless I *do* find out, this lad is going to be in very bad shape indeed. You can help him if you'll talk to me."

"Just what do you mean by bad shape?" she asked.

"He'll be locked away for life in a mental institution," Sidney said.

She crushed out a cigarette, took a fresh one from a lacquered Chinese box and lit it.

"I thought I might come to that myself once," she said. "Would it really help this boy if I stuck my neck out and told you about Howard?"

"It most probably would," he said, "but you won't be sticking your neck out."

"Don't be too sure of that," she said. "Howie can be nasty and vindictive. A really ugly customer. But—oh hell. Anyway, I was once married to Howie, as you know. We had a smashing new house up near Otter Loop, by Lawrence and Avenue Road. There was a picture story about it in *Chatelaine*. A singer's marriage and career piece. I traveled a lot and kept odd hours, and I kidded myself that I had all the answers. Until some new questions came along."

"What sort of questions?" Sidney asked.

"Weekends. Howard went away every weekend. Fishing or hunting or something, with some friends. Vague friends. Where did he go? Oh, different places. Bobcaygeon, Galt, Ste. Adèle. Well, little Sharon dreaded those stories in the paper about a rift in the happy marriage, so she did a little quiet detective work, hoping to get rid of her rising jealousy."

"Detective work, eh?" Sidney said. "How did you go about it?"

"The speedometer," she said. "Take the mileage off his big station wagon on Friday evening, check it again Sunday night or Monday morning. Interesting. Mileage always the same, near as makes no matter. Never less than two hundred and eighty-four, never more than three twenty. Usually two ninety odd. So I figured all these weekends were spent at the same place. But where? So I did more detective work. When his gasoline bills came, I steamed them open with the teakettle and checked the gas receipts. Any gas bought on those weekends was bought on Highway 400 or Highway 11. And the farthest north point of purchase was Bracebridge. Also, if ever he bought gas on Saturday or Sunday, he bought it in Bracebridge. So..."

"So, his hideaway was in the Bracebridge area," Sidney said. "Miss Willison, you would make a formidable detective."

She smiled wanly. "If that ever got out, I'd never get another husband," she said. "But anyway I was curious about these weekends, naturally, because they went on winter and summer. And then I did a Bluebeard's wife. I peeked into the forbidden cupboard."

"He had one of those, did he?"

"Yes," she said. "In the basement recreation room. Yale lock. Mustn't touch. Secret business papers. So one Saturday I called in a locksmith and got him to open it and give me a key. And what did I find? Films. In cans. Sixteen millimeter and eight millimeter. And boxes of stills. Mr. Grant, they were the sort of pictures which nasty, elderly men or naughty schoolboys leer over. I borrowed a projector and ran off a film. I couldn't describe it."

"Blue cinema?" Sidney said.

"I think that's what it's called. The kind of films that men show at stag parties, I believe. Well, in this film a burglar breaks into a house and finds a woman all alone. He holds a knife to her throat and—well, it was all very frank and revealing. In the end, she is so pleased with his attentions that she calls for an encore, which is shown in clinical detail.

"Well, I was just sick. Now you may believe what you like, but I played several films. Some of them in color, and there were outdoor sequences. White pine trees, rocks and girls. Typical Muskoka scenery. The indoor shots were all in rooms with high ceilings, and there was a large entrance hall with a curving staircase. I could only conclude that they were taken in one of those big, old cottages on Lake Muskoka and that Howard was spending his weekends making them. You see, he is a clever technician and knows something about films and sound equipment."

"A pretty dangerous business," Sidney said.

"Oh, long stretches in the penitentiary for anyone that gets caught having *any* connection with that sort of business. The police sort of keep an eye on film producers and photographers. When I was younger I was always being invited to do artistic poses for some photographer—in the evening somewhere. Well, I had the goods on Howie, but I was scared. Like Bluebeard's wife. I took the projector back, and then I packed up everything I owned and moved right out. I stayed in New York. I was scared stiff. But Howard followed me. He caught up with me at the St. Regis. He wanted to know why I had left him. I told him some lies, but he knew. You see, he had some photographic device in that cupboard which told him that it had been opened, and finally he accused me point-blank. So I admitted that I knew. And honestly, his face terrified me.

"He said that making those films brought him in a nice, steady income, and not another soul in Canada knew anything about it. I think he borrowed or bought old equipment from this commercial film outfit he was connected with and took it up north on the weekends, and then the finished products were smuggled into the States.

"Well, Howard said that his business associates were certain American gents who didn't fool. He said that if ever I opened my mouth, it would never be safe for me to cross the border again. He said they would get me in Buffalo, Cleveland, Chicago, New York or Los Angeles. He asked me if I knew how acid affected a person's complexion. He said maybe I should talk to Victor Riesel. He said he had taken the precaution of moving all that stuff away from the house, and nobody would ever find it.

"Finally I agreed to divorce him and not ask for any settlement, and I swore I would never tell a soul, so he let me go. And now I've told *you*. So now you know where Howard got his spending money."

"I can see the pattern," Sidney said. "I came across a case where Gadwell wanted to distract somebody's attention so he arranged an accidental-on-purpose striptease. The man is trying to build sex as a spectator sport."

There were many other questions, but they brought forth nothing of positive value. On the negative side, Miss Willison knew of no connection between Gadwell and Ralph Paget.

Had Wes Beattie somehow stumbled on Gadwell's secret, through attending a stag party or paddling about in Muskoka? A possible new motive had appeared.

❀ ❀ ❀

After leaving Miss Willison's apartment, Sidney called Bob Duffy and warned him that he might receive some sort of threat, and then called June to caution her against revealing the name "Gadwell" to her brother if she should succeed in seeing him. Then he headed for St. Clair Avenue and caught Dr. Milton Heber just as the psychiatrist was leaving his office.

"Mr. Grant!" Heber said. "The young lawyer who, as I recall it, undertook to get in touch with a certain woman witness. How did you make out?"

"Dr. Heber," Sidney said, "I have news for you. The weird world of Wes Beattie is even weirder than you thought. There is actually some substance to it. Wes *was* framed on the purse theft. I'm convinced of it."

"Splendid!" Heber said. "And it was very wise of you to come for immediate psychotherapy. Would you like to be admitted to the Psychiatric, or would you prefer Homewood?"

"Sorry, no dice," Sidney said. "Now, Baldwin Ogilvy tells me you have proof that Wes's murder-night alibi is all lies. I would like to see your proof. By the way, Ogilvy said..."

"Yes, he called me and asked me to let you have anything you wanted. Well, it's very simple. I persuaded Wes—much against his will—to take heavy sedation. Sodium pentothal. So-called truth serum. He wanted to know why, and what did I intend to ask him under the truth serum. He was frightened of it. He obviously had guilty secrets he was afraid of spilling."

"Who hasn't?" Sidney asked.

"Oh, agreed, absolutely. But an innocent person charged with a crime is more likely to welcome any form of truth serum or polygraph test. However, after some days of persuasion, Wes agreed. And I was able to put on tape an interview in which Wes went right through his alibi story in meticulous detail. And, unlike his wild and improbable stories of the conspiracy, this was as skillful a piece of lying as I have ever heard. And psychiatrists hear plenty."

"You mean it's possible to lie under this truth serum?" Sidney asked.

"Yes. That's why 'truth serum' is a misnomer. What Wes did, I believe, was to rehearse and rehearse his story until he had it taped, and all the rough edges rubbed off. It's possible that he actually believed every word of it himself. Under certain circumstances I believe that a person with delusions could fool the polygraph lie detector."

"Then, if this was such skillful lying, how do you *know* it was lying?" Sidney demanded.

"Well, externally, for a start, we know that on that evening Wes Beattie left his fingerprints on a telephone at his uncle's apartment. This has been proved quite objectively. His movements in the preceding days have been checked out most carefully, and the only time those fingerprints *could* have been put there was on that evening. His alibi for all other times is only too well substantiated."

"Yes. But that is begging the question to the point where you are *petitio princi—pie-eyed*," Sidney said. "What about *internal* evidence?"

"Even better," Heber said. "Wes nerved himself to face the ordeal by pentothal, and he was clever about it, but not clever enough. He knew he would be asked to describe the apartment to which he claimed he had been lured. He knew he had to have details. So he formed a mental picture of an apartment. He furnished it in his mind until he could string off all sorts of things—pictures on the walls, books, records and such like. On this background he superimposed a story about being lured away by a girl, with whom he had an affair—also described in quite astounding detail.

"But here's the catch. Wes has never known any sort of house or apartment that *didn't* have good pictures, carpets and *objets d'art*. He put together the sort of apartment where you might conceivably make love to a lady of considerable taste, assuming that her taste could descend to Wes in the matter of men. But the *girl*. You should hear her. I have no doubt she is a real girl, with whom Wes at some time has had a sordid affair. She was obviously raised on bubble gum and movie fan mags and comic books. Her vocabulary is revealing. She says, if I recall correctly, 'Honey boy, I know that God intended you and I for lovers.' Wow! If the girl is real—and I believe she is—Wes probably knew her at a cheap hotel. She absolutely does not fit the background he has given her. She could not possibly live in the apartment that Wes furnished for her.

"The girl talks like an uneducated waitress in a cheap restaurant. Yet she has a Modigliani in her dining room, a Renoir in her bedroom, a modern abstract in her living room, books by Ivy Compton-Burnett, Proust and Agatha Christie, a hi-fi with no rock, cha cha or cowboy guitars— only Haydn, Stravinsky and Broadway musicals. Wes allowed himself to get very drowsy, but he kept enough grip to recite these things in a very convincing manner. Now, what can you make of that

—coupled with those fingerprints? There is a sort of insane cunning in it, even allowing for the fatal error."

"May I have the tape?" Sidney asked.

"Certainly. If you haven't got a machine, you can rent one on Yonge Street. But beware of being sucked into the weird world of Wes Beattie, or you'll find yourself occupying the next bed at the Psychiatric."

Sidney took the tape recording and went home, feeling somewhat depressed. He toyed with the theory that the technically clever Gadwell *had*, in fact, invented a method of transferring fingerprints photographically, but he quickly rejected it.

His reverie was interrupted by a phone call from June, who said she had news for him, and he agreed to meet her at the Park Plaza to hear all about it.

"Well," June said, when they had been furnished with whisky sours, "I got in to see Wes with very little trouble. I found a nice young intern who took me straight up. I expected to find Wes in a padded cell with barred windows, but lo and behold, there he was in the TV lounge, chatting with fellow patients, and apparently perfectly rational. I upset the applecart, I'm afraid. Tremendous emotional outbursts, tears, clingings to sisters' necks and all that. Why had I deserted him, why hadn't I come before? I told him I'd been warned off. No family. So he burst into a tirade about conspiracies.

"We went to his room, and I told him Mr. Ogilvy was going to withdraw. He sneered horribly and talked about rats leaving the sinking ship. I think he enjoys the romantic feeling of being alone against a hostile world. I told him to shaddap and let *me* talk. I said Mr. Ogilvy was being a real prince about the whole thing. I told him that, whatever Gran or Uncle Ralph might say, he had a right to appoint his own lawyer, and I recommended you. I said you had made certain helpful discoveries, but did not specify. He said, 'Is he on the trail of the gang? Tell him to watch himself! They got Uncle Edgar.'

"I asked him if he had any slightest inkling of a clue why anyone should want to ruin him, and he came out with a brilliant theory. He said, yes, he'd worked it all out. 'This is an international gang, see?' he said. 'And when they're going to pull some job in the big time, like New York or Chi, they try it out here, like Moss Hart and Lerner and all that mob tried out *Camelot* in Toronto before they opened on Broadway.'

"I thanked him prettily for this brain wave and we talked of other things. He wanted to know all about you. Was I sure you weren't in the gang? How old, how tall? I told him older than Bruce Kidd and shorter than Goose Tatum. I told him your nickname, and he was charmed. He started referring to you as 'the old Gargoyle.' Gee, the old Gargoyle would soon have him off the hook and round up those guys. So I left him pedaling madly on his manic cycle and rushed to tell you. Oh, by the way. He wrote a note appointing you as his counsel, and borrowed a dollar from me, which he gave me back to hand to you as a retainer. He said to say he would pay you plenty more, but pull-enty more, as soon as you spring him on this rap. Now where do we go?"

"There are two roads open," Sidney said. "I have to get a tape machine and listen to a depressing tape, and I want to do some exploring in Muskoka. My own car is a heap..."

"Oh, I have a Citroën," she said. "It goes like a bomb. Do you want it? But what do you want to explore in Muskoka?"

"I want to look for an old summer cottage. A big old frame one that's been winterized. It is a hideout, I believe, of Howard Gadwell's. I've been thinking about it, and the more I think, the more I want to find it. And it's got to be this weekend or not at all. Also, I may have to do a spot of breaking and entering. And tomorrow I will have to interview my new client and see if he can give me any help."

"So when is your Muskoka safari?" she asked.

"By golly, I'd like to go tonight," he said. "Night would be the best time to locate the place. Look, this is dynamite, so quiet, eh? Gadwell used to go to this joint every weekend.

Probably still does. It would be easier to locate the cottage at night if there were lights showing. And once I've found the place, I can go back up there and explore at some time when I know that Mr. Gadwell isn't at home."

"Just what do you mean, you want to look for a cottage? Muskoka is lousy with cottages."

"Well, this one is special. Big, high ceilings. Probably off by itself. Very private."

"On an island, then," she said. "Sounds like Little Pittsburgh to me."

"Little Pittsburgh? Who he?" Sidney asked.

"Sort of a section of Muskoka Lake," she said. "Before all the millionaires moved to Texas, they used to grow them in Pittsburgh. Steel, coal, that sort of thing. Well, some of these millionaires discovered Muskoka. They bought islands, back around the turn of the century. They built huge, gingerbread frame cottages and boathouses, and they really lived it up. There used to be Mellons up there..."

"Watermelons?" Sidney said.

"No, idiot. Two-L Mellons, like Carnegies and so on. Most of them have sold out or died out, but the cottages are still there. Some have been turned into lodges, I believe. But, Sidney, you could flounder around for days. What have you to go on?"

"Dead reckoning," he said. "I have a fairly exact distance from a point in Toronto, up 400 and 11. The turnoff appears to be Bracebridge. Couple that with the description of the cottage, and where does that put you?"

"Along the Port Carling road, almost for sure," she said. "And it sounds very much like Little Pittsburgh. But if it's on an island, you've had it. The place is crawling with islands."

"Suppose a person were going to an island up there in winter," Sidney said. "Would he drive over the ice to it?"

"I imagine so," she said. "The ice is good and thick at least till April."

"All right," he said. "Now suppose I set out on that route and drove the exact number of miles I figured on. That should bring me to a landing stage. Right? Supposing it's an island we're looking for."

"Yes, that makes sense," she said. "Maybe the big wharf at Beaumaris or something like that."

"Okay. Well, suppose you got out and searched about with a flashlight on the ice. Maybe you'd find car tracks, eh?"

"Sure, complete with trolley wires and streetcar stops," she said.

"Don't be smart, Miss Smarty," he said. "If people *do* drive up on the weekend, there might be tracks, eh? So if you got a direction to go, well, you might drive along and see lighted windows. And maybe the gas station nearest the turnoff would remember about cars going in there at this time of year."

"Crazy. Mad. Mixed up," she said. "You don't know Muskoka. Why, your friends draw maps for you showing *exactly* how to get there, and you still get lost. What gives with this cottage anyway?"

"I don't really know, June," he said, "but everything in this case is so elusive. If I hadn't followed some pretty slender threads, I'd be nowhere. I want to find that cottage, soon, fast. I've got to explore Gadwell's activities. It's the only lead I've got, really."

"Like to go tonight? In all this cold snap?" she said.

"I can't wait for tennis weather," he said. "Frankly, yes. I can't waste time. At least I can try the experiment."

"All right," she said. "You've got yourself a car and a driver. What else do you need?"

"Maps," he said. "Muskoka county maps. Flashlights. Warm clothes. Thermos flask filled with coffee, well laced with brandy. And I'd like some means of making an illegal entry, in case I decide to."

"I can get the maps," she said. "And the thermoses and their contents. I will also round up some flashlights."

"You think this is a harebrained scheme?" he said.

"Yes. But I *like* harebrained schemes. Please, please, let me come? Don't say 'We don't want no girls in this gang.'"

"All right," he said. "Go home. Eat a big meal. Get your stuff collected and stand by. I have other arrangements to make."

The first arrangement was a further call on Sharon Willison, who was getting ready to go to the studio for further checking of her figures. "Just ask my agent if Sharon doesn't know her arithmetic," she said, and produced the actual book in which she had recorded her husband's mileages.

The absolute minimum round-trip mileage for Gadwell's Muskoka expeditions came to two hundred and eighty-four and a bit, but this figure appeared no less than four times— all, according to the record, in the summer. The lowest winter mileage came to a shade under two hundred and ninety.

"Hey, look at that!" Sidney said. "The minimum goes up in winter! Why? His hideaway is on an island and in winter he can drive right to it over the ice. A shade more than two miles. Miss Willison, you are a true scientific detective. Science is measurement. This minimum in summer must be the exact distance between your old house and the landing stage where he left his boat."

"Golly! I never thought of that," she said.

All that was needed from the songstress after that was the address of the house where she had lived with Gadwell, and, having obtained it, Sidney headed for the southeastern quarter of the city to make his other arrangements.

Nine

DURING HIS BRIEF CAREER at the bar, Sidney Grant had pleaded few cases before juries. The most successful of these had been a case before a county court jury involving one Snake Rivers, who had been charged with burglary.

The crux of that case had been Sidney's cross-examination of Inspector Frank Young, of the Metropolitan Toronto Police, concerning a search the police had made of Mr. Rivers's dwelling. The cross-examination had proceeded thus:

Q. "You obtained a search warrant and went to the accused's house?"

A. "Yes."

Q. "Did you discover anything of significance during this search?"

A. "No."

Q. "You had some purpose in making this search? You expected to find something?"

A. "Well, we thought we might."

Q. "You thought you might find stolen goods?"

A. "Well, maybe."

Q. "Or burglar tools?"

A. "Perhaps."

Q. "You had received information that these things were in the house?"

A. "We were acting on information. Yes."

Q. "But this information was incorrect? You found nothing there that in any way implicated the accused?"

A. "Well—well, no. He..."

Q. "Never mind that. You found nothing at all. That is all."

To the jury, Sidney was able to point out that the evidence against his client was extremely insubstantial and consisted solely of a chancy identification. He was thereby able to save Snake Rivers from a fourth term in jail.

After leaving Sharon Willison's apartment, Sidney sought Snake Rivers in a low beer hall which he was known to patronize of a Saturday night.

The regular customers of the place eyed Sidney with some suspicion as he wove through the crowded aisles to Snake's regular table, but Snake greeted him with boisterous affection.

"Gee, nice to see you, Mr. Grant," he said. "Let me buy you a couple of beers."

"No thanks, Snake," Sidney said. "I've got work to do. I hope you're keeping out of trouble these days."

"I sure as hell am," Snake said. "Listen, I've had all the stir I want, see? I got an honest job that pays real good— turning back speedometers on used cars up on the Danforth. No more of that old jazz for me."

"Good," Sidney said. "Can I talk here?"

"Sure. Just come close," Snake said.

"When the police raided your place," Sidney said, "they'd had a tip from a stool pigeon that you had illegal instruments in the house. Right?"

"Sure thing," Snake said. "But they didn't find nothin', like you said."

"Well, if you ever possessed tools of that sort, you won't need them again, will you? They might just tempt you to use them one night."

"Yeah, that's right. But I'm through. No kidding. Next time up I'm liable to get twenty years."

"All right. Can you tell me where I might get hold of some tools of that type? I may want to get into a house during the owner's absence."

"Gee—don't do it," Snake said. "They'll get you sure as hell."

"I'm looking for evidence—not loot," Sidney said. "And I don't intend to get caught."

"Who does?" Snake said. "Gee, I can tell you where to pick up them things, but I don't like it. Where's this job?"

"Up north. Miles from anywhere."

"Huh! This summer cottage jazz," Snake said. "I know guys that used to go after outboard motors and stuff. You've got to watch out in case they got some local farmer watching the place. Listen, how about taking me along? You need experience on a job like this."

"No," Sidney said. "If *I* get caught, I'll be all right. But you can't afford to be remotely involved in anything. Where can I get this stuff?"

"I'll have to line it up for you," Snake said. "When I give you the green, you drive east along Dundas from here, turn right at the fourth street, then down half a block and turn left up the lane. Only before you turn up the lane, pull up on the right and park. A kid will come past and throw something over your license plates. You gotta have your lights out. Then pull into the lane, fast, with the lights out, and stop at a stable. It's on the right-hand side of the lane. Make sure your trunk is open. Someone will throw the stuff in your trunk, and when you hear it slam, drive out fast, turn right and go about fifty yards and stop. Another kid will take these rags off your license plates and give you the go sign. Then start up, switch your lights on and belt the hell out of there."

"Sort of elaborate, isn't it?" Sidney said.

"Sure. But we figure the police know them tools is in the loft. They got a stoolie watchin' for when they leave. We been meanin' to get them out of there and dump 'em, so it's all set up. Cost you twenty bucks for time and labor. Now you run through the drill and see you got it straight. If you follow instructions real close, you can't go wrong."

Sidney repeated the instructions twice and told Snake that he would have to phone for his transport.

"Don't call from here," Snake said. "Take the outdoor booth at the corner of Dundas, then go one block west to meet your car."

Sidney went to the corner, leaving Snake at the table, and called June.

"Look, Juney, this thing is a bit risky," he said. "How about bringing the car down here and going back in a cab? I've got to do a lot of cloak and dagger work. Real underworld stuff."

"The heck with you, young Gargoyle," she said. "After collecting maps and flashlights and laced coffee, I'm not going to be bumped off the flight. You just tell me where to pick you up. Will it be really truly underworld?"

There was no arguing with her, and Sidney, whose conscience told him he should drop the whole thing, gave up. "Okay," he said at last. "You're as stupid as I am."

And he gave her instructions as to where to meet him and told her to be sure the trunk was unlocked.

❀ ❀ ❀

"All right, pull up on the right here," Sidney said in a level voice. "Now, lights out. Watch this kid—Lord, they start them young down here —the little devil is as casual as all get out. Just look straight ahead, dearie. Okay, lights still out, pull ahead and swing into that lane. Go."

June, who was a superb driver, gunned the Citroën into the narrow lane. A two-story brick structure loomed on the right.

"Stop. Right here," Sidney said.

In less than ten seconds they heard the trunk slam. "Go girl, go," Sidney said. "Swing right at the end. Good. Now pull over here."

June stopped at the curb, and another boy, apparently about twelve, strolled past. He took something from the front of the car and continued on his way. But at that instant the rear door opened and somebody slid into the back seat. The door slammed.

"Okay, now drive. Go. Get the hell out of here," a voice said. "Keep the lights off for a bit."

Sidney's blood froze, but June already had the car in motion. Sidney turned slowly and saw the features of Snake Rivers in the back seat.

"I decided to come," Snake said. "You're going to need a pro. Once you got out of that lane without your license being took you were okay."

Sidney caught a picture of Snake Rivers being sent up for twenty years and June Beattie joining her brother in the criminal ranks, but they were under way, and there was no turning back.

They drove to the house where Gadwell and Sharon Willison had lived and recorded the mileage, and then June headed the Citroën up Avenue Road toward 401 and 400.

She was enchanted by all the hocus-pocus that had gone on in the lane, and Snake Rivers was happy to explain it all.

"See, one night I got word the cops were going to put the arm on me," he said. "They was working on a tip. Well, I grab a suitcase and head out, and whoever is watching the joint follows me. That gives my chum enough time to get this stuff out the back way and dump it in the loft of that old stable. So I was arrested with an empty suitcase on me, and they raided the house and didn't find nothing, so Mr. Grant was able to spring me."

"I don't want to know about this, Snake," Sidney said. "I merely pointed out to the jury that the evidence against you was inadequate."

"Okay, Mr. Grant, so you don't need to listen, but the young lady was innarested..."

"Yes, Sidney, you just shut up and let Mr. Rivers talk. I want to hear about this."

"Okay," Snake said. "Well, we got to know that the police knew the tools was in that loft. So they put somebody to watch the joint and report when anybody took them out. Well, okay, so we had that stuff under police protection till we wanted to use it. This stoolie could phone in and maybe give the license number of the car that drug the stuff away. Well, okay, we had it fixed to cover the plates and move fast. A set of tools like this is worth eight, nine hundred bucks."

"But you assured me that you were through with burglary," Sidney said.

"Well sure, but this stuff may be useful to some other guy," Snake said.

Sidney suddenly felt a little unhappy about the morality of helping to snatch a set of burglary tools out from police surveillance, but June, who had never met a burglar before, was far too interested in the mechanics of the craft and questioned Mr. Rivers closely about methods.

The learned discussion continued while the Citroën snaked its way northward on the almost deserted highway, cruising comfortably at eighty-five.

"Easy, girl," Sidney said. "We don't want to get pulled for speeding with that stuff in the trunk."

But June was almost incapable of going easy on a clear four-lane highway, and the Citroën pulled into Bracebridge in less than an hour and three quarters after leaving the city. It was nearly midnight, and the town was asleep.

It was a cold moonlight night, without a breath of wind, but Sidney was appalled to note that there was a thin layer of new snow over everything. They stopped for coffee at an all-night eatery and learned that the snow had stopped falling and the sky had cleared less than an hour before.

"If our friend came up last night, there's not much chance of finding any tracks," Sidney said. "Let's look at the map and figure out where the mileage will bring us to."

June produced her map, and they spread it on the table. After a little arithmetical work, June stated that the end of the journey would come several miles before Beaumaris.

"There are some wharves along there," she said. "We might pick out the right one, but driving out on the lake will be hopeless."

"Having chased the wild goose this far, we might as well go on," Sidney said. "We could see lights at quite a distance."

They resumed the journey, but when they reached the Port Carling-Beaumaris turnoff, Sidney suggested that June pull off to the right of Highway 11 while he studied the snow on the Port Carling road.

It was a very light snowfall which the first wind would blow away. Sidney cleared a patch of road with his foot. Beneath the new snow the asphalt surface was clean. No car had passed along the Port Carling road in either direction over the smooth white surface, and as he stood beneath the stars in the awesome northern silence, Sidney began to feel a little silly about the whole business.

Miles away he heard a farm dog bark, and not so far away he heard raucous laughter and the slam of a car door. A Saturday-night party was breaking up. He heard a car start and drive away somewhere, then utter silence.

Ahead of him, to the west, two searchlights stabbed into the sky, wobbled and described a brief arc, then disappeared. Sidney watched them idly, vaguely wondering what search-lights they could be, when they shot up again, and he realized they were the headlights of a car going uphill. They continued to shoot up at intervals, moving from left to right, never reappearing in exactly the same direction as the last time, and then, far off, he heard the snarl of an engine.

He turned and looked back at the Citroën, where June and the burglar were in the midst of an animated conversation. Suddenly the cold got through to Sidney's bones and he shivered.

He turned and started back toward the Citroën, but the snarl of the approaching car caused him to look back, and he saw its two headlights wink at him from a hilltop and disappear. The Port Carling road was hilly and winding, and the engine noises rose and fell as the car moved from hilltop to valley. It was moving fast.

"June," he called, "turn your lights out."

She rolled the window down and called, "What did you say?"

"Lights out," he replied.

The Citroën went dark, and Sidney walked to the side of the Port Carling road, where he chose a station beside a tree. The headlights winked, half a mile away, then disappeared, but the engine noises were now continuous. In a few seconds the headlights came again, illuminating the whole stretch of road between Sidney and the approaching car. He turned his head away to avoid being blinded. A truck was approaching from the south, changing gear noisily, and now its headlights also became visible, just as the big car from the west slowed down at the approach to the highway.

It was a Cadillac, and it swerved slightly as the driver braked, but he controlled it skillfully. It came to a stop and waited for the truck to pass, and the truck's headlights flickered over the driver's face. He was leaning forward anxiously, waiting his chance to turn onto the highway, and Sidney had no difficulty identifying him. It was Howard Gadwell. The truck passed. The Cadillac started up and swung to the south, leaving behind it a clear set of tracks on the new-fallen snow.

Sidney walked slowly back to the Citroën and got in beside June.

"Don't tell me. Let me guess," she said.

"You've already got it," Sidney said. "That was our little pal. So, if you will get moving before the snow clears, we can find out where he's been."

"Sidney," she said, "I've always heard that it's better to be born lucky than rich. You must have been born with a horseshoe round your neck."

"Don't talk, woman, drive!" Sidney said. "You can only be lucky if you play it that way. We might still be sitting in Toronto saying that the whole expedition is impossible if we weren't a bunch of lucky fools."

The track of the Cadillac stood out clear and black, and there was no difficulty in following it, especially since it had insisted on staying on the road. Sidney did a countdown on the distance, and exactly three-tenths of a mile before the dead reckoning position of the landing stage, the tracks turned down a side road to the left through the bush.

June eased the Citroën down the bumpy side road, which led to a dilapidated boathouse with a long wharf in front of it. At that point the Cadillac tracks turned off onto a small bay beside the bathhouse, and from there out to the ice of Lake Muskoka.

"Lights out," Sidney said. "Mr. Gadwell may have left pals behind. We can follow the tracks by moonlight."

The tracks veered away to the southwest, through a narrow channel between two islands, swerved to avoid another island, then moved across an open stretch and finally reached a high, rocky island covered with what looked in silhouette like white pines. On the south side of the island the tracks turned into a small bay and up to a beach, from which further progress was impossible.

As they crossed the bay, they could see above them a huge gingerbread frame cottage in the moonlight.

June shuddered. "I'm going back right now," she said. "Sidney darling, get me out of this! I just saw Alfred Hitchcock's shadow on the rocks."

When the engine stopped, the silence was ghastly. On their own level, all was inky blackness. Above them the moonlight played on mansarded roofs and gingerbread woodwork.

"I know it," June said. "That house is crawling with mastiffs, their vocal cords cut, and they leap out on one silently. There are deaf butlers in ancient evening clothes, carrying decanters on silver trays to elderly recluses. There are hatchet-faced housekeepers putting black widow spiders in the bed linen and trap doors that open in every corridor. I won't go near it."

"All right, chicken," Sidney said. "You stay in the car where it's warm."

"What's that? You'd leave me here, with Boris Karloff creeping through the woods from his grave? You swine! If you move *one foot* from me, I will utter one piercing shriek and go mad. It runs in my family. My brother..."

"Shut up," Sidney said. "Let's go. Can you get us in there, Snake?"

"Nothin' to it," Snake said. "But we gotta watch out for alarms and wiring systems."

"Alarms and wiring systems," June said. "That's all I need. When we trip the wire, mad gorillas are released in the grounds. I see one now." Her fingers were firmly gripped in Sidney's arm as they walked up the rocky path to the broad veranda.

"Lord, what a place!" Sidney said quietly.

"Part of Little Pittsburgh, all right," June whispered.

At the top level the rock had evidently been blasted off to make a lawn and garden, and it was possible to imagine the place in summers of long ago, with Chinese lanterns over the lawn and men in white ducks walking among the rose arbors with the dark-eyed beauties of Pittsburgh. But with the temperature at zero, it required a fair force of imagination.

The windows were all stoutly shuttered and the doors were boarded over. Snake, an expert in choosing the path of least resistance, found a likely-looking window and went back to the car to get the proper implements for opening it.

"Intrepid fellow!" June whispered. "I wish I'd never seen *The Cat and the Canary.*"

Snake Rivers worked calmly, with truly professional skill, and in a few minutes had the shutters open and the sash raised. Sidney went in first, followed closely by June, who immediately seized his arm again, and Snake came in last.

The house was completely furnished in the grand manner, but everything was old and dilapidated and covered in thick dust. They found the great entrance hall with its curved staircase and balcony, and turned their flashlights on ancient carpets and brocaded chairs. They went up the stairs and turned along a corridor with sixteen closed doors. June nearly stopped the circulation in Sidney's arm.

"They're lurking behind those doors," she said. "I know it. Butlers. Evening clothes. A mad lady, still in the wedding dress she wore the day her bridegroom was killed."

Heavy electric cables lay along the floor of the corridor and turned into a bedroom, where two modern-looking twin beds were set up in one corner, with a vanity table of modern design beside them. Elsewhere in the house the ghosts of Gadwell's film industry were to be seen, but it quickly became obvious that the house had been unused for a long time.

They found a basement, hewn out of solid rock, that had evidently once been a wine cellar, but in more recent times had been used as a film laboratory.

"Look!" June said. "Movie makers! I told you Hitchcock had been here."

But the house was cold and deserted, and there were no indications of recent human activity.

"Gadwell certainly hasn't been spending the weekend here," Sidney said.

They emerged by the same window that they had entered, and Snake made everything fast.

Back at the Citroën, Sidney cast about and found where the Cadillac had parked on the snow-covered beach.

"Ah, here we are," Sidney said. "He went *that*away."

The footprints led along a different path, right across the island to a two-story frame boathouse with a spring-locked door.

Snake looked the place over and went round to the side, where he climbed a tree and let himself in by an upstairs window, returning via the stairs to admit the other two.

"Warmth," June said. "That's what we need."

The temperature in the boathouse was far from cozy, but after the near-zero weather outside it felt relatively comfortable. There was an oil space heater on the lower level, which came on at the flick of a switch.

In the lower portion there were two modern outboard boats with Fiberglas hulls, and an old-fashioned mahogany launch pulled up on the dry floor, and at one side there was a long workbench. Upstairs was a comfortable apartment where somebody had recently had a meal of beans and bacon. There was also a glass, still smelling of rum.

"Now why would Gadwell come all the way up here to eat beans and drink rum?" Sidney asked. "The business end of this place hasn't been working for months."

June produced a thermos flask from the pocket of her coonskin coat, and they all had a drink of hot coffee, laced with brandy.

"He evidently never went near the big house," Sidney said. "He came straight here. I wonder what he was doing."

They searched the apartment without finding any clue and went downstairs again to the boathouse and workshop. It was admirably equipped with tools, which might have been used in servicing film equipment. While Sidney and Snake Rivers were looking at the bench, June suddenly stooped down to the floor.

"What have you got, June?" Sidney asked, looking at the spot illuminated by her flashlight.

"Something very, very strange," she said. "Water."

There was a moment of silence as the three people examined a small puddle on the floor, and then the silence was broken by a sound which froze all three conspirators in their tracks.

It was the hum of an engine, which suddenly became audible in the darkness outside.

"Quick—flashlights out," Sidney said.

They stood in total darkness and silence. The engine continued its hum, softly, insistently, getting no nearer and no farther, and then Snake burst out laughing.

"It's the diesel that runs the electricity," Snake shouted. "She switches on automatic. Turning on the heater done it."

They all laughed and resumed their study of the tiny pool of water.

"Look," June said. "This air isn't warm, but it's warm enough to thaw *that*." She pointed to an artifact which was leaning against the end of the bench.

"What is it?" Sidney asked.

"It's an ice drill," she said. "Ever go ice fishing?"

"Sure," he said. "Of course! You drive out on the ice, drill a hole for your fishing line then climb back in the nice warm car and wait for the fish to bite."

"That's right," she said. "So our friend came up for a spot of ice fishing. See, he brought the drill back in here with ice on it, and the ice has melted."

"Well I'm blowed," Sidney said. "Ice fishing. All alone."

He stood thinking for a minute, than walked to the door and went out. June and Snake Rivers stood looking at each other.

"Come out here, and bring your flashlights," Sidney called a few minutes later. "Maybe I've got something."

June and Snake found him on a path outside, stooped over and looking at a footprint. "Faint," he said, "but we can follow it. Mr. Gadwell went this way on his fishing expedition. Look, it leads out to the lake."

Bending over as they walked, they followed the footprints out onto the snow-covered surface of the lake. The trail continued for about two hundred yards, where there was a trampled patch of snow. June went down on hands and knees and started brushing the surface.

"Here you are," she said. "This is Mr. Gadwell's fishing hole. It's frozen over again."

She stood up and stamped her foot, cracking the thin layer of ice which had formed over the hole.

"No fishing hut, no car. He just stood out here and fished in the wide open spaces," she said. "What a weird character!"

"Like something Wes would dream up," Sidney said. "June, what if he *wasn't* fishing? What could he be doing? Getting rid of something? It would make a dandy place to dispose of evidence."

"Weird, utterly weird," she said. "So now what do we do?"

"Damn it, there's nothing we *can* do, except mark the spot maybe," Sidney said. "Another hour and it would be lost forever."

"What's the point in marking it?" she said. "And how would you go about marking it anyway?"

"If Gadwell wanted to lose something, we might as well mark the spot," Sidney said. "Say, Snake, how about nipping back to the boathouse and getting an oar? If we stick an oar through the ice it will freeze right in solid in case we want to find the place."

"It sounds really kooky to me," June said. "But your kookiest ideas seem to pay off."

Snake went back at a fast lope and returned with an oar, which was rammed through Gadwell's fishing hole and left there, standing upright, like a flagstaff left by some polar explorer.

Thereafter the party adjourned rapidly. A light wind had come up, clearing patches of ice on the lake and making it difficult to follow the tracks back to the landing stage. But June navigated with considerable skill, and less than an hour later they were wolfing ham and eggs in Harry's All-Nite Restaurant near Sparrow Lake Road.

It was nearly six o'clock on a cold March morning when they got back to Toronto.

Ten

SIDNEY WAS DREDGED FROM the depths of sleep early Sunday afternoon by the jangling of a telephone bell. He cursed and dragged himself up to answer it. It was Inspector Frank Young of the Metropolitan Police calling.

"Oh, Sid, I just wanted you to know that you have a job," the inspector said. "We have arrested your client, Mr. Herman Rivers, again. You know, Snake Rivers? I like to keep you gainfully employed."

"What has Snake been up to now?" Sidney said.

"He says *you* will explain everything. And Sid— remember how you cross-examined me about certain burglar tools? Your client had them smuggled out of his house, and hid them in a loft. We were keeping that loft under surveillance. Well, last night the tools were spirited away, in one of those foreign cars. A Citroën, it sounds like. And Mr. Rivers couldn't be found all night in any of his usual haunts. You see, there was a big job in the East End last night. Electronics warehouse. Big haul. Safe blown. We picked Snake up, arriving home at seven this morning. He'd better have a good alibi."

"He has," Sidney said. "He was with me, and I can prove it."

"Sid," the inspector said, "I wouldn't like to see a guy like you land into any trouble."

"I won't," Sidney said. "My strength is as the strength of nine, because my heart is relatively pure. I—I will bring a witness of unimpeachable integrity who will clear him. Just give me a little time."

It had suddenly occurred to Sidney that the incriminating tools were still in the trunk of the Citroën and would have to be put away safely before June's name could be mentioned.

"Snake and I were eating ham and eggs at four-fifteen A.M., a hundred miles north of here, at Harry's place on Highway 11," Sidney said.

Inspector Young remained dubious for some time, and it was late in the afternoon before Snake Rivers was set free.

By that time, the burglar tools were carefully stowed away in the basement of Robert Duffy's home, and June was able to come to headquarters and confirm the alibi.

"Gee, it all worked out perfect," Snake said. "The cops were watchin' me so close they forgot about certain other characters. I heard they made a real good haul."

"Snake," Sidney said, "I admonish you as your legal and spiritual adviser to sever all connections with those certain other characters. Twenty years is a long time."

"Oh, sure, I'm through, no kidding," Snake said. "From now on, I want no part of nothin' like that, except maybe in an advisory capacity. Just hang onto them tools till I tell you where to deliver them, will you?"

But Sidney's conscience was already black with guilt because he had acted as a red herring, and he arranged to purchase the tools outright for five hundred dollars. "Which your brother will pay," he explained to June, "as part of the investigation costs. And probably well worth it." He had intended to spend the afternoon with his client at the Psychiatric, but, by the time he had settled the burglar's problems, he decided it was too late, and he spent a lonely evening at home writing notes on the various aspects of the case.

In particular, he mused over the role played by Ralph Paget, and he racked his brains for some means, any means, to find out if there was any sort of link between the ultra-respectable Paget and the ultra-disrespectable Gadwell.

❀ ❀ ❀

But on Monday morning he had other things to think about. He located the film-studio island on June's map and wrote to a lawyer in Gravenhurst to find out who owned it. He set June to work calling friends who had Muskoka cottages, in order to find what local gossip had to say about the place. He sent Miss Semple out to rent a tape machine so that he could play the recording lent to him by Dr. Milton Heber, and he called an acquaintance on the morality squad of the Ontario Provincial Police in order to get the low-down on the obscene film racket.

The last inquiry turned up a piece of interesting information. The FBI in Washington had sent an emissary to Toronto some months before to try to locate a production center for obscene films, which, they claimed, were being made in Canada and exported to the United States. They had rounded up several distributors and captured a number of films, and they claimed they had effectively stopped the traffic, which was tied in with every other racket from dope pushing to the numbers game. But the Canadian authorities had been unable to give them any help at all. Even usually reliable underworld sources had never heard of such a racket in Canada, and check-ups of commercial studios had proved fruitless.

It was after one o'clock when Sidney dragged himself away from his office for a bite of lunch, and the second editions of the evening papers were on the newsstands. Sidney glanced at the black top line as he passed the corner; then he stopped and read it carefully. Finally, with trembling fingers, he fished a quarter from his pocket and bought both evening papers and did not even bother to collect his five cents change.

Under the big headlines the face of Sam Black, parking lot attendant at the Midtown Motel, was on display, three columns wide, and the headlines told about the finding of his body.

Sidney ducked into a cafeteria to read all about it as he munched on a sandwich.

At eight o'clock on Monday morning—according to the newspapers—one Steve Setti came on duty at a car park on King Street, near the business heart of the city, and noticed a car parked at the back of the lot which had been there all day Saturday. On Sunday, the lot had been unattended. Setti pointed the car out to his mate, who had been on since seven, and said that the car had certainly been there when he arrived.

There were many bars in the area, and it was not unusual for a gentleman to decide to leave his car on the lot all night and take a cab home, but he usually came back for it in the morning.

The windows and windshield of the car were heavily frosted over, and all the doors were locked. So Setti called the police, and in midmorning they came and towed the car to a garage. At about eleven the frost had melted from the windows, and a mechanic, chancing to glance in, saw a man's face on the floor of the front seat. Police were called at once, and the car was opened. The man inside it was very dead indeed, and frozen completely stiff.

He was taken at once to the morgue, where he was identified as Sam Black from papers found on the body. He had been shot twice at close range, through the heart.

Police learned, from neighbours, that Mrs. Black was away visiting a daughter by a previous marriage. Reporters had gained access to the Black bungalow through the good offices of a neighbor who had the key, and had lifted certain portraits and family groups, which were spread generously through the editions.

Diagrams on the front pages of both papers showed the parking lot and the position of the car, and one paper was able to point out that the murder spot was in plain view of its city-room window.

"Well, well, well," Sidney said. "And that explains the ice fishing!"

He gulped his sandwich and coffee, called Miss Semple and told her he would be delayed, and hurried down to King Street to have a look at the scene.

On the south side of King Street there were two large parking lots, running back to a lane that paralleled the street. The lane went west, behind a row of shops and the Prince George Hotel, which stood on the corner. Black's car had been parked at the rear of the most westerly lot, right beside the lane.

Sidney looked along the row of shops between the parking lot and the hotel: Lichtman's, who handled all the newspapers and magazines in the world; an old book store; Goldstein's, where Sidney sometimes bought a fine Havana cigar when he was feeling rich; the Press Club, haunted by newsmen and their pals; a pipe store; and then the Embers Restaurant, which had its own entrance on King Street, but was really part of the Prince George Hotel.

He stood on the north side of the street and looked, until he was frozen through, but before he crossed the road he thought he had the solution to the crime. Police were still searching the ground in the parking lot as he crossed over. He bumped into a newspaper friend on the south side, and gratefully accepted an invitation to have a drink at the Press Club, and he phoned June from the club to invite her to join him at four—after which hour ladies were admitted to the premises.

In the meantime, after combating the cold by means of a double Scotch, he made a brief foray to the Embers Room to complete a small piece of research.

The headwaiter greeted him politely, but with a puzzled look, not knowing whether he was a late luncher or an early diner.

"Sorry," Sidney said, "I've eaten. I just want to ask you a question. Can you recognize this gentleman?"

He pulled a five-by-seven glossy photograph of Howard Gadwell from his briefcase and held it out to the man.

"Sure. That's Mr. Gadwell," the waiter said. "He eats here a lot."

"Did he eat here on Friday?" Sidney said. "Friday evening?"

"Friday?" the headwaiter said. "Sure, I think it was Friday. One of the gentlemen couldn't have a steak because it was Friday, and they were kidding him. Yeah. He had a party of four gentlemen, Friday night, sort of late."

"Thank you," Sidney said. "You've been an immense help."

At four o'clock June Beattie joined Sidney and his newspaper friend at the Press Club, where there was much speculation in progress about the murder. The body had frozen so quickly that it was not possible to determine even the day of death, but the evidence of the parking lot attendants suggested it must have been Friday—late in the evening.

When Press Club conversation swung away from the murder to the evening's hockey game, Sidney slipped away with June to the Simcoe, where they could be more private.

"It's terrific!" he said. "Our friend Black became Black Mailer. He put the bite on Gadwell, and Gadwell killed him. I'm afraid we signed Black's death warrant, or at least I did, when I gave him Gadwell's name. And I think I know how it was done. Notice the way phone calls and parking lots keep cropping up?

"A blackmailer always has to meet his victim privately, but he's always afraid of really remote places because a blackmailer is liable to be murdered more than any other type of man. Gadwell cunningly suggested this parking lot because it would seem so safe, being close to a busy street—especially around here on a Friday evening. He told Black to pull in right to the rear of that lot, just after ten. The attendant goes off at ten. He told him to park there, turn the lights out and sit in the car.

"Then he invited three men to have late dinner with him at the Embers. At the right moment he excused himself to go to the men's room. He went out the back of the restaurant into the hotel corridor. Maybe he left his coat at the hotel check room instead of in the restaurant, or maybe he went out without a coat. He went out the York Street entrance, up the lane behind the hotel, made sure nobody was just parking or leaving, and then stepped out and yanked open the door of Black's car. Black had his left side to the lane, and he was probably looking out toward King Street, waiting for Gadwell's car to turn in. Gadwell had probably promised to turn up with much, much money in small bills.

"Gadwell pumped two rounds into him, probably using a silencer, shoved the body over onto the floor, then locked all the doors. You can reach over from the back seat and lock the front door in that model.

"Then he pocketed his weapon and returned to the hotel, having been gone less than five minutes—possibly as little as three. Very bold, very successful."

"And was it the gun he was throwing through the ice up north?" June asked.

"Of course. He hid the gun Friday night, but when the body wasn't found all day Saturday—it just sat there in the car, with the windows all frosted—he decided to dispose of it, but good. It was an easy run to Muskoka after dark on Saturday, and it put the gun away where it could never be found."

"Never?"

"Never," Sidney said, "except for the long, long chance that someone might find his hole in the ice before it froze over properly. June, the five hundred for Snake Rivers was money well spent."

"But can the gun be found in that deep water?" she said.

"I have an idea for some ice fishing that might do it," he replied.

The murder of Black had put certain other events of the day in the shadow, but June at length came round to them. Ralph Paget and old Mrs. Beattie had learned that morning of Baldwin Ogilvy's withdrawal from the case, and Paget had called June to give her what for.

"His rage surpassed all measure," she said, "and Gran is absolutely furious. Uncle Ralph says he has certain serious matters to discuss with you as well."

And so the day passed, and Sidney Grant had still not met his most important client.

Just because a little delay would have been useful, the proceedings of the assize court accelerated. An accused man committed suicide in jail; another, scheduled for trial, pleaded guilty; and Sidney suddenly realized on Tuesday morning that the case would probably be called against Wes on the following Monday.

Tuesday was also the day when Sidney's appointment as Wes Beattie's counsel was published. When Wes was brought up in the magistrate's court for remand, Baldwin Ogilvy stood up and made a brief statement.

"Your Worship," he said, "until now I have been appearing for the accused, Wesley M. Beattie. But I have so many pressures and commitments that I feel compelled to withdraw from this case. My withdrawal does not reflect any change in my attitude to the accused or his case, and I am happy to know that his defense will be in very competent hands."

"Then who is appearing for Beattie?" the magistrate asked.

"I am, your Worship," Sidney said.

The accused stood in the dock and goggled at his new lawyer. It was their first meeting, and Wes did not appear to be impressed. Sidney turned and grinned at him as the magistrate said, "Remanded in custody."

Their first conversation was held a few minutes later in the corridor before Wes was hustled away to the hospital.

It was too brief to add much to Sidney's knowledge of the case, but it was memorable nevertheless, because Wes and his weird world had come to dominate Sidney's life, and the central figure of this cosmogony was therefore per se a figure of surpassing interest.

And, as Sidney looked into the light blue eyes and the slightly anxious face, he found himself wondering again: "Could this boy kill?" But the annals of crime were too richly studded with baby-faced killers for Sidney to put much store in appearances. And he himself had seen the face of an angel contort into a visage from the road show of Dracula.

Which left him still in a terrible quandary with regard to the defense. He could trace the skilled hand of Gadwell in Wes's affairs to a point, but at that point the tracks faded away. The question, as Sidney put it to himself, was: Did Edgar Beattie really believe Gadwell—as Paget asserted— and did he really give up the pursuit? If so, it was a strong possibility that Wes, in utter frustration, had killed the man he worshiped. If, on the other hand, Edgar had been pressing forward with his investigation (and if Wes knew it), there was no chance on earth that Wes would have attacked him. Another question: Had Edgar tested and tempted Wes by *telling* him he had given up the search for Mrs. Leduc?

And then a new and comforting theory began to form in Sidney Grant's mind: Edgar had insisted to Gadwell that he was going to continue to track him and Mrs. Leduc down, until he met them face to face, and so Gadwell came to Edgar's apartment and killed Edgar, and Wes, who had been hanging around to hear the results of the interview, went up to the apartment, let himself in and found the body. He started to call the police, but suddenly he felt that his own position might be precarious. He hung up, looked again at the body, and the horror of it blotted everything from his mind.

Yes, that was it, Sidney decided. There was a hypothesis that could be taken into court. It would be a dandy hypothesis, founded partly on evidence and partly on conjecture.

With this comforting thought in mind, Sidney was about to leave his office on Tuesday afternoon when the telephone rang and Miss Semple called out that it was Mr. Ralph Paget.

Sidney cursed, but picked up the phone. Mr. Paget wished to see him and give him some information that would be of immense help to him. Could Sidney come to his office at once? Sidney toyed with the words "Climb a tree," but agreed to go and see Mr. Paget instead.

Mr. Paget's office would have served admirably as the almoner's office in some medieval monastery. It had the right discreet mixture of God and Mammon, with steel engravings of church towers and arches to give the religious note, and the corporate seal of the company (a fine antique machine, with the look of a thumbscrew about it) to lend the secular touch.

Mr. Paget, however, was all business.

"Mr. Grant," he said, "my wife's nephew, in his all-seeing wisdom, has decided to appoint you as his counsel in place of Mr. Baldwin Ogilvy. Since it is his own neck that is in jeopardy, he certainly has the right to appoint anyone he chooses. And you, as Wes's lawyer, are planning, if I mistake not, to alter the line of defense chosen by Mr. Ogilvy. This, too, is right and proper. But I feel it is my duty to point out certain facts which I had rather you learned now than in the middle of the trial."

"Thank you. Pray tell me, sir," Sidney said.

"Well, first of all, it was a great blessing, we thought, that the Crown Attorney more or less agreed to accept the insanity plea. Because Wes actually confessed to two witnesses, and the Crown is holding those witnesses in reserve."

"He *confessed?*" Sidney said.

"Yes. You didn't know that, did you? *I* knew, and I told no one. I considered it too dangerous a thing. It was the confession which compelled us to seek the insanity compromise."

"Did Baldwin Ogilvy know about the confession?"

"No. I was tipped off in strict confidence that the Crown held this very damaging evidence. I had to protect my informant."

"Well, let's hear about it. What did he say exactly?" Sidney said, noting that the pit of his stomach had entirely disappeared.

"Oh, it's simple enough," Paget said. "After the police interrogation Wes was questioned by various psychiatrists. His behavior was getting more and more neurotic; they had to give him sedation and all that sort of thing. Well, the question arose then as to where Wes should remain in custody. The Attorney General's department had the final say, but they decided to consult an official of the Department of Reform Institutions on the question of security. This official is a respected civil servant with a certain amount of psychological training."

"With a certain knowledge of brain surgery," Sidney said. "A pilot with a certain knowledge of aviation. Pray, sir, continue." Paget suppressed a certain irritation. "Now this man went to see Wes in the Psychiatric Hospital, and he questioned the doctors and nurses there in order to see if Wes was a danger to fellow patients, or a security risk escape-wise. He also interviewed Wes, with a hospital orderly present. Now this man knows something of psychology, but he has had enough experience of looking after criminals that he doesn't hold with a lot of coddling or beating around the bush. So he spoke out quite firmly to Wes. He's rather military in appearance, and..."

"Okay, okay," Sidney said. "Now I know who you're talking about. So his mustache bristled, his face turned purple and then he said...go on."

"Well, you may be right about that," Paget said, "but this gentleman said to Wes: 'The reason for all this stupid, scatty behavior of yours is simply because you're trying to escape from something, isn't it?' Wes replied, 'Yes sir.' 'And what you are escaping from is the knowledge that you killed your uncle. You're responsible for his death, aren't you?' Wes again replied, 'Yes sir.'"

Sidney leaned forward and saw that Paget was reading the details from an *aide-mémoire* on his desk, but Paget covered the paper until Sidney leaned back again.

"Then the major—er—this gentleman—said: 'You killed him, didn't you? Isn't that it?' and Wes said, 'I guess you could say so. Sure.' And then he sobbed and sobbed and this gentleman and the orderly quietly left the room."

"Now let me take it from there," Sidney said. "So Major Hale went out and wrote down the conversation at once. Later, the orderly was summoned to Hale's office, and, after having his memory refreshed from Hale's notes, he corroborated the whole thing in an affidavit and has since been given a good government job as a prison official."

"You may be right. That I don't know. Of course I was silly to try to conceal the name. You are perfectly right on that. But, Mr. Grant, this is admissible evidence..."

"Is it, my Lord?"

"Wes had been arrested, charged and warned. It was a voluntary statement made without any inducements or threats."

"And did Wes, by any chance, get the idea that this was another psychiatrist he was talking to? Notice his words. This is not an unequivocal confession. Wes might well mean that it was his stupidity and weakness that killed Edgar, not his hand holding a blackthorn stick. So Major Hale faded away quietly and whipped the orderly witness out of reach and recommended to the A.G. to leave Wes in the Psychiatric, and then proudly handed the A.G. this clinching piece of evidence, gained because the major got a C in second year pass psychology in 1921 and now knows more about it than Jung. Sir, thank you, thank you, I am most grateful for this knowledge. I suppose Wes just never felt it was worth telling his defenders that he had made this confession."

"He may well have forgotten it," Paget said. "But you see, it will never be produced if the insanity plea is used."

"Oh, won't it?" Sidney said. "In other words, the Crown Attorney knows it stinks, so he won't use it unless he has to. Well, that's dandy. I've always wanted to get Major Barnaby Hale in the witness box, so at least I've achieved one minor ambition."

"Mr. Grant, great heavens!" Paget said. "After what I've told you, you surely are not going to go ahead with your plan! Don't you *care* whether your client hangs or not?"

"Oh yes, I care very much. But sir, why have you kept this knowledge so close to your chest?"

"In order to protect my informant, as I said before. I was told in strictest confidence. But the other point, also very unfortunate, is that I am certain to be called as a witness for the Crown against Wes if you follow your plan. And that would be most painful and embarrassing for me."

"You—a Crown witness?" Sidney said.

"Yes. Unfortunately I was perfectly frank when the police questioned me about wills, and it seems I will have to tell about the contents of Edgar's will, and I will have to state that he intended to change the will and cut Wes out. You see, these things were told to Wes in my presence and are therefore admissible."

"Splendid," Sidney said.

"But I *can't* say *why* Edgar planned to change his will," Paget said brightly. "You can object to that, I'm sure, because it brings in Wes's previous criminal record. I'm sure you can keep *that* out."

"Goody for me," Sidney said.

"Now then, old man," Paget said, suddenly a pal, "don't you feel that, really, Mr. Ogilvy had the right approach, in the light of everything? Can I perhaps arrange a little meeting between you and a representative of the Crown Attorney?"

"No thank you, Mr. Crown Witness," Sidney said. "I will now say thank you and good-bye, and I'll see you in court."

"You're a god..." Paget began, half-rising, then shrugged and sat down.

Eleven

"**W**ES," SIDNEY GRANT SAID, "you've got to come back to earth. Earth, man. Your situation is serious."

Sidney was seated by his client in Wes Beattie's small private bedroom in the Psychiatric Hospital.

"But, gee, I feel so good. I mean now somebody believes me, after all the time I kept screaming at them, trying to tell them, and nobody would listen."

"But you're not out of the woods yet," Sidney said. "I now know who the people were who had you charged with theft. It looks to me as if they really worked an elaborate gag to frame you. I haven't found any reason why they *should* frame you. Something very fishy was going on—but what?"

"Search me," Wes said.

Sidney handed him two lists of names, one male names, the other female.

"Read those names out loud," Sidney ordered, "and then tell me if you know anybody by those names. Tell me if they mean anything at all."

Wes read the names slowly, but neither Howard Gadwell nor Janice Swann Wicklow, who were included on the lists, meant anything to him.

"No dice," Sidney said. "Well, now. Here is our problem. If you were being tried for that theft, we could get you acquitted without difficulty. But you are being tried for murder. If you plead insanity, two psychiatrists will swear that you have lost your marbles, and you'll be locked away in an institution 'at the Queen's pleasure,' as we say."

"I hope the Queen gets a lot of pleasure out of it," Wes said.

"On the other hand, we can claim that you did not kill your uncle. We can probably show the existence of a conspiracy against you. We can also, probably, show that your Uncle Edgar was interested in tracking down these conspirators. We can put forward the hypothesis that the conspirators killed him and framed you a second time. But unless we explain how your fingerprints got onto that telephone, we may be stumped.

"We say: 'Our story is that we were lured away by a woman in the pay of these conspirators, that she lured us to an apartment. We don't know where the apartment is, not even what district it's in.'

"That is going to sound pretty feeble. And the Crown Attorney is going to say that *he* knows the apartment, that it was Edgar Beattie's apartment, and he's going to produce *your* fingerprints to prove it."

"I can't help that," Wes said. "This gang—they're pretty cunning. It's like they can change the truth."

"But Wes, they can't transfer fingerprints. Now then, a psychiatrist heard your account of your evening at that apartment. He is a highly trained man. He thinks the story is false."

Wes was on his feet, quivering. "Oh sure!" he said. "So they give you truth serum and then say you're lying. What was wrong with the story?"

"Discrepancies," Sidney said. "Now what about the girl? Where did you meet her?"

"Picked her up. Downtown," Wes said. "She came and sat at my table and shot me a line and all that, and we made a date. So she picked me up in her car after dark and drove me to her apartment. I wasn't noticing where we were going, and, well, you know how it is. We fooled around in this apartment, had a couple of drinks and— well, she was a pushover, frankly. Then she said her husband was coming home and she drove me downtown and dumped me."

"And what was the apartment like?" Sidney asked.

"Well, like any other apartment," Wes said. "Sort of ordinary. I wasn't there to look at apartments, don't forget."

"But under sedation you described it in detail," Sidney reminded him.

"Well, maybe that was my unconscious mind that sort of noticed the details."

"Dr. Heber thinks you made those details up to lend verisimilitude to an otherwise bald and unconvincing narrative."

"There you go again!" Wes said, his voice rising. "All the time I'm lying, lying. They said there was no gang, and you found them."

"This apartment story is true?" Sidney said.

"Yes!" Wes screamed.

"Well, it was the third story you told them," Sidney said. "Which doesn't help at all. I wondered if there was perhaps a fourth story that you haven't told yet."

"Like what?" Wes said, shooting him a cautious glance.

"Like Wes Beattie behaving like a lame-brained idiot, and being afraid to tell the truth. It's happened before."

"Yeah? What are you getting at?"

"Oh, Uncle Edgar got a call from this man. The man told him to lay off. Uncle Edgar said, 'Never. Not till we meet face to face.' The man made a date to come and see him on that Friday night. Wes suspected that it would happen, so he figured it would be Friday, the day Uncle Edgar returned from the road trip. He hung about, away down the street. Saw a man go in—too far away to recognize. Figured it was the man. Saw the man come out two minutes later, and went along to investigate. Found the door open and walked in. Saw the body. Edgar had admitted his visitor, and had gone to sit down while the man took off his coat. The man seized the stick and cracked him unawares. So Wes found the body. He was horrified, started to phone the police, heard Flo Churcher call out. Suddenly got frightened and ran away.

"Maybe Wes had had a key to the apartment for years. Maybe Uncle Edgar lent it to him once, and he put it on his key ring and forgot it. When the police discovered it, he thought it was too incriminating, so he lied—he was accustomed to lying. He remembered the way he had been framed before and tried to work out a similar frame-up for the murder which would explain the key being planted by the decoy woman. But he forgot that he'd left those fingerprints, and he was stuck with his story and couldn't explain them. He felt that admitting he'd been near the apartment would be putting his head in the noose, because the conspirators were so elusive."

Wes Beattie sat staring at him wide-eyed. "Gee, how did you figure it out?" he said. "You know something? That's exactly the way it happened. I saw this guy go in. The dame was waiting out on the street in a parked car. The same dame that was a witness against me. I crept up close enough to look at her when she lit a cigarette. While I was watching, this guy came down and jumped in the car, and they drove away."

"And you took the license number?" Sidney said.

Wes stopped in full flight. "Yeah," he said. "I memorized it, but I didn't have a pencil or anything, and I forgot it afterward. Then I went up, and it was just like you said."

"And this is now the truth, and nothing but the truth?"

"Yes," Wes said.

"And you were extremely angry just now when I told you that Dr. Heber thought you were lying."

"Gee, I'm sorry," Wes said. "But you know..."

"The story of this girl and the apartment? You made it up?"

Wes paused, and doubt flickered across his face. He hung his head guiltily.

"Yes, I made it up," he said.

"How about the description of the apartment. The details. You made them up?"

"Yes."

"Tell me some of them."

"Well, I said—" Wes thought hard, with his eyes closed—"I said there was a Modigliani and classical records and stuff, like ikon paintings."

"And you wanted to let on this came from your unconscious, that you couldn't remember it when you were wide awake?"

"That's right. I knew about this heavy sedation bit."

"Dr. Heber thought you were clumsy. You described an elegant apartment furnished with some taste, and a girl with a comic-book mind."

Wes looked puzzled. He sat and thought that one over for a full minute. "Yeah. That's sort of funny, isn't it?" he said. "But I don't see what's wrong with it. See, this woman was a decoy for the gang, so it really wasn't her apartment. It was some joint they planted her in."

"But you said you made her up. You said it was a lie."

"Oh sure," Wes said. "But the way I made the lie up, I meant it to seem like it wasn't her apartment."

"Wes," Sidney said, "to change the subject, did you ever confess that you murdered your uncle?"

"No, certainly not," Wes said. "Never."

"Someone says you did."

"Well he's a goddam liar."

"A big fellow, with a military mustache. He came in with an orderly."

"Him?" Wes said.

"Him."

"Oh, God—does he say I confessed?" Wes stared at Sidney in horror.

"Yes."

"Well I didn't," Wes said, and his voice was rising with excitement. "I—they had a lot of headshrinkers examining me. I thought—gee, he said I could confide in him. He said it would be better, I'd feel better, if I admitted it. I said I didn't kill Uncle Edgar, and he said something about me really being responsible, and I said yes. Oh, God—not him."

"What else did you say?"

"Well, he said you could really say I killed Uncle Edgar, meaning on account of my stupidity, and I said sure or something, sort of to get rid of him, see, he bugged me, this guy. He was sort of like the magistrate that sent me up the river. Colonel Blimp kind of. He can't…"

"He can," Sidney said. "So, my young friend, you are going in to bat on a sticky wicket, as the Limeys would say. I will have to move all hell to get as much evidence in the record as possible to show the existence of this conspiracy. Then I have to decide whether or not to put you in the witness box. How do you feel about it?"

"Swell," Wes asserted. "I'll just tell them the truth, like I told it to you…"

"Wes, the Crown Attorney is going to cross-examine you, and if there is any little inconsistency, he will tear you apart. Now listen, my boy. If this is the truth, the whole truth, and nothing but the truth, it will stand up to all the Massinghams in the world. It will be indestructible. But if it's a lie—God help you. Now think it over. In any case, I may just decide to present your story as a hypothesis, to create reasonable doubt in the minds of the jury and keep you out of the witness box. You're a bad witness."

"Why?"

"When I asked you if you took the license number of that car, you thought it over and decided you didn't have a pencil to write it down. As a matter of fact, you didn't get near the car, did you? Maybe you never saw a car. Wes, whatever embroidery you may wish to add to the story, forget it. Stick to the solid truth."

"Okay, Gargoyle," Wes said.

"And don't call me Gargoyle. Call me Mr. Grant. And we'll get your hair cut and brush you up a bit, and remember to sit up straight in court and look dignified. Cut out all the smiles and grimaces and try to act grown up."

"Yessir," Wes said, looking astounded.

Sidney shook his head thoughtfully as he walked away.

The last days before the trial raced past in a welter of activity. There were witnesses to subpoena and details to check out about Flatiron Island, where Gadwell had operated his film studio. The title to the island was registered in the name of a man in Cleveland.

Sidney took a flock of pictures to show to Wes, including one of Howard Gadwell, but Wes didn't recognize it as anyone in particular.

The search for a motive was becoming desperate, because without a credible motive the conspiracy was simply part of the weird world of Wes Beattie. But nowhere could Sidney find any link between Ralph Paget and Howard Gadwell, or between Paget and Janice Wicklow.

Had Paget met Janice, perhaps, during a night on the town in Montreal? Had he offered her money to frame Wes, and had she brought Gadwell into the picture?

The only course of action open in the time that remained was to follow up the leads on Gadwell.

Sidney went to the Metropolitan Police and to the Ontario Provincial Police, and stated that he could possibly locate the murder weapon which had killed Sam Black. He said that, owing to the nature of his practice, he sometimes had access to information from the underworld, and he felt it his duty to place it before the authorities.

He also assured the morality squad that he had located the studio which the FBI believed existed in Canada, and he said that, in due course, he would be able to name the Canadian agent of the mob.

He got action on both scores. A federal agent flew in from Washington, and Sidney had to waste a valuable day going to Muskoka to show the agent the cottage on Flatiron Island, and to locate the oar, which was still standing like a flagstaff, frozen in the ice. The FBI man confirmed that the man in Cleveland who owned the cottage was, in fact, doing a long stretch in a federal prison.

The provincials were extremely dubious about trying to find a weapon in the depths of Lake Muskoka in March, but Sidney suggested a powerful permanent magnet lowered on a stout fishing line, and they agreed to try it.

"Try various weights on the line," Sidney said, "and keep casting away. If there is a weapon there, it may be lodged in a hole, and you might not get it in the first hundred tries. But a fisherman has to be patient."

The threat that the Metro Police would try it if the provincials didn't was sufficient to settle the matter, and Sidney returned to the city in a fast cruiser to make his final arrangements for the defense. Poor Miss Semple had been handling a load of detailed work almost unaided.

Naturally the Crown Attorney learned about the information which Sidney had given to the police, and he demanded explanations. Sidney gave him the name of Howard Gadwell—a name not unfamiliar to Mr. Massingham—and suggested that Gadwell be kept under constant and discreet surveillance until further developments.

"I'm rather busy on another matter at the moment," Sidney told him.

"So I understand," Massingham said. "You are defending Beattie. Am I to understand that you will not plead insanity?"

"That is correct," Sidney said.

Massingham's answer was to have Wes transferred promptly from the Psychiatric Hospital to the Don Jail. It came at an unfortunate time. The hospital authorities reported that Wes's condition had deteriorated after his lawyer's visit. The mood of gaiety and optimism had vanished. Once more he was moody and withdrawn, inclined to turn hysterical at the slightest excuse. The relative comfort of the hospital had given him a feeling of security. The return to the harsh world of prison was unlikely to help him.

Twelve

MRS. BEATTIE HAD BEEN taught as a girl that it was polite always to leave something on the plate, and even the rigors of two wars had never cured the habit.

This had worked out well for Betty Martin, who, after her orphanage upbringing, could never resist polishing off the delicacies left by her mistress.

Even on that fateful Sunday, the day before the trial, Betty gobbled up the remains of the deviled kidneys on the breakfast tray, as soon as Mrs. Beattie swept grandly into the bathroom, and then hurried the tray to the back stair in order to destroy the evidence.

In due course Mrs. Beattie emerged from her bath, and Betty, as was her custom, helped her to dress, but she jammed zippers, failed to make the correct junction between hooks and eyes, and was guilty of much hair pulling during brushing operations.

Mrs. Beattie remained icy calm through all the blunderings, but wondered aloud in an ominous manner whether Betty were not getting a little too old for such work, which only upset Betty and decreased her efficiency still further.

Marcia Paget appeared and wanted to know if her mother wished to be driven to church in the Jag, but Mrs. Beattie said she would not be attending divine worship that morning. Claudia came in to ask what right Marcia had to take the Jag, and flounced off in a temper when she got no satisfaction. When the toilet was completed, Mrs. Beattie stood up and said to Betty: "You may call me a taxi."

"Where shall I say you're going, Mum?" Betty asked.

Mrs. Beattie did not answer. She appeared not to have heard the question, and Betty, crushed, went to do her bidding. But Betty had her methods.

When the taxi arrived, she helped Mrs. Beattie down the steps and took such a time tucking her into the cab that the driver had time to ask, "Where to, lady?"

It would have been infra dig to ignore the question and let Betty know for sure that her mistress was going on a secret mission, so she spoke up loud and clear. "To the Don Jail," she said. "Do you know the way, driver?"

"A hell of a sight better'n I know the way to the York Club, lady," the driver said, and Betty had to hustle away into the house to avoid giggling.

The driver's eyebrows shot up, but, sensing a distinct chill from the back seat, he drove off in silence.

But already Betty was racing to the bedroom, where she seized the telephone and dialed with trembling fingers.

"Oh, Miss June, Miss June," she said, when the connection was complete, "a terrible thing is happening and Miss June only you can stop it. Mrs. Beattie has gone to the jail."

"God, not another in the family," June said. "What's she charged with? Keeping a disorderly house? Claudia at it again?"

"Oh, Miss June, Miss June, you mustn't joke, there was such a to-do. Mr. Paget is in the kennel again, I mean the doghouse, and Mrs. Beattie says he is an officious fool and she says Mr. Grant is a Charlotte Anne and a Mounty Banks, and she is the only one in the family that can do anything right, and now she's gone down to bully poor Mr. Wes and make him go to the lunatic asylum. Oh do get Mr. Grant and go and head her off, Miss June. Oh I'm sorry about waking you but you must, you must.

"All right, here we go again," June said.

A wild mink coat and blue-tinged hair will often open doors which are normally closed to anyone not having a proper pass. Besides, Mrs. Beattie's supreme self-confidence bordered on the faith that moves mountains. She was therefore able, with little difficulty, to obtain a Sunday morning interview with her grandson.

"Oh Wes, Wes, my poor boy Wes, what are they doing to you?" she said, and the warder withdrew to a tactful distance and averted his gaze.

Wes, his eyes filled with fear, stared at her.

"You have retained Mr. Grant, an inexperienced lawyer who is terribly anxious for notoriety," she continued. "What becomes of *you* is no concern to *him*. He will have had his picture in the papers. He will have argued a case before the assizes. He will have produced sensations. He has decided to ring in something about a guilty couple who were having an assignation at that motel, and this will make a Roman circus of the trial for the evening papers. He will put you in the witness box and subject you to merciless cross-examination. How will you stand up to it? Will you get excited and hysterical? Will you make an exhibition of yourself?"

"No, no, I won't, not this time," Wes said.

"How do you know? You are in no state to endure this ordeal," she said. "And for all the sensational material which Mr. Grant can produce, Mr. Massingham will bear down with remorseless logic on the plain facts."

"Well, the plain facts, Gran..." Wes began.

"Spare me, please," she said. "I am not in the best of health. I came here this morning to make one final appeal to you—to your own good sense. Wes, dear, if it would help you, I would permit myself to be photographed doing the Twist with Mr. Grant. You are the only one who matters. Now—it is still not too late to use the earlier plea which had been decided upon. Mr. Ogilvy, of course, will have nothing to do with the case, but we can get another lawyer. Even Mr. Grant might be persuaded to handle your plea of—mental disturbance. You will go to a reasonably comfortable institution, and at a later date we may be able to free you."

"You mean fifty years from now?" Wes said.

"But if you persist in this folly," she said, ignoring his remark, "we can expect a sensational trial and a dubious end to it. Think how a jury will react. You are almost bound to be convicted. You will be forced to stand and hear that ghastly sentence—possibly from a judge who has dined at our house. Then there will be appeals and petitions for clemency. But— others have gone to the gallows recently, and the present government would be frightened politically of commuting the sentence for a member of a prominent family.

"I hope I will not live until the final, dreadful scene— the ghastly ceremony which will take place in this building— shortly after midnight. I dread the night I may have to spend on my knees, praying for the soul of my little Wes. Oh, protest, cry, do what you will. The facts are to be faced."

Wes was struggling to speak, but no words would come, only tears.

"Now then, I must go, Wes," she said. "You may never see me again."

There were thrush notes of emotion in her voice, all the more effective because they were used with moderation.

"This is your last chance," she said. "Public humiliation and a terrible end—or the path of reason. Wes, let me get you a new lawyer. Change your plea. Do it for Gran."

"All right, all right," he sobbed, "but let me alone, will you? Just stop it. Oh, God, they said the truth would make me free, but nobody believes me, not even Sidney Grant. He thinks I'm lying like everyone else. It's true—he only wants to have a murder case."

"Of course it's true," she said. "Well, darling Wes, we'll have you back in the hospital tonight, and I will tell Mr. Grant that you don't require his services any more."

"Good. Tell me now, Mrs. Beattie," Sidney Grant said.

She swung around and saw Sidney and June, who had just entered the visitors' room. Extreme irritation showed on her face.

"Very well, Mr. Grant, I will tell you now. Your services are no longer required. My grandson is making other arrangements."

"Is this true, Wes?" Sidney said.

Wes looked at him in anguish.

"I—I don't know what to do," he sobbed.

"You have made a wise decision. Stick to it," Mrs. Beattie said.

"Perhaps your grandmother is right, Wes," Sidney said. "If you killed your Uncle Edgar, she *is* right. Plead insanity, and I will pull out with the greatest pleasure."

Wes sobbed incontinently, his head bowed over, and then he looked up and between sobs said: *"I—didn't*—kill—him. That's all I know. I'm frightened of hanging, I admit it, but I'd rather have it over than spend a hundred years in a looney bin. Juney, what should I do?"

"Follow your lawyer's advice," she said. "If you killed Uncle Edgar, fire Mr. Grant and plead insane. If you didn't kill him, tell our revered grandmother to go jump in the lake."

Wes sat up and stared at her with his mouth open.

"Go on," June said. "Tell her to go jump in the lake.. That's what you need. Bust this thing wide open, now. She's got you, boy! She's an enchantress, like Circe. She ties you up in knots. She's utterly selfish and unscrupulous. She's the guilty one all through the piece. Her own convenience means more than anything. Now brace up, boy, and tell her, before she sells you to the funny farm."

Wes was awestruck, almost paralyzed, and then he shuddered.

"Go on, say it," June said.

"Gran, go jump in the lake," Wes said, like a man in a trance.

Mrs. Beattie rose from her chair, like Nazimova making an exit.

"I forgive you, Wes," she said. "It was your sister, not you, who said it. You are a poor, weak, impressionable fool. *She* is her mother again. I regret, June, that I ever dragged you from the gutter where you learned your manners." And with that she swept from the room.

"Sorry, Wes," June said. "I don't normally advise young men to be rude to old ladies, but this was a purely therapeutic measure."

Thirteen

SIDNEY CONSIDERED SEEKING a remand, stalling for time in order to check out some more facts, but a conversation with Massingham, the Crown Attorney, which took place on Monday morning, convinced him that delay could be psychologically disastrous.

Massingham, a very large man, drove Sidney into a corner, and, speaking with considerable sweetness, gave him a piece of his mind.

"I now know what your game is, Grant," he said. "You've been buzzing about quite a bit. Well I, too, have made some investigations, and I am here and now giving you a friendly warning. You got to hear about Wes Beattie's delusions. You thought it would be amusing to substantiate them. You worked on his sister to get yourself appointed and elbow Baldwin Ogilvy off the course. Then you had a great slice of luck. Black was murdered. At first I didn't see the connection, but when I learned that Black had once been a witness against Beattie, all became crystal clear."

"Oh—you get the picture, do you?" Sidney said.

"I most certainly do. Black was a crook. He left large bank balances. It was a typical gang-slaying effort, but it served your purposes very well. From some underworld source, you gained possession of the weapon which killed Black. Also, from underworld sources, you learned about Howard Gadwell's obscene film racket. What a splendid opportunity! You decided to fabricate a conspiracy against Beattie, along the lines of the one he imagined. Gadwell became your scapegoat.

"Fortunately, I checked into certain activities of yours. You—and June Beattie—gave an alibi to Snake Rivers, a known burglar. The police were keeping an eye on the spot where Rivers had hidden certain illegal tools. Those tools were spirited away in a foreign car. I have talked with the informant and ascertained that the car was a Citroën. You, June Beattie and Rivers went to Muskoka in a Citroën. You took the murder weapon which had been given you to dispose of. You used Snake Rivers to break into the boathouse at Flatiron Island. You took the ice drill, bored a hole in the ice, dropped the gun, then marked the spot with an oar.

"Then you went to the police and claimed to have 'certain information.' The police would find the gun, and you would suggest that Gadwell dropped it there. You would say that Gadwell killed Black to shut his mouth—that Black had committed perjury as part of this alleged conspiracy. Then you would claim that Wes was framed because he *knew* something about this film racket—something he had stumbled on in the bank. It is a beautiful thought, Grant. But I'm giving you fair warning: don't try it!"

"That's most ingenious," Sidney said. "You're away ahead of Wes at concocting conspiracies."

"Oh, am I?" Massingham said. "And perhaps ahead of Mr. Sidney Grant as well. Now then, it appears that you are an accessory after the fact in the murder of Black. For some criminal client, you have diverted suspicion to Gadwell. You— and June Beattie, your dupe—cooperated with a burglary syndicate to divert the attention of police from that big job in the East End. In due course we're going to wring Snake Rivers out, and June Beattie, and your promising young career at the bar will be finished. I have a good mind to interrupt this trial and commence action against you *now*.

"For your own ends, you are throwing Wes to the wolves. For sheer notoriety. Wes had a good chance to avoid trial and go to an institution. *You* are going to hang him. Once he is convicted, it will be almost impossible to have his sentence commuted. However, since he obviously killed his uncle, and he will be no loss to society, I have decided not to intervene at this stage. But I want you to know that you and June are going to pay for what you did, and you might as well realize it."

"Massingham," Sidney said, "all I can say at this moment is that you're wrong. Dead wrong. And I'll warn you, too. If you allow Gadwell to slip through your fingers and get away to Brazil, you'll regret it. Keep an eye on him, and if he attempts to leave town, grab him."

"Oh, we will, we will, never fear," Massingham said. "He may be a key figure in certain proceedings against a young barrister— and I will personally vouch for it that he won't slip away."

"Thank you," Sidney said, "that's all I wanted to know."

It wasn't all that he wanted to know, but it was something.

Sidney found that the pit of his stomach had disappeared. He had a sudden vision of June Beattie in the dock, charged with aiding and abetting. Massingham turned away.

"By the way," Sidney called after him, "did the provincials find the weapon? How did the fishing go?"

"They found it all right," Massingham called back over his shoulder. "A thirty-eight-caliber automatic fitted with a silencer. It took them two days, but they got it, and the ballistics experts say it's the gun that killed Black. But of course I don't need to tell *you* that."

And, when court convened, Sidney Grant in his black gown felt sick through and through.

The case had sensational aspects, and the courtroom was crowded, even though the opening of the trial was bound to be mere routine. The press box was full, and a caricaturist was busy sketching the principals in the trial, drawing the burly Massingham like some medieval bishop in his black robe, and Sidney Grant as a small and demoniacal acolyte. Miss Semple, who had handed over the office to a telephone answering service, was beside her employer, and her amazing red bouffant did not escape the caricaturist's eye.

In the front row of the spectators' section Ralph Paget, anxiety peeping through his calm exterior, sat next to Claudia Beattie, large and aggressive. Next to her, smartly turned out, but on her best behavior, was June, who sent a little smile in Sidney's direction, and Sidney found it difficult to smile back. Beside June, well supplied with Kleenex, Betty Martin sat with her eyes glued to the back of Mr. Wes's neck.

Wes, in the dock, tried to sit straight and be calm, but there was terror in his eyes.

Mr. Justice Blaine entered and took his seat on the bench, and the crowd rose and became silent. An official intoned the time-honored words: "Oyez, Oyez, Oyez, all persons having anything to do before my Lord the Queen's Justice of the Supreme Court of Ontario at its sittings of Assize and Nisi Prius, Oyer and Terminer and General Gaol Delivery draw near and give your attendance. God Save the Queen."

At that moment it would have been difficult to believe that the city of Buffalo, New York, was only sixty miles away as the crow flies.

Events moved slowly at first. Selecting a jury occupied the whole of the first day, and the second day was taken up pretty well with routine evidence. There was an autopsy surgeon, who gave the cause of death and described the probable nature of the blow—a very powerful blow from behind. He identified the blackthorn stick as the probable murder weapon, and it was introduced as an exhibit. Sidney, in cross-examination, asked him if he had examined the accused. The surgeon said no, but he had seen him.

"Did he appear to be a powerful man?"

"No."

"Was he the sort of man one would expect could deliver such a blow?"

"Well, frankly, no, but..."

"That is all," Sidney said.

But Massingham had more questions.

"Would you say it was possible for the accused to deliver such a blow?"

"Yes sir. Under strong emotion—anger, fear or some such—I would say he was quite strong enough to deliver the blow."

The surgeon was followed by police witnesses. One of them was a fingerprint expert, who said that the only prints on the blackthorn stick were those of Miss Churcher, the housekeeper, and those of Edgar himself. But he told about lifting latent prints from the telephone in the apartment—it was entered as an exhibit—and identified them as the prints of the accused. In his opinion the prints had been made within the few days preceding the murder.

Then a police inspector read statements made by Wes Beattie after his arrest. The effect was pitiful. Wes could not help squirming as the inspector's voice droned on: "Well, these guys I was with were called Pete and Al. I met them in this beverage room. I'm not sure which one it was. Down Jarvis or Sherbourne maybe." And later: "Well no, it wasn't true. See, that's what I told my grandmother when I got home, but in fact I was out with this girl. At her house, see? Her parents were out. No, I won't tell you her name." Still later:

"Well no, see, she wasn't a girl, she was a married woman, and honest, her husband would kill her if he ever found out."

The jury looked at the boyish prisoner in the dock and exchanged smiles.

Finally, Wes's statement about the mystery gang was read, and the jurors shook their heads.

Sidney Grant did not oppose the introduction of any of the statements. It was useless. But the effect of the statements on the jurors was even more damaging than he had feared.

The police witnesses were followed by two women and a man who had seen Wes lurking near the scene of the crime. Two said they had seen him there on the fatal Friday evening; the other had seen him "several times" during the preceding days. One woman saw him at the outer door of the apartment, trying to open it with a key, and when she stopped and stared, he turned and walked off furtively.

Sidney was keenly aware that the police had selected the three witnesses from a couple of dozen volunteers. In every murder, people come forward to report suspicious things they have seen. Imagination usually plays a large part in their evidence, and they are always prepared to fight off cross-examination with great hostility.

It was scarcely worth attacking them, especially since Wes was prepared to admit that he *had* hung about the place. Sidney passed these witnesses over lightly. But he knew they had caused further damage. Once he turned and caught June's eye, and she looked at him from a face drained of emotion.

After the people who had seen Wes lurking came a witness who showed that Massingham was determined to touch every base. His name was Alfred Rimmer, and he was a plant wire chief with the telephone company. Mr. Rimmer was as pinstriped and perfect as Ralph Paget himself, and he had obviously completed the course in public speaking offered by the Junior Chamber of Commerce.

In the witness box, he drew the neatly folded handkerchief from his breast pocket and patted his brow, then replaced the handkerchief with great care. In answer to questions, he stated that the telephone in the murder apartment was of a type called the oval-based handset, an obsolescent type that had not been used for many years in new installations. In fact, he said, it was a comparatively rare instrument. He said that the telephone on exhibit in court was certainly the instrument which he had removed from the apartment at the request of police, doing the work himself because of the importance of the occasion.

Company records showed that the original installation in the Beattie apartment had been an oval-based handset, and that it had never been changed.

"Your witness," Massingham said.

"The phone was never changed by the company?" Sidney asked.

"No sir," Rimmer said, speaking with precision.

"Somebody else might have changed it, without the company records knowing it?"

"Yes sir. But..."

"Just answer the questions, please," Sidney said. "Now, is it possible for a private citizen to get possession of a phone like this?"

Rimmer thought carefully.

"Yes or no."

"Well, yes. Station equipment of this type could be purchased from our own suppliers."

"Station equipment?" the judge said testily. "We're talking about an apartment."

Rimmer smiled sweetly. "In the company terminology, my Lord," he said, "telephone instruments and other plant installed on the subscriber's premises are referred to as 'station equipment.'"

"Are they really?" the judge said.

"Now then," Sidney continued, suppressing a smile, "suppose somebody installed another oval-based handset in that apartment. Is there any serial number by which you could detect the change?"

"Well, no sir," Rimmer said.

"In short, all you can say is that this piece of station equipment is of the same type as the one originally installed in the apartment?"

"Yes sir."

"You can't swear that it's the actual one?"

"No sir."

But Massingham was not letting that go. He ascertained that oval-based handsets had not been available from the supplier for years and that it was most unusual for private citizens to own "station equipment."

"Ordinarily, *all* equipment on a subscriber's premises is company property," Rimmer said.

Whereupon Sidney had a go at him again. "Are there certain classes of citizen who *do*, to your knowledge, own telephones?" he asked.

Rimmer looked uncomfortable

"Come, come," Sidney said. "I refer specifically to bookmakers and boiler-room operators. By boiler-room operators I mean operators of stock promotion outfits who solicit prospects by telephone. Don't they sometimes have their own phones?"

"Don't answer unless you know of your own knowledge," Massingham said.

"Have you ever followed a police raid into a bookie's office?" Sidney said.

"Yes," Rimmer admitted.

"Did you find telephones there, connected to company lines, which were not company property?"

"Yes sir."

"And have you encountered the same thing in these so-called boiler rooms?"

"Yes sir."

"Thank you."

Massingham sat glowering for a minute, but then a slow grin spread over his broad face, and the grin became a chuckle. He looked like a man who had just watched an enemy fall into his trap.

"Call Mr. Ralph Paget," he said.

❊ ❊ ❊

The laws of evidence are to a large extent bound up with the doctrine of hearsay, which is not evidence. Broadly speaking, a witness may not repeat on oath something that he has heard someone say, but there are large areas of exception. He may repeat what he heard the accused say, or something he heard someone say in the presence of the accused. But remove the accused from earshot, and the witness can report no more of the conversation.

Massingham carefully established that Edgar Beattie had twice discussed his will in detail with Wes Beattie, in the presence of Ralph Paget, and therefore it was possible for Paget to repeat the entire conversations in the witness box, and he did it in a most businesslike way, standing very straight and looking directly ahead of him.

He made it entirely clear to the jury that Edgar had willed a sum of money to Wes and that the sum had been multiplied by stock market gains. He also made it clear that Edgar had informed his nephew that he meant to change the will, and there were nods of understanding in the jury box as the jurors got the message. Jurors glanced at Wes, who was squirming. The motive was established once and for all.

Sidney rose to cross-examine, and Paget turned his head forty-five degrees, ostentatiously avoiding his questioner's eye.

"Did the deceased, Edgar Beattie, give any reason for this proposed change?" Sidney asked.

"Yes sir," Paget said. "He stated that he was displeased with the conduct of the accused."

"Did he state specifically the conduct that had displeased him?"

Massingham half-rose, looked at the judge, then glowered at Sidney.

"Yes sir. He said that the accused was a thief, and he wanted no part of him."

"Ah! And did he give any grounds for this statement that the accused was a thief?"

"Yes sir. He said that Wes had been convicted of theft in court and could no longer expect decent people to have anything to do with him."

The jury gasped and glared at Wes, the spectators gasped, the judge glared at Sidney and Massingham was plainly nonplused.

At that point, nothing could have been more damaging to the defense.

Sidney blandly ignored the furor. "Oh," he said. "Now, do you, of your own knowledge, know if this statement of the deceased's was true? Had the accused been convicted of theft?"

"Yes sir."

"Were you present in court when he was convicted, and did you hear the evidence?"

"I was, and I did."

"My Lord," Massingham said, "I am sure the jury is interested in hearing about the previous criminal record of the accused, but all of this is wildly irrelevant."

"On the contrary, my Lord, in due course I will show that this is all relevant and vital."

"I hope you will," the judge snapped. "Pray continue."

"You remember the witnesses in that case? Apart from police witnesses, there were two—a man and a woman."

"I recall them."

"And the name of the man, the male witness in that theft case?"

"Sam Black."

"And the nature of his evidence?"

"He said that he caught Wes Beattie with a woman's handbag concealed under his coat, having just removed the handbag from a parked car."

"And is that the same Black who was recently murdered in a King Street parking lot?"

Massingham jumped up and protested, but the damage was done.

"And now, do you recall the woman witness?" Sidney asked.

"I do. She gave her name as Mrs. Irene Leduc, of Sudbury."

"Now I show you a photograph and ask you if you can recognize the woman whom it portrays."

Paget looked carefully at the glossy print of Mrs. Wicklow and nodded. "That is the woman," he said. "The woman who called herself Mrs. Leduc."

"My Lord, I wish to enter this photograph as an exhibit," Sidney said.

The photograph was duly marked and entered. "Now, Mr. Paget," Sidney continued. "At that conversation, where Edgar told the accused that he intended to change his will, did the accused make any statement concerning his conviction for theft?"

"Yes sir. He said that he had been innocent, but had been convicted as a result of a frame-up."

"Did he say anything specifically about the evidence given by the woman who called herself Mrs. Leduc?"

"Yes sir. He said she was part of a conspiracy against him. He claimed she had given a false name in court."

"This woman had said that the accused stole her handbag?"

"Yes."

"And did the deceased, Edgar Beattie, make any change in his plans after hearing this statement of the accused's?"

"Yes sir. He said he would trace the woman, Mrs. Leduc, and talk to her, before he altered his will."

"You were familiar with the character of Edgar Beattie?"

"Yes sir."

"If he made a promise like that, would he be likely to keep it?"

"If it were at all possible. He was a man of his word."

"And do you know if he succeeded in tracing this woman?"

"No sir. I know that he tried..."

"One moment. How can you *know* that?" Massingham interjected.

"Sorry," Paget said.

"And did he, before he met his death, change his will?" Sidney asked.

"No sir."

"He couldn't very well change it *after* he met his death," the judge said.

"I am in your Lordship's debt," Sidney said, with a little bow. "Now, Mr. Paget, did Edgar Beattie later tell you, in the presence of the accused, that a man phoned him and advised him to stop searching for this woman?"

"Not in the presence of the accused," Paget said.

Massingham was again on his feet. Question and answer had been sneaked in so neatly that it was scarcely worth protesting. Seeds, tiny seeds, had been sown.

But, opposed to the weight of evidence which the prosecution was building, they were as nothing.

The motive had been made clear, and the opportunity—for the police had produced the key to the apartment, which had been found in Wes Beattie's key container. Then there were the fingerprints, and the damning statements made by Wes.

Finally, on Thursday morning, Massingham called Major Barnaby Hale to the witness box. He looked the old-fashioned gentleman. There was a suggestion in his dress that he had just left a fashionable wedding. His mustache was an aggressive thing. His manner was authoritative.

The Bible was handed to him.

"Do you solemnly swear that the evidence which you shall give between our Sovereign Lady the Queen and the prisoner at the bar shall be the truth, the whole truth, and nothing but the truth, so help you God?" the official intoned.

"I do," the major replied in a resonant voice.

He then, under questioning, recounted how he had had occasion to talk with the accused in the presence of another, and how the accused had admitted to him that he was responsible for his uncle's death, and repeated the words, "So you really killed him, didn't you," which he had used, and Wes's reply, "I guess you could say so."

The major was a prominent figure. As a government official, he had frequently come out boldly in favor of the strap, the lash, the cat-o'-nine-tails and the noose. He was a believer in punishment, almost for its own sake. He was against the coddling of criminals, against the use of psychotherapy and sociological techniques. It had been said that he was born to play the Mikado, and when Sidney rose to cross-examine him, he looked rather like Ko-Ko before that stern ruler.

"Now Mr. Hale," Sidney began.

"Major Hale, if you please," the major corrected.

"I'm so sorry, major. Where did this meeting take place?"

"In the Psychiatric Hospital, where the accused was being held for observation."

"And what was the occasion of your visit?"

"The Attorney General had asked for advice on the type of custody in which the accused should be kept. I was investigating the security of the hospital in relation to the prisoner."

"And when you entered his room, did you tell the hospital authorities you were going to?"

"No. I didn't want to bother them. I got a man on the cleaning staff or something to take me up."

"Did you bribe the man to take you up?"

"I most certainly did not!" the major roared.

"Well, did you tip him?"

The major thought a moment. Sidney Grant had insisted that James Dunlay, the corroborating witness, be excluded until called.

"Hum. Yes, I might have tipped him."

"I don't want to know what you might have done," Sidney said. "I want to know what you did."

"Yes, I tipped him."

"How much?"

"Oh, I'm not sure. I can't remember."

"Well, was it silver money or paper money?"

"I don't like the attitude you're taking," the major said. "You are insinuating..."

"No. I'm asking. Silver or paper?"

"Hum. Haw. Paper, I believe."

"A bill, eh? Now, was it a dollar bill or larger?"

"Oh, I can't remember," the major said.

"So it could have been larger. Was it as large as a ten?"

"Certainly not."

"You remember that much. Might it have been a five?"

"Yes, it could have been a five. Possibly."

"Not a ten?"

"I told you that. I remember now. It was a five."

"You're quite sure?"

"Positive."

"I'm happy to have restored your memory so thoroughly. Now, do you usually tip five dollars to people who show you upstairs?"

"Well, it would depend on the circumstances."

"I'm sure it would. Major Hale, you have an area of responsibility for prison administration. Suppose a minor employee of a prison took a total stranger to see one of the prisoners without reporting the fact to his superiors. And suppose that the man accepted five dollars for taking him. Would you say that the man had been bribed?"

"No. But that's different..."

"Is it? If such an incident were reported to you, would you not discipline the man?"

"It would depend entirely on the circumstances."

"I'm sure it would," Sidney said. "Now then, having tipped, but not bribed, this Dunlay with a five-dollar bill, you went to the room where the accused was under observation. Did you then state your name and your business?"

"Well, no. I said 'How do you do?' and chatted about the weather."

"Did you at any time tell him your name and why you were there?"

"I—no, I don't believe so. I said—after certain preliminaries—'You're a very unhappy boy, aren't you?' He said yes, and I said he could tell me why, and that led up to his confession."

"Did you use the words 'You can confide in me'?"

"I don't remember using such words."

"Are you prepared to swear that you *didn't* use them?"

"Oh, I may have said something like that, having no inkling, of course, that he was going to confess."

The major was becoming more and more uncomfortable.

"Did you let him believe that you were a psychiatrist?" Sidney asked.

"Well, I never said *what* I was. I can hardly tell what a person thinks."

"But you didn't tell him you were acting as a high-level stool pigeon?"

Sidney apologized to the court and to the major. He withdrew the question, and butter wouldn't have melted in his mouth. But the purple explosion of the major had made it all worth while.

Thereafter he forced the major to admit that he left the hospital without reporting the conversation to the authorities there, that he went back and betrayed the confession—the major objected to the word "betrayed," and altered it to "reported"—to the Attorney General's department, that he sent for Dunlay and discussed the overheard confession with him, that Dunlay impressed him as a superior sort of chap, which led the major to offer him a job. In general Sidney exposed the major's action for what it was.

Later he made a complete monkey of the unhappy Dunlay and demonstrated that he was a near-moron and incompetent to handle the job he had been given.

But he failed utterly to shake the *fact* of the confession. No matter how equivocal it might have been, no matter how dishonorable the means of getting it, it was there, in the evidence, and the jury believed it. Belief was writ plain in their faces.

And the prosecution case, built with great care, was coming to its close, after only four days. The last witness, Miss Florence Churcher, had been saved until the end because of her physical condition. She had not come to the court until Thursday afternoon, and she had to be helped into the witness box.

Nevertheless she spoke up well and was a good witness. She got across. There was a sweet resignation in her manner and great courage. She described her actions on the night of the crime, and the finding of the body, in a high, clear voice, without undue emotion.

But her most important contribution was in connection with the telephone. She absolutely identified the instrument on exhibit as the telephone which she had dusted for years in Edgar's apartment. She pointed to paint splotches of various colors and told how they had got there during various paintings of the hall. She pointed to a telephone number scratched on the Bakelite and recalled that Edgar had scratched it there on an occasion when he had no pencil or paper.

If Mr. Grant wanted to make anything of the telephone man's failure to identify the telephone absolutely, Miss Churcher's evidence would give him something to think about.

It was the final thrust of the prosecution, and Massingham smiled broadly as he handed the witness over to his opponent.

The jury was getting impatient. They had reached their verdict, and the rest was mere formality. In the morning Sidney would start building the defense, and it would be uphill all the way, and in the end he would face a terrible decision—whether or not to put Wes into the witness box.

He stood by the lectern and looked at the thin, bent old lady with her face of pure goodness, and he wished devoutly that there were some way he could score one point on cross-examination. To bully her was unthinkable, and would have been disastrous.

"Miss Churcher," Sidney said, groping in darkness fathoms deep, "there was only one telephone in the apartment?"

"Yes sir," she said.

"And you never at any time had an extension?"

"No sir."

"So you never had occasion to send for an installer or a repairman from the telephone company?"

"No sir."

Sidney paused. "So, to your knowledge, there was never a telephone repairman in the apartment during your stay?"

"She's already answered that question, Mr. Grant," the judge said. "I trust there's some point to these questions?"

"Is that correct?" Sidney said.

Excitement rose in Sidney, but he forced himself to be calm, for the witness appeared to be in doubt.

"But my Lord, I *didn't* answer that question," Miss Churcher said. "You see, I said we never had occasion to *send* for a repairman. But I know a repairman *came* there once."

"But you didn't send for him?"

"No sir. Somebody else reported that our line was out of order, so the company sent a man. These people tried to phone us, and they couldn't get through, so they reported the line out of order."

"And *was* the line out of order?" Sidney asked.

"Yes, it was. But I didn't know it until the repairman asked me to test it. Then I tried it, and it was dead. There wasn't that buzzing you get..."

"The dial tone?" Sidney suggested.

"That's right. No dial tone," she said. "So the man said he'd have it right in a jiffy, and he did. There was no more trouble."

Massingham was getting impatient, and so was the judge.

"Now can you tell us," Sidney said, dreading the reply, "about when this call was made by the repairman?"

She thought deeply.

"Well, it's hard to say," she said, "after all this time. But it wasn't long before poor Edgar was killed. It was during that week, because I told him about it when he got home, and he thought it was very funny."

"Funny?" Sidney said. "What did he think was funny about it?"

"Oh, not funny peculiar," she said. "Funny ha ha. Edgar was a terrible tease. You see, the repairman told me our line was dead, and I said no it couldn't be because I'd been talking on it not five minutes before."

"Miss Churcher," the judge said gently, "you must not tell us what people said to you."

"But, my Lord, I promised to tell the whole truth," she said. "And anyway, I *had* been talking just five minutes before, because this young lady called up from the Alfred Curry Studios and said, 'Congratulations, you've just won two weeks' free dancing lessons.' That was the part that Edgar thought was funny, because I told her dancing lessons were no good to me because I'm well over eighty and have arthritis, but not because I disapprove. We were Methodists, but we danced and played cards, and I've even done the Charleston..."

The jury and spectators were enjoying it, and the judge, in spite of his exasperation, was amused.

"Miss Churcher, you must just answer the questions. You must not volunteer anything."

Sidney's heart was pounding violently in his rib cage. "Now how did your conversation with the Alfred Curry Studio end?" he asked.

"Well, this young lady was so persistent, saying that all kinds of people dance today, that finally I just hung up and went about my work."

"Now then. The repairman. Did you get a good look at him? Would you recognize him again?"

"Oh, I think so," she said. "I don't see many people, and I remember faces very well. My eyesight and hearing are quite good, but I have to wear glasses."

"Now did this man ring the front doorbell, and did he tell you through the speaking tube that he was a telephone man?" Sidney asked.

"No, I don't think so," she said. "I think he just knocked at the door. He must have come in as someone was going out."

"Thank you. That is all," Sidney said.

"No further questions," Massingham said.

And as court adjourned, Sidney watched Massingham make a dive for Mr. Rimmer, the telephone company witness, to find out what in blazes was wrong with the company records.

Sidney himself made a dive for June and booked her for drinks and dinner.

Fourteen

"I'VE BEEN AN INCREDIBLE IDIOT," Sidney said, after the drinks arrived. "I should have known better. I really solved this case at the seminar, when I heard Dr. Heber talking about it. All the answers came to me then, I mean the principle of the thing. I'm like Shaw's Saint Joan—I should have believed my voices. I started looking for what was credible, instead of recognizing the truth. And your brother Wes is so damn impressionable, so easily dominated."

"Stop being Delphic," she said. "What are you yattering about?"

"Your brother," he said. "The principle of the thing is this: Wes is an experienced and competent liar. Given half a chance, he can construct a credible lie. Nobody believes him, of course, which is the penalty liars pay. Once they are known, their best efforts are rejected. The whole point of Wes's conspiracy story is that it was incredible. As a lie, it was much below the Wesleyan standard.

"Look. He was arrested. On the theft charge. He lied, hastily and not too well. He lied again. He was caught. He couldn't lie his way out of the predicament, which he instinctively tried to do. So he hesitantly tried the truth. And it was so fantastic that nobody believed it. Then he was arrested for murder, and it was the mixture as before. One, two, three lies—then the truth. And nobody believed it. That was the message I got from Dr. Milton Heber's little dissertation. Deep down inside I believed it from the start, but my superficial critical faculty kept rejecting it.

"And finally I conned Wes into abandoning the incredible truth and seizing on a credible lie. Thank God I saw the light in time—if it is in time."

"I just don't get it," she said.

"Someone is framing Wes. Someone who knows him. Someone who is clever. Someone who knew that he would try to be credible rather than truthful, and that someone therefore dished him up a helping of truth that no one would believe. Until now, that someone has held all the cards."

"But what can we do?" June said.

"I have a tape recording," he said. "It was made by Wes under sedation. It is the full story of his alibi. Dr. Heber said it was full of inconsistencies which damned it. Then Wes, bless him, admitted that it was all a lie, to fool Heber—and I believed him. But Wes was clever enough to point out that Dr. Heber's alleged inconsistencies are not inconsistencies at all. Now, believe it or not, I have never listened to that tape, because it seemed worthless. So as soon as you drink up your dinner, I'm going home to do it. June, through this awful week, I have seen the prison bars opening up to admit you—and me. I couldn't summon up enough nerve to tell you. I've been paralyzed, but now I'm in action again."

"Tell me about the girl. How did you come to meet her?" Dr. Heber's voice said from the tape machine.

Sidney Grant, clutching a brandy, lay back on the sofa and listened.

"Well, I met her downtown," Wes's voice said. "In this place where I used to always eat. I didn't like eating with the agency guys. I went to this place where I didn't know anybody and read a book, and this girl came and sat at my table. I edged over and kept on reading, but I could feel her staring at me. She said I must think she was rude, staring like that, but she couldn't help it because I was the spitting image of a boy she used to know. I said no kidding, and she said no kidding, when she first saw me she nearly rushed over and kissed me. Wouldn't that have embarrassed me in public, she said. I just glared at her cold and hard and thought how kooky can you get? She said sorry, I ought to know better and she smiled and looked hurt. I said forget it—I just like my privacy at lunch. She said, oh, pardon me for breathing, now I'll crawl away. I said heck, I didn't mean it like that, I just meant I like reading. She said 'Oh, you're just like him in every way. You value your dignity and privacy. You like to read. You can be cold and cruel to people that like you. I'll bet you'd do just like he done, if the same thing happened.' I tell her I'm not cold and cruel, but a person has to protect themselves, and I ask her what happened and what this boy did. She says she can't really tell me, a perfect stranger, but it was just that this boy ran out on her when they'd been going steady, and she humbled her pride and groveled in the dirt to try to explain, but he wouldn't look at her again. And she said she knew I would be the same way. No matter how much a girl loved me, if she made one little mistake that would be it. Proud men won't forgive a girl, she said. Well, part of me knew her line wouldn't be good enough to make Ann Landers or a confession mag, but by this time I'm kind of looking at how she's made, which is pretty good and all female, and my critical faculty isn't so hot. I said it would depend on what mistake a girl made. I said I could always forgive spelling mistakes and she says, 'Oh yes, I knew it, you can laugh at other people as if they hadn't got no hearts, because you haven't got one yourself. It wasn't a spelling mistake I made.' I said what was it. She said it was the worst mistake a girl can make. She said she was going steady with this boy Ross, and then her girl friend told her she saw Ross at Wasaga Beach with this blonde that was married, and he was there all the weekend. And she was so jealous, she wanted to make him jealous, so she went on a party with this other boy, a real wolf type and a regular octopus with eight hands, and Ross is there but he just looks contemptuous. Well, she felt so bad, she let this boy give her too much to drink, and he also slipped her some tranquilizers, with the result she went right off the deep end, and of course this wolf type bragged about it all around town, and Ross just walked right out on her and went away and joined the navy. And she cried and wrote and begged for forgiveness, but he wouldn't answer her letters."

"The swine," Sidney said, sitting up and pulling at his brandy.

"Anyway by this time I'm getting kind of interested," Wes's voice continued. "Like she was pushed over close and talking very quiet into my ear and almost crying. And her thigh was touching mine and when she leaned over I could sort of see, well, she was really stacked, and she had this perfume. So my voice was a bit shaky and I said, 'So what? A girl is liable to make that mistake. Why should a guy be so tough on her?' She said what was so awful, she had always said no to Ross, and now she wanted him that way, but he was gone forever, but when she saw me she thought for a minute I was him, and... well, anyway I was getting ideas, and I said maybe I could take Ross's place. And she said there, men, they're all the same. They only want a girl for one thing, and I was like all the rest. She said no girl would mind that, if only she could feel that there was anything more, like a little tenderness and love, and I said well, how about a date, and we could see how she felt about me.

I said she'd find I wasn't like these guys and all that stuff. And anyway the upshot was she said, 'Oh, I wouldn't mind anything if you'll only be kind!' Holy cow, I make a date. She says don't say anything to anyone, but keep every evening clear. It might be Friday, Saturday or Sunday, but she would phone me for sure and tell me where to meet her.

"She said she had to be careful because she made an even worse mistake. After this party, and after Ross walked out, she found she was in trouble, and she had to marry this wolf type, and he was mean as hell to her and kicked her around, but like all these wolf types he was jealous as anything about her. I said what about the kid, and she said she lost it, she had a miscarriage after she got married. She got my phone number at the office and said to stay downtown for dinner Friday, because probably Friday she would call me, and she squeezed my hand under the table. So anyway I fell for this line."

"Okay, Wes, okay," Sidney said. "I understand perfectly."

The tape droned on, and Wes recounted how he had waited, all of a tremble, for his big date. Most nice girls didn't want any part of him, as an ex-jailbird, and the girls at the office all went with account executives or clients. Then on Friday she called and said, "Tonight is our night, dearest," and told him to meet her at the Ladies' Beverage Room entrance of a hotel on Jarvis Street. She told him to meet her at the rear entrance, the one coming in off the parking lot.

Sidney sat up at the term "parking lot." Parking lots had already loomed large in the case.

Wes met the girl at the doorway. He had parked his car in the lot, which was unattended—a car which his grandmother had bought for him when he came home from jail. But the girl was in terror. She said they couldn't go in—some friends of her husband's were in there—they would have to go somewhere else. She told him to leave his car and come in hers. She couldn't leave it there. Her car was parked on the side street, and they got into it. It was a Ford or something like that. She drove away, but didn't say where they were going.

"I was sort of fooling with her in the car," the voice went on. "She said how could she drive if I did *that*, but she didn't get mad. I kept looking at her and I didn't have a clue where we were going, turning every which way, and first thing I knew we were in a lane, and she turned into this garage with an overhead door and turned the lights out. She jumped out and pulled the overhead door down; then I caught her and she said, 'Not here, honey boy.' We walked through a little yard, all dark, and went in the back door of this old apartment house and up the wooden stairs, and then we were in the kitchen of this apartment. She said, 'See, honey boy, my husband is away, out of town, and the night is ours.' I grabbed her, but she said she wanted a drink. I said I would have rye, and she wanted a rum and Coke. She looked in the fridge and said damn it, no Cokes. She said would I call the drugstore and order a couple of cartons of Cokes and a carton of Matinee cigarettes. I was cursing. She said the phone was in the hall, but leave the kitchen door open and there'd be enough light. The hall bulb was gone. She said call the drugstore, the number is Walnut 9-0962. I called and the number was busy. I tried it again and still busy. I called out the line is busy and she said oh, skip it, she'd found some Cokes in the ironing cupboard and she still had a full package of cigarettes. I went out and she had the drinks all poured and I started to fool around and she said not here..."

The drowsy voice went on, recounting how the lady, whose only name was Gail, led him to a bedroom with a Renoir above the bed, and how certain events took place which fully occupied Wes's attention for several minutes. And then Wes, wearing only his shorts, wandered out of the room and through the apartment, carrying his stillunfinished drink, and how the girl called to him to come back, and eventually pursued him, and he asked her about the abstract painting in the living room and the Modigliani in the dining room, and she said her husband was an awful square and his mother and his aunts gave him all these things because his father was dead so his mother gave him his father's books and all.

Then they went to the kitchen and had another drink, by which time Wes wanted to see the Renoir again. So they returned to the Renoir, and once again were very happy and preoccupied, and she told him not to touch anything, because her husband would notice if anything were out of place, and he walked around and looked at the books and records, and then the phone rang. The girl answered and listened a minute, and she appeared to be terrified.

A girl friend had phoned to say that she had seen Gail's husband drinking downtown. He hadn't gone out of town. He might be trying to trap her. She told Wes to get dressed as quickly as he could, and they both dressed and rushed out, through the dark yard and into the car. The girl pulled up the overhead door, then told Wes to lie down with his head in her lap, in case any neighbor might see them leaving the lane, and he lay there as she drove away, and it was so comfortable that he fell asleep, and when he woke up they were back in the side street beside the hotel, and she shook him and said quick, get out. She said, "Honey boy, I know God intended you and I for lovers," and promised to call him again. And there he was on the pavement feeling woolly and drowsy, and the girl had gone.

"And Dr. Milton Heber is a plain damn fool," Sidney said aloud when the tape had finished.

Sidney had become drowsy during the recital, but now he was wide awake.

As Wes had said, suppose the girl were acting as a decoy—why should she fit in with the décor of the apartment? Viewed in that light, the whole thing became credible.

Sidney played the tape again, speeding it up at times and skipping portions, but making careful notes of all the bits of description—paintings, books, records, furniture, china and glass.

But the point which struck him with the greatest force on the second run was the telephone call to the drugstore. If Wes were lying, why would he include such inconsequence? Was it his attempt to hint that he had put his fingerprints on the telephone during the evening —fingerprints that were to be transplanted to another telephone by magic?

If he were telling the strict truth, on the other hand, the thing was of the greatest significance. Under those circumstances, the girl was an actress, acting out a scenario prepared by that obscene impresario Howard Gadwell. No detail would have been overlooked. Would she really have run out of Cokes? If so, would she really have asked Wes to phone for some?

If the idea was to cut Wes off from the world, would she let him call a real drugstore? Suppose the call got through, and he said "Send up some Cokes"? Then the drugstore would have asked for the address. If they failed to get it, they might remember the call. It would be a complete breach of security.

That being the case, the call must have been part of the scenario, and its only possible use was to get Wes's fingerprints on a telephone. So she told him to call the drugstore—she called out the number to him. Did she just pick a number at random? That might have been dangerous. The person answering might have said "Peachtree Restaurant." Some slight conversation might have followed—which might have been remembered later. It wasn't the sort of detail the conspirators overlooked. No, Sidney reasoned, it must have been a prearranged number. Possibly the apartment of some member of the conspiracy, maybe the home of a friend, who had been asked to leave the telephone off as a gag, in order to ensure that Wes got a busy signal.

Sidney Grant was pacing back and forth in his attic room, but suddenly stopped and stood still. Something had exploded in his brain.

Under sedation, Wes Beattie might have dredged up the *actual* number from his unconscious mind. He had rattled it off very glibly, without thinking. If it were an actual number, it could lead to a member of the gang or an accomplice or to somebody who had been asked—last September—to leave the phone off for an hour.

It was a thin chance.

Sidney looked up Gadwell's number, but it was definitely not the one. And Gadwell lived in one of the ultramodern apartment houses on stilts, up on Avenue Road. It certainly could not have been the decoy apartment.

Sidney turned back the tape and listened, checking the drugstore number that the girl had given to Wes. Walnut 9-0962. He walked slowly to the telephone and dialed it. A woman's voice answered after several rings.

"Hello?"

"Hello, can you send me a cab right away?" Sidney said.

"Oh, I'm sorry. You must have the wrong number. This is a private residence," the voice said. It was a cultured voice.

Sidney hung up. Not a drugstore.

He called a friend at police headquarters, where, in spite of his practice, he had many friends.

He gave the number, Walnut 9-0962, and asked his friend to find out from the telephone company whose number it was. The police would find out faster than he could.

The answer came back in five minutes. The number belonged to Dr. E. Neil Whitney, at an address in Moore Park.

It was nearly eleven o'clock, and Sidney was tired. It was hardly the time to make social calls, but time was precious.

Sidney called a taxi, and drove to Moore Park.

Dr. E. Neil Whitney lived in an old-fashioned apartment house like many others in the area. Sidney sat in the cab and studied it until the driver said, "That's ninety cents, Mac." Sidney was feeling in his pocket when he saw some people emerging from the building, and then he bent his head over and hid behind the front seat.

"Don't get sick in this cab, Mac," the driver warned.

"No danger," Sidney said. "I just want to stay here until those people go."

The people were Ralph Paget and his wife Marcia, the same Ralph Paget who had been so cooperative as a witness the day before.

They stepped into a parked Jag and drove off.

It was a link that Sidney Grant had been looking for, provided it was the Whitney apartment that they had been visiting.

Sidney paid the cab and walked into the lobby. He found the Whitney bell and pressed it.

"Who is it?" a woman's voice asked.

"Mr. Grant. A lawyer. May I see Dr. Whitney for a minute?"

"At this hour?" the voice said.

"I apologize for the hour. I won't stay a minute," Sidney said.

There was a dubious silence, but then the buzzer sounded, and Sidney quickly opened the inner door.

As he rode up on the slow automatic elevator, he racked his brain for an opening to the conversation. He couldn't just say, "Did Ralph Paget ask you to leave your telephone off the hook last September?"

Mrs. Whitney was framed in the doorway of her apartment as he approached it.

"Are you Mr. *Sidney* Grant?" she said. "My husband says you were probably looking for Ralph Paget. The Pagets just left, not five minutes ago."

Which settled one question.

"No. You are Mrs. Whitney? I wanted to talk to you and Dr. Whitney about the Wes Beattie case."

"Such a frightful thing!" Mrs. Whitney said. "My heart bleeds for Ralph and Marcia and the poor old lady. Do come in."

She led him through a dark, narrow passage which opened into a large living room, where the bridge table was still set up with cards and score sheets spread over it, and Dr. Whitney was just sitting down with a fresh drink, which he had evidently poured while his wife was occupied.

"Not another one, darling?" she said. "This *is* Mr. Sidney Grant. My husband. We've been talking about you quite a lot this evening. Were your ears burning?"

"Here, sit down, Mr. Grant, and let me buy you a drink," the doctor said. "What can we do to help the great defense?"

Sidney sat down, facing a white-on-white abstract painting that hung above the sofa, and agreed that he could use a Scotch and water.

"Paget is very worried about the course you're taking," the doctor said. "But he tells me you really dragged poor old Hale over the coals."

Sidney watched Dr. Whitney go into the dining room, where he saw, hanging above an Italian inlaid chest, a portrait of a lady with a long neck. He stood up and walked to the archway leading to the dining room and saw some bright blue and gold ikon paintings on the opposite wall. At first he merely had the feeling of entering a vaguely familiar house, but as he swung about and checked the positions of various objects, his head began to swim.

"Aren't you feeling very well?" Mrs. Whitney said. "Here, come and sit down."

He sat down and allowed his eyes to wander, inventorying the apartment, while Dr. Whitney, looking puzzled, pushed a drink into his hand.

Everything was in place, everything was right. The olive-green rugs, the inlaid dining-room chairs, the pictures were all as Wes had described them on the tape recording. When Sidney's brain began to clear, it suddenly occurred to him that if you want to make sure of getting a busy line, the simplest way is to dial your own number.

This was the apartment where Wes had spent the night of the murder, with a girl called Gail.

"Tell me," Sidney said, shaking himself, "has Wes ever been to this apartment?"

"No, not that I know of," Mrs. Whitney said. "Neither June nor Wes. We're great friends of the Pagets—Marcia and I were at school together—but the only place we ever met Rupert's children was at old Mrs. Beattie's place."

"Oh," Sidney said. "Well, you're going to think this is very strange, but I am going to ask you the traditional question. Where were you on the night of the murder?"

He grinned, and the Whitneys both laughed, a trifle dubiously.

"We've got a cast-iron alibi. We were in England," the doctor said.

"We went over on one of those seventeen-day tours," Mrs. Whitney added.

"And this apartment was vacant then?" Sidney asked.

"Why, no, it wasn't, as a matter of fact," Mrs. Whitney said. "By great good luck we managed to sublet it for two weeks. It helped no end to meet the cost of the trip."

"Nothing of the kind," the doctor said. "It just *increased* the cost by three hundred dollars, or more, if the truth were told. It made my wife feel too prosperous."

"Uh—do you mind if I ask who you sublet it to?" Sidney said.

"No, not at all. It was a Mr. Beauclair, Aubrey Beauclair, an Englishman. He had to spend two weeks in Toronto, attending company meetings, and his wife simply *loathes* hotels. She has a regular *thing* about it. He said that a hotel suite would cost them at least forty dollars a night, and she would hate it, so he would much prefer to rent our apartment while we were away."

"Is this Mr. Beauclair an old friend?" Sidney asked.

"No—a complete stranger. We only met him—no, we never *did* meet him. Somebody, at some cocktail party, told him about us. He had said to this person that he was going to advertise for the sublet of an apartment, and this person said why not call the Whitneys because we were going away. He took down our name, but he couldn't for the life of him remember who recommended us. One never *does* remember names from a cocktail party."

"But how could you rent it to him without seeing him?" Sidney asked.

"Oh, that was very funny. He was just heading for Malton to catch the plane to Montreal and meet his wife, who was coming by ship, and he wouldn't return until after we'd left. But he seemed so *anxious.* He suggested that I should get some form of agreement, satisfactory to me, drawn up, and leave it with my bank manager, together with the keys. He would satisfy the bank manager and give him the rent, for deposit to my account, and he would post any bond necessary against breakages, et cetera. Well, it seemed a bit odd, but an extra three hundred isn't to be sneezed at when you're traveling."

"No, I suppose not," Sidney said.

"But Mr. Grant, what's all this got to do with Wes Beattie?" the doctor said.

"Plenty," Sidney replied. "Will both of you promise me that you won't say a word—not even to the Pagets—if I tell you how this fits in?"

They both promised secrecy.

"All right," Sidney said. "Your Mr. Beauclair was, I believe, either the murderer of Edgar Beattie, or an accomplice. He rented this place so that he could lure Wes here at the time of the murder."

"You must be mad!" Dr. Whitney said.

"But it's impossible. Mr. Beauclair comes from a fine old English family," Mrs. Whitney said. "Why would he..."

"Darling, you never met the man," the doctor said. "Have you got some reason for saying this?"

"Yes," Sidney said. "Wes gave a most detailed description of the apartment where he claimed he was taken on the night of the murder. Everybody, psychiatrists included, thought he had made up some sort of composite apartment. But every single point of description fits *this* place. Right down to the Modigliani in the dining room."

"But it *isn't* a Modigliani," Mrs. Whitney said. "It's *me*, painted by Grant Macdonald, although I'm *sure* my neck isn't so long and swanlike."

"You say Wes has never been here?" Sidney said.

"Never. All kinds of people have mistaken that painting for a Modigliani," she said. "Heavens—are you sure there isn't a mistake?"

"Almost certain," Sidney said. "So only your bank manager saw this Beauclair? Who is he?"

"Herb Jackson," Dr. Whitney said. "He isn't a manager any more. He was promoted to be a superintendent at head office. Want me to call him?"

"Sure," Sidney said, "if it isn't too late."

Dr. Whitney made a phone call, but returned to say that Jackson was away in Vancouver, but was coming in on the jet flight and would be at the office in the morning. "How far are you from Edgar Beattie's old apartment?" Sidney asked.

"Five minutes' walk, no more," the doctor said.

Sidney was taken on a guided tour and saw everything from the overhead door in the garage to the Renoir in the bedroom. He arranged that Dr. Milton Heber and a fingerprint expert should visit the house in the morning, and departed, still trembling from the almost physical shock of walking straight into the weird world of Wes Beattie in the most prosaic section of Moore Park.

One of the most significant finds had been a halfempty carton of Cokes—untouched since September, a legacy from Mr. Beauclair. Mrs. Whitney had remarked to her husband on the strangeness of the aristocratic Beauclairs drinking soda pop.

Fifteen

"**N**OW YOU'RE quite sure this is the truth?" Sidney said

"Sure. Gee!" Wes said. "He was lying on his side, and you could see where his skull had…gosh, I don't like to talk about it. I can see it right now. I grabbed the phone and started dialing—then I heard Flo call out. All of a sudden I realized the fix I was in…"

"Wes, you tell it fairly well," Sidney said. "And it is a great big fib. I don't blame you. I put the words in your mouth."

"Are you calling me a liar?" Wes demanded angrily.

"Yes, Wesley, dear," Sidney said. "But this is nothing new. Do you even *know* the truth? Wes, I've found the apartment

186 John Norman Harris

where your little girl friend took you, and it's all as you described it."

"You *found* it?"

"Yes. *Now* what is the truth?"

"You found it! It *was* true, see? But I gave up hoping anyone would ever believe it. Gee, Mr. Grant, you're..."

"Please! Now tell me, did you ever tell your Uncle Ralph about that apartment?"

"No. Just the police, and the headshrinkers. I never really talked much to the family after I was arrested."

"Hum!" Sidney said. "Well, now I have to talk to a banker. Ever hear of Herb Jackson in the banking business?"

"Sure, he was my boss," Wes said.

There was a long, long pause.

"Okay, okay," Wes said. "He was my boss—manager of my branch. Why are you staring at me like that? What's the trouble? Hey, Mr. Grant..."

It was some minutes before Sidney recovered his speech.

"Don't worry about me, Wes," he said. "The smell of jails before breakfast sometimes hits me that way. Now, we were talking about Herb Jackson. I want you right now to tell me all that you know about Herb Jackson. How you met him, all your dealings with him. It is now eight-fifteen. I will ride with you in the paddy wagon to City Hall. But talk."

"Old Herb?" Wes said. "Gee, he was a swell guy. A great friend of Grampa's. Gramp used to curl with him— Gramp was skip of the rink and Herb was vice. I often heard Gramp say what a wag old Herb was, and I kind of wished I could work under a manager like that."

"Oh, you did, did you?"

"Yes. Well, see, I heard that his branch needed a junior. So I went to the accountant at my own branch and said I wished I could get a transfer to Mr. Jackson's branch. Well, he really came through. He said, 'Wes, if you wanted a transfer to the North Pole, I'd help you get it.' So I landed in there, just a while after Grampa died.

"Anyway, you don't go running to the new manager and say you're a grandson of his old friend. I mean that would be like real posterior saluting, so I never said a word, but I got to like this Herb character. He would come around and say, 'Hi, Laddie. How're things going?' and kid along with the girls and make everyone feel good. But the accountant, my immediate boss, was a sourpuss sort of guy, always riding hell out of you and chewing you up. So I never told Mr. Jackson who I was until this check came along."

"This check," Sidney said. "There was, I take it, a check."

"Oh, sure, and it was a very funny one. It was stale-dated, see? I mean it had been drawn the previous September, and this was about May, for gosh sake. And who do you think drew it? My grandfather, no less! See, there was this stupid girl. She brought the check to me and said, 'What do I do with this?' I looked at it, and it was made out 'Pay to a lucky stiff called Ed Gowan,' and it was signed by my grandfather—for a hundred and eighty bucks, yet!"

"And he was dead?"

"Sure. See, what happened was this. Grampa had lost this money to this man when he was recuperating in Arizona. I guess the guy was a Texas millionaire or something, and to him it was just peanuts. So after the poker game he stuck the check in his wallet and forgot it— maybe he was away in Europe or something for a while. Anyway, one day he must have noticed it and deposited it in his account in Phoenix, Arizona, in the Valley National Bank, I think it was. So it trickled through slowly to Toronto, via New York. But this girl said there was no account of Grampa's, which was natural, him being dead.

"Well, I looked up his account in the closed-out accounts, and sure enough he'd had this current account which he closed out in January. He'd had a big overdraft, which he paid off— nearly four thousand bucks—and he closed the account the same day.

"So anyway the accountant, Mark Carter, was away, and I took this check right into the manager's office and gave it to Mr.

Jackson. I said I didn't like to return this check 'No Account,' and should we inform the executors maybe and get the estate to pay it? He said okay, leave it with him. I said if it would be any help I would call Uncle Ralph and save a lot of trouble, and then he looked surprised and asked did I know this Mr. Beattie. Well, he was really surprised when I told him I was his grandson. He said, 'Come in here and sit down, fella,' and shook my hand and told me what a great old guy Grampa was, and he ended up taking me to lunch at the Victoria, where they have a buffet and you eat all you want, hot and cold. I wasn't twenty-one at the time, but he bought me a Martini and a bottle of beer with my lunch and he told me all sorts of stories about Grampa."

"And what did he do with this check?" Sidney asked.

"You'd never believe it," Wes said. "He had the check with him, and he burnt it, right there in an ashtray. He said he felt he owed it to Grampa, because he'd bet him two hundred bucks that Argos would go right through to the Grey Cup, and of course Grampa was so sick by Grey Cup time that he never got a chance to pay up. He said he'd pay the check himself and give twenty bucks to the Salvation Army in Gramp's name and then he'd feel a lot better. Gramp always liked the Sally Anns. Then he told me all about Gramp, and what a real sport he was. Grandma never went for this stuff, but Grampa was always playing the horses and the markets and betting on the World Series and the Stanley Cup, sometimes as much as a thousand bucks on a game, and he used to play poker at the club for big stakes and bridge for a dime a point and all that jazz. And the reason he kept this private account at our branch was to keep his gambling activities separate. Whenever he was down, he would run an overdraft till quarter day and then pay it off, so Gran wouldn't know about it, and when he knew he was dying, he made arrangements to pay off his overdraft and close the account, because he figured it would hurt Gran to know he'd been keeping her in the dark."

"Wes," Sidney said. "During all your troubles, when we were looking for someone with a motive for ruining an obscure bank clerk, did it never occur to you that *this* funny little deal might have been at the root of it?"

"Well, I thought about it a couple of times," Wes said, "but see, there *couldn't* have been anything wrong, because there wasn't any *money* in that account for anyone to steal. See, there was only an overdraft of about four gees, and that was paid off. I checked back through the account, and it *never* had a credit balance of more than fifteen hundred bucks or so. Actually, when I was checking through the account, Mr. Jackson came along and helped me and showed me like where Gramp had lost a thousand bucks on Philadelphia Eagles or won a thousand on Montreal Alouettes."

"So you didn't have to tell Uncle Ralph about that account?" Sidney said.

"Oh, heck no. He would have gone straight to Gran and spilled the beans. You know what an old fussbudget *he* is. Mr. Jackson said we really owed it to Gramp, like any other customer, to respect his wishes about privacy. He said it was one of a banker's basic responsibilities. He said I had a great banking career ahead of me, and it was important that I grasp the fundamental principles right from the start, and the first one was that you just don't gossip about customers' business, period."

"Oh."

"He told me about a kid in the bank that was handling paper from the local jewelry store, and what does he come across but an installment payment bit for his sister's engagement ring! He goes home and tells his sister that her fiancée bought the ring on installments, and she promptly breaks off the engagement. So then the fiancée sues the bank."

"A fascinating story," Sidney said. "Mr. Jackson seemed to be very keen on keeping this account away from Uncle Ralph."

"Sure. Because he would feel it his duty to tell Gran, which was what Grampa wanted to avoid. So I said don't worry, Uncle Ralph would never know. Gosh, he was acting like a real pill at the time, always nagging me. I said it wouldn't hurt if Uncle

Edgar knew, because he and Gramp were the same about this betting and stuff. He was away on the road at the time."

"And did Mr. Jackson agree with that?"

"Well, he said it certainly wouldn't hurt if Uncle Edgar knew, Edgar being a real sport, but still as a matter of principle it was better not to discuss it."

"And just when did all this take place, Wes?" Sidney asked. "In relation to your being framed up on a theft charge?"

"Oh, a week before, maybe. About a week, I guess."

"Wes," Sidney said, "I see the gentlemen want you to go for a ride in the paddy wagon. All I wish to say is this: there is no gull so gullible as a chronic liar. When you have wedded yourself to the truth, once and for all, you will learn to recognize it, and its opposite. You will learn that nice, smooth-talking men are often your enemies, that nasty guys who bully you and make you do your job are often friends. You will recognize sweet reasonableness and flattery and mere superficial credibility for what they are, and you will know that truth is truth because it's *true,* not because it's agreeable. Now, where was that branch of yours? I won't ride with you—I'll take a cab."

Wes gave him the address of the branch, and was led away, and Sidney hurried down to the jail office and phoned for a taxi.

Sidney rang the bell and was admitted to the bank, which was not yet open. He found Mark Carter, Wes's old accountant, in the manager's chair.

"Mr. Carter," Sidney said, "I'm in one hell of a rush, and I need your help. I'm Sidney Grant, and I'm defending your ex-employee Wes Beattie. Wes's grandfather, Charles Beattie, kept an account here—a current account—which he closed out shortly before his death. He closed it out by paying off an overdraft of about four thousand dollars. Your predecessor, Jackson, was most anxious that Beattie's relations and executors should know nothing about that account. I can't see—any more than Wes can—how you could steal money from an overdrawn account, but..."

"Mr. Grant," Carter said, "I am a banker. I have been a traveling auditor. I know that the faintest smell of anything queer *always* means something. In the situation you mention, my first move would be to look at the securities ledger and find out how that overdraft was secured. One moment, please."

He pressed buttons, and people appeared. He asked for documents and ledgers, and one by one they arrived, while Sidney sat and fidgeted.

"Now then," Carter said, "that account was closed out on Friday, January 13. The overdraft was secured by thirty thousand shares of Minerva Mines Limited, lodged with the bank—market value fourteen cents a share. Partially secured, I should say. Mr. Beattie's name was good for several times that figure. I would guess that Mr. Beattie lodged those shares just for someplace to leave them. Jackson would have let him have the money on his signature."

"So the shares were worth about four thousand dollars," Sidney said.

"Were. I see you're not a fan of the mining market," Carter said. "Minerva, even in the present lousy market, is over nine bucks. It hit a peak of close to sixteen dollars. Now, if you want a suspicious circumstance, Minerva took off, as we say, on a famous Friday the thirteenth, when everybody along Bay Street was mourning because they hadn't bought some. On that day, the stock rose from nineteen cents to over a dollar in the last half-hour of trading, and it opened at two dollars on Monday morning. By Wednesday it was trading at seven dollars. Is this what you want?"

"It sounds like it," Sidney said.

"Now Mr. Beattie's shares, I see, were sold on Tuesday, January tenth, at fourteen cents, and the proceeds deposited in his account on Friday, the day the check came through."

"That was pretty unlucky," Sidney said.

"Unlucky? Mr. Grant, you have suspicions. So have I. My predecessor was a great personality boy and a great spender. He was up to his ears in debt—always kiting checks before payday.

All the symptoms. About a year ago he became prosperous. He wasn't smart enough to conceal prosperity. He went to the Breakers at Palm Beach for a spring holiday. New clothes, new car. He said his wife had inherited money. He built himself up to a big promotion in the bank. He is now our chief liaison with the mining industry.

"I don't quite see how this ties in with poor Wes Beattie's troubles, but you are in a hurry, so I'm going to stick my neck out and tell you just how this little swindle was engineered. To me it's clear as a bell. Wasn't old Mr. Beattie paralyzed at this time?"

"Yes," Sidney said.

"Well, on that fateful Friday, Herb Jackson hears at three o'clock that Minerva has taken off. He checks into the rumor, discovers that an announcement is coming over the weekend. Several drill holes have produced high-grade copper. Monday there will be a buying panic. So he phones some crooked broker friend..."

"Howard Gadwell?"

"You said it, sir, I didn't. But I won't deny the distinct possibility. He calls him and suggests back-dating the sale of Mr. Beattie's Minerva to the previous Tuesday and bringing in a check right away to liquidate the account. We are open late hours on Friday. He bungs the check through, and the account is clear. So, at their leisure, Mr. Jackson and his pal sell Minerva close to the peak. They would clean up a couple of hundred thousand each, and you are looking at a mug who should have caught them. Ha! Look here!"

"What is it?" Sidney asked.

"I remember this deal," Carter said. "I was joint custodian. I asked Jackson what authority we had for selling this stuff. I was new at the branch, and I had never met Mr. Beattie. Jackson said he had a letter of authority. He had it in his desk somewhere and would send it down to attach to the card in the security file. Read it."

It was on the letterhead of the Superior Trust Company, and it said:

Dear Sir,

I am acting on power-of-attorney for Mr. Charles L. Beattie, who is unable to handle his affairs owing to a paralytic stroke. Mr. Beattie wishes to sell the 30,000 shares of Minerva Mines Limited, held by you as collateral, at market, the money to be credited to his current account, which he wishes to close out. We shall arrange payment of any outstanding debit balance, or if there is a credit balance, please remit for deposit in Mr. Beattie's account with us.

Yours truly,
RALPH L. PAGET

"Then Paget was a party to the deal," Sidney said. "But Wes said Jackson was very anxious that Paget shouldn't be told about it."

"He was? Maybe he was afraid that Wes would blurt the whole thing out at the dinner table. I suppose that when I goaded Jackson into demanding authority, he got Paget to write this letter to stick in the file. So there were three shares at something above a hundred thousand apiece. Well, Mr. Grant, I was deeply suspicious, and it was silly of me not to see that this account was the origin of Jackson's sudden prosperity. I've stuck my neck out by talking to you, and now I'll have to call our chief inspector at once. I hope you will use this information with some discretion?"

"I'm very grateful, and I'll do all I can to protect you," Sidney said. "Tell me one thing. Wes left here early one day, and was picked up for stealing a purse. Do you remember that?"

"I certainly do. Wes had been borrowing money from everybody and his brother, and the boys had lowered the boom on him. He came to me this day and said he wanted to leave early—he had some big deal on. I told him nix, he could just get back to his desk and think about work for a change. And then

Herb Jackson came back—I was in this office, relieving him, that week—and gave me the old soft soap. You know, a kid is only young once, why did I want to be so tough? So I said that if he wanted to let Wes go early he could, but I was against it, and Wes dashed away."

"You were relieving him? How come?" Sidney asked. "Oh, Herb was our great mining guy, and he was spending the week at the mining convention in the Royal York Hotel."

"Good-bye," Sidney said. "You've been wonderful."

And he raced all the way to City Hall, arriving just in time for the opening of court.

Sixteen

AS SIDNEY ENTERED the courtroom, Massingham approached him and drew him to one side. He looked puzzled and distressed.

"Grant," he said, "we've arrested Gadwell. He got restive last night. He sneaked away from his apartment and holed up in a cheap hotel—under a false name. Then he sneaked away from there at midnight and went to Malton. He had booked a flight to Idlewild. He was carrying a large amount of cash. We're holding him on the false name bit, but we can't hold him long. Tying him down on the obscene film business may be—difficult. Uh—if you can give us any help, I might alter my views slightly on your own—er—activities."

"I will certainly give you all the help I can," Sidney said. "But not because I'm frightened of any action you've got in mind. Where is he?"

"Police headquarters."

"All right. Arrange to stick him in a line-up. I'll send a witness to identify him. Just clear the decks for me. Once my witness has identified him, you can hold him and never let him go."

"Good man," Massingham said, a trifle huffily.

Sidney sat down beside Miss Semple.

"Grab your book and write, Georgie dear," he said. "You're going to be busy. When you leave here, get a subpoena for one Herbert Jackson, superintendent at the head office of the Modern Bank. Then arrange with St. John's Convalescent in Willowdale for Miss Florence Churcher to be got up and rushed to police headquarters, where she is to try to see if she knows anybody in a line-up. If she does, get her down here. When you've lined up the Churcher bit, go to the bank and serve that subpoena. Let Jackson think we want him as a character witness if he's very curious. I'd like to serve him as late as possible, but I don't want him to slip away. The ideal thing would be if we could serve him just when he's finishing lunch and bring him straight here without any warning."

"Is that all?" Miss Semple said.

"No ma'am," he said. "Before you go to the bank, phone Dr. Milton Heber, who should be cooperative. Ask him to take a cab straight to the apartment of Dr. E. Neil Whitney in Moore Park and look around. Ask him to note any similarities between that apartment and one that was described to him by Wes, then to get down here to court as fast as he can. And call Sergeant What's-his-name, the fingerprint bloke, he's an old pal of ours. Ask him if he'd mind going to the same apartment and see if he can find a print of Wes Beattie's on one of the l.p. records. Wes said he thumbed through the records."

"Anything else?"

"Oh yes. Damn it, so many things today. Subpoena Dr. and Mrs. Whitney. On second thought, don't try to serve Jackson yourself—get servers on the job. Serve Heber too. Go, girl, go!"

Miss Semple arose with great dignity, just as Massingham finished telling the judge that the prosecution case rested.

Sidney stood up and called Tex Wicklow to the witness box.

After he had been sworn, Sidney showed him the photograph of his missing wife, already marked as an exhibit, and asked him if he recognized her.

"Yes sir, that is my wife, Janice Swann Wicklow," the geologist said.

"Did you ever know her as Irene Leduc, of Sudbury?"

"No sir."

"Were you aware that she went under that name?"

"No sir."

"Mr. Wicklow, we have heard evidence that the woman represented by that photograph, giving the name Irene Leduc, went into court and gave evidence against the accused, Wes Beattie, in another matter, last May 12. Can you tell us where you were at that time and what you were doing."

"I was in St. Michael's Hospital, in a coma, as a result of being struck by a taxi on Front Street."

"And where were you and your wife staying at the time of this accident?"

"We were staying at a suite in the Royal York Hotel. We were attending a mining convention."

"Can you tell us what you were doing when you were struck by this taxi?"

Wicklow grinned. "I was trying, unsuccessfully, to dodge," he said. "But apart from that, my wife and I were returning to the hotel after having dinner at the Rathskeller."

"Oh. Now had you and your wife been dining tête-à-tête, or were you with a party?"

"My Lord," Massingham said, "this seems to be pretty irrelevant."

"It's extremely relevant, actually, my Lord," Sidney said.

"We were at a dinner party, and our host was Mr. Howard Gadwell," Wicklow said, before the judge could make up his mind about Massingham's objection.

"Ah! Mr. Howard Gadwell!" Sidney said, registering the name as thoroughly as possible. "Now, sir, can you tell us the present whereabouts of your wife?"

"No sir, I haven't seen her since last September."

"Have you made efforts to locate her?"

"Yes sir, and so have you. The Bureau of Missing Persons, the R.C.M.P. and the Association of Credit Bureaus are all looking for her, but there's no trace of her."

"Thank you. Your witness."

But Massingham had no questions, and Sidney called the man from the car rental agency, who testified that a woman giving the name of Mrs. Irene Leduc had rented a black Dodge, and the number of the driver's license she had shown was such-and-such. Then he called a policeman, who said he had arrested Wes Beattie at the Midtown Motel and had checked the driver's license number of the woman witness, Mrs. Leduc. It agreed with the number quoted by the car rental man. He also identified Mrs. Leduc from the photograph.

Next came a man from the motor vehicles department, who said that the license bearing the serial number in question had been issued to Mrs. Irene Ledley. The address of Mrs. Ledley was 28 Bayview Circle. The official gave it as his expert opinion that an amateur could have altered the address to 428 Baylie Circle well enough to deceive an unsuspecting person.

Mrs. Ledley then gave evidence. She said that she had never altered her license, that she had never rented a car and that she believed her license had been stolen while she was visiting a mining convention at the Royal York Hotel. The date of the theft, she thought, was one day prior to the arrest of the accused on a charge of theft.

"I trust this is leading us somewhere, Mr. Grant?" the judge said.

"My Lord, Mr. Paget gave evidence that the deceased was trying to trace Mrs. Leduc at the time of his death," Sidney said. "We now see that Mrs. Leduc was, in fact, Mrs. Wicklow, who gave evidence against the accused under a false name. Mr. Paget said that the accused claimed he was the victim of a frame-up, and he also said that the deceased was investigating that frame-up."

"Very well, carry on," the judge said.

Massingham turned and stared at Sidney, like a man who was beginning to see the light, but through a glass, darkly.

Sidney turned and saw Dr. Milton Heber entering the court. Since Massingham had no questions to ask Mrs. Ledley, Sidney promptly called Heber to the witness box. Heber was sworn, and qualified himself as a practicing psychiatrist.

"Now, Dr. Heber," Sidney said, "I believe that you were present in this court during earlier proceedings, and you heard certain statements made by the accused which were placed in evidence."

"I was and I did," Dr. Heber said.

"I refer in particular to a statement by the accused in which he said that, on the night of the murder, he was lured to an apartment by a woman."

"Yes sir."

"Now then, did you conduct certain examinations into the mental state of the accused after his arrest, and did you, in the course of those examinations, ask him to describe in detail the apartment to which he claimed he had been lured?"

"Yes sir."

"And he said that he had no idea where that apartment was?"

"That is correct."

"Since that time, have you seen an apartment similar to the one he described to you in detail?"

"Yes sir. I have just returned from visiting an apartment which corresponds in every detail with the description given by the accused." He gave the address of Dr. Whitney's apartment and the name of the tenant.

Sidney then questioned him in detail about the description—about pictures, books and furniture. "And was each of these details in agreement with the description given by the accused?" he asked.

"Yes sir—except that the accused described one painting as a Modigliani, but in fact it was painted by Grant Macdonald. I mean that there was a painting in the apartment which was by Grant Macdonald, and the accused described a similar painting but said it was by Modigliani."

"Now, sir, what is your opinion with regard to the apartment described by the accused, in relation to the apartment of Dr. Whitney?"

"I believe that the accused was describing Dr. Whitney's apartment from firsthand knowledge," Dr. Heber said.

Massingham, who was looking more and more baffled, tried to make something about the error in identification of the painting, but only succeeded in eliciting the fact that Dr. Heber, too, had mistaken it for a Modigliani.

Sidney next called Mrs. Whitney, who said that she had met the accused, but to her knowledge he had never visited her apartment during her tenancy of it. She stated that, at the time of the murder, the apartment had been sublet to a Mr. Aubrey Beauclair, whom she had never met, and she told about handing over the keys to her bank manager, Mr. Herbert Jackson, with instructions to give them to Mr. Beauclair.

As Mrs. Whitney left the witness box, Miss Semple returned to the court and made her way to the counsel table. Sidney walked to her side and whispered, "How goes it?"

"I've never been in such a rat race," she said. "Subpoenas, phone calls—but the sergeant found a fingerprint, and Miss Churcher made an identification. We brought her down in an ambulance. They're helping her up the stairs now. And I absolutely demanded that the police bring the man along under guard. I felt sure you'd want him."

"You were so right," Sidney said.

Howard Gadwell was just entering the court, accompanied by a husky detective. He looked pale and frightened.

"We have reached the hour of the noon adjournment," the judge began, but Sidney interrupted him.

"My Lord," he said, "I have one more witness this morning. I am recalling Miss Churcher as a defense witness, and in view of her condition, I would like to have her heard now."

"Will this take very long?" the judge asked.

"No, my Lord."

At that moment Miss Churcher, assisted by a nurse, entered the court and was conducted straight to the witness box. Being already sworn, she was able to answer questions at once.

"Miss Churcher," Sidney said, "you told us that a telephone repairman came to the deceased's apartment shortly before the murder, and you thought you would recognize him again if you saw him. Have you seen him since that time?"

"Yes sir," she said. "I saw him this morning. He was in a line-up of men, and the policeman asked if I recognized anybody, and I said yes, the fourth man was the telephone repairman who came to the apartment. I knew him at once."

"Will Mr. Howard Gadwell stand up?" Sidney said.

Gadwell, at the rear, stood up, as did the detective beside him, and it was obvious that the two men were handcuffed together.

"Do you see the man in court, Miss Churcher?" Sidney asked.

"Yes sir," she said. "It's that rather sallow man with the mustache, standing up there."

"This is the man who came to the apartment and told you he was a repairman? A telephone company repairman?" Sidney said.

"Oh, yes sir, I'm quite sure of it," she said.

Massingham had no questions, and court adjourned, amid a feverish buzzing of conversation. Sidney went out quickly with Miss Semple and returned to his neglected office, where they had sandwiches and coffee sent up.

"It's all so confusing," Miss Semple said. "All of a sudden everything has changed. I got Sergeant Reid and had him go to the apartment with Dr. Heber. He took Wes's blown-up prints with him, and he says he has a perfect latent print of Wes's which he found on a new Stravinsky recording. Will that help?"

"It will get Wes right off the hook," Sidney said. "Lucky I was able to duck out before Massingham caught me. How about Jackson?"

"Well, I discovered that the bank is having a big all-day meeting of senior officers, and Mr. Jackson is in it," she said. "They will all have lunch in the directors' dining room, and they will be coming out at two."

"How did you find that out?"

"I have my sources, Mr. Grant! I called Gertrude Jessup, who is a member of my bridge club, and she is also secretary to the general manager of the bank. *She* has arranged with the head steward in this dining room to let her know when Mr. Jackson is leaving, and she will then alert the elevator starter, who will show our process server how to intercept Mr. Jackson on his way back to the committee room. Is he a key figure in the case?"

"He is *the* key figure," Sidney said. "And here comes another one."

June Beattie was just entering the outer office, with her uncle, Ralph Paget, in tow.

"Hi!" she said. "Say, that's a smart idea having sandwiches sent up. Gargoyle darling, can you get any for Uncle Ralph and me? I'm fam."

"Let me know what you wish, and I shall telephone for it," Miss Semple said. "There is an excellent delivery service on Melinda Street."

June called for a ham and swiss cheese on rye and black coffee, and Paget thought he would like a chicken salad on brown, and milk. He looked as baffled as Massingham. Miss Semple went to her own office to phone.

"Mr. Grant," Paget said, "I simply can't understand how Neil Whitney's apartment comes into this thing. I've known the Whitneys for years. Helen is a very old friend of my wife's."

"Never mind that," Sidney said. "You've got a question to answer. Did you write to Herbert Jackson, authorizing him to sell old Mr. Beattie's shares in Minerva Mines, just before Mr. Beattie died?"

"No, I did not. Furthermore, Mr. Beattie didn't *own* any Minerva. Edgar made an absolute killing in Minerva, and he had tried to urge his father to buy some as well. But..."

"But?" Sidney said.

"But...he was dissuaded. Very well, *1* dissuaded him. I am always opposed to gambling in these penny stocks, and I told Edgar it was absolute nonsense. Mrs. Beattie supported me, and old Mr. Beattie said, 'All right, I'll be a good boy.'"

"When was that?" Sidney asked.

"Oh, four or five years ago. Edgar hung on and made a killing, and of course I never heard the end of it from my wife."

"Mr. Charles Beattie was *not* a good boy," Sidney said. "He bought thirty thousand shares of it and sold it three days before it left the launching pad. Herbert Jackson's authority for selling it was a letter from you, on Superior Trust letterhead, saying that you were acting under power of attorney and you wanted the stock sold at market—to close out Mr. Beattie's account."

"That is a goddamned lie!" Paget said.

"Uncle Ralph, Uncle Ralph," June said, "if the rector could hear you, he'd ban you as a sidesman for six months. You wouldn't be allowed to take the collection..."

"Shut up, June," he said. "Mr. Grant, you be damn careful..."

"I will," Sidney said. "Either you are lying, and you will be hanged, or Herbert Jackson forged your signature. Did you *ever* write to him on Superior Trust letterhead?"

"Yes, I did. I had power of attorney. I wrote to ask him if my father-in-law had an account in his branch; they had been good friends at the club, and I thought it possible. We were trying to get things in order because the end was approaching."

"And what did Jackson say?"

"I don't remember exactly, but it was to the effect that Mr. Beattie had no account at that branch."

"Then, sir," Sidney said with a sweeping gesture of the arm, "I apologize for the dark suspicions I have been harboring. By golly, your chicken salad on brown has arrived. Georgie, pay for it from petty cash and put it on Wes's bill, multiplied by ten. Mr. Paget, it's all over but the shooting."

Seventeen

MR. HERBERT JACKSON WAS known as a real salesman, a man with personality, a great kidder, a hot sport and a number of other things. When he appeared in the corridor at City Hall he looked merely like a worried man with gray hair.

"Mr. Grant," he said, seizing Sidney by the arm, "I wish I could help you, but I don't think there's really anything I can do. Wes was a great boy until he went off the rails, and his grandfather was a curling buddy of mine..."

"I thought you might be a character witness," Sidney said.

"Oh, great!" Jackson said. "But honestly, I don't see how it can help. I mean, he was no great shakes around the bank...I can only say that he never actually borrowed from the till."

"Even that will be useful," Sidney said. "They've built a powerful case against him. You will be excluded for a few minutes, and then we'll call you. There's a room for excluded witnesses to wait in."

Long meetings of the senior executives were one of the occupational hazards of the bank, and Mr. Jackson had not had time even to read the early editions of the papers.

"Go with him and keep him in conversation," Sidney whispered to Georgina Semple. "I want him to come to the witness box fresh and innocent."

Miss Semple smiled archly and followed Jackson to the witness room.

The court room was unusually hushed as proceedings opened for the afternoon. The defense evidence had, up to that point, proved nothing, but suggested much. Massingham looked blank, the judge was puzzled, the jurors and spectators were ready to hang onto every word.

Sidney recalled Sergeant Reid, the police fingerprint expert, who produced a new Stravinsky recording and said he had found it in the apartment of Dr. E. Neil Whitney. He had found on it a latent print of the right forefinger of the accused, Wes Beattie, during a visit to the apartment during the morning. The record was entered as an exhibit.

Dr. Whitney was then called, and he stated that the recording had been purchased the day before he and his wife left for England in the previous September. Since Wes Beattie had been under arrest since before their return, the conclusion was obvious to all, namely, that the print had been made during their absence.

Massingham did not question either witness.

And then Sidney Grant called Herbert Jackson, who entered the court with Georgie Semple. He was a grayhaired man, with a certain distinction, and a nose which proclaimed his long attachment to good whisky. He had a certain urbanity, and he nodded in a friendly fashion to the accused in the dock, but the most casual observer could have seen that he was under a great strain.

When he had been sworn, Sidney commenced to examine him in a businesslike way.

During his days as a branch manager, had he had as a customer Mrs. E. Neil Whitney?

Yes.

In the previous September had he sold her some American Express traveler's checks and made other travel arrangements for her?

Yes.

Had he written a letter of introduction to the bank's London, England, branch for her?

Yes.

The air of anxiety increased steadily when Jackson saw the direction in which Sidney Grant was heading.

"Now, before she went away for her trip to England, did Mrs. Whitney leave some keys with you, and did she give you instructions as to their disposal?"

"Yes sir," Jackson said.

"And did you, acting on those instructions, pass on those keys to another party?"

"Yes sir."

"Do you remember the name of this other party?"

Jackson couldn't remember exactly. Beauchamp, perhaps, or some such name. He could only vaguely remember the man's appearance. Tall, fair, English. The man had given him money to deposit in Mrs. Whitney's account. Had he also posted a bond? Well, yes, at least he had satisfied Mr. Jackson as to his financial responsibility, and he had returned the keys to Mr. Jackson two weeks later.

"Very good," Sidney said. "Now did you also have, as a customer, Mr. Charles Beattie, grandfather of the accused?"

"Yes sir."

"And did you hold certain stock certificates belonging to Mr. Beattie as collateral security against an overdraft?"

"Yes sir."

"And did you sell those shares and credit the account of Mr. Beattie with the proceeds?"

"Yes sir."

"On whose instructions did you do that?"

Jackson looked at Ralph Paget, stern-faced in the front row of spectators, and he was like a trapped animal. "We always have power of attorney to sell stocks held as collateral," he said. "In case the stock is dropping on the market, we can sell out—that's the way we can secure our loan."

"Very good," Sidney said. "Now, did the accused question you about this account of his grandfather's which had been closed out, at a time when the accused was employed by the bank in your branch?"

"We discussed it, yes."

"And did you tell him that he should not discuss it with the executors of his grandfather's estate?"

Jackson was trembling slightly, and he glanced at Wes in the dock.

"I believe I told him that any information should be passed through official channels and not in an informal way."

"Did you ever write to Mr. Ralph Paget, telling him that Mr. Charles Beattie did not have an account at your branch?"

"Yes sir. After the account was closed, I wrote to Mr. Paget, in reply to a letter from him, and told him we no longer had an account in old Mr. Beattie's name."

"Did you say 'no longer' or did you just say that he had no account?"

"I don't remember the exact wording. But I certainly told him that there was no account in Mr. Beattie's name at that time."

"Now, at a later date did the accused bring you a check for one hundred and eighty dollars, drawn on that closed-out account by Mr. Charles Beattie before his death?"

"Yes sir."

"And did you burn that check in the presence of the accused, and did you pay it out of your own pocket?"

"Yes sir. Mr. Beattie and I were great friends. I had made a bet with him, which I hadn't been able to pay. So that was the way I paid it."

"Very creditable," Sidney said. "Now then, in May of last year, did you attend, as a representative of the bank, a mining convention at the Royal York Hotel?"

"Yes sir."

"And on Tuesday evening, May ninth, did you go to dinner with some of the delegates at the Rathskeller restaurant?"

"I believe I did. Yes."

"And who was your host at that dinner?"

"Host? I'm not sure. I think I picked up the tab myself."

"Was Howard Gadwell a member of that party?"

"Howard Gadwell? Yes, I think he was with us."

"Will Mr. Wicklow stand up, please?" Sidney said. "Was this gentleman on the party?"

"Yes sir."

Sidney walked to the registrar and asked him for the picture of Mrs. Wicklow, which he handed to Jackson.

"Do you recognize this woman?" he asked.

Jackson studied it carefully, but his hand was trembling.

"Yes sir. I think that's Mrs. Wicklow," he said.

"Was she on the party with you?"

"Yes, I guess she was."

"And did you conspire with Gadwell and Mrs. Wicklow to steal a driver's license, lure Wes Beattie to the Midtown Motel and make it appear that he had stolen Mrs. Wicklow's purse?" Sidney said, raising his voice.

"No, of course not. How—how dare you suggest such a thing?" Jackson tried to be indignant, but it didn't quite come off.

"On the Thursday of that week—the day on which the accused was arrested for theft—you returned briefly to your branch from the convention. You were there when the accused asked for permission to leave early. The accountant wouldn't let him go. You overruled him. You gave the accused permission to go—and be framed up on a theft charge. Why?"

The judge looked at Jackson's face and started to intervene, but checked himself.

"I—the boy seemed anxious to get away early," Jackson said.

"Now then," Sidney continued, lowering his voice, "we have heard evidence to the effect that Mr. Howard Gadwell, posing as a telephone repairman, went to the apartment of Edgar Beattie on the morning of the murder or the morning before that."

Jackson's face fell apart.

"Did you conspire with Gadwell to remove the telephone from Edgar Beattie's apartment during that visit and substitute a similar oval-based handset, owned by Gadwell for his boiler-room operations? And did you conspire with him to install the telephone from Edgar's apartment in the apartment of Dr. Whitney, which you rented to Gadwell, who was posing as Mr. Aubrey Beauclair? And did you arrange for a woman to lure the accused to the Whitney apartment, and to get him to put his fingerprints on that telephone in that place? And did you and Gadwell then remove the telephone and return it, complete with the accused's fingerprints, to Edgar's apartment? And did you murder Edgar on that same visit, when you were returning the telephone? Did you, or did Gadwell?"

"Gadwell did it!" Jackson screamed. "I had no part in it. He never told me why he wanted the Whitney apartment."

"Did you sell Mr. Charles Beattie's stock to Gadwell, and did you take half the profit on it?" Sidney said.

"It was a legitimate deal. Charley told me to sell it. I had a perfect right to buy it."

"*Charley* told you to? He was paralyzed. Didn't you forge Ralph Paget's name to a letter ordering you to sell that stock?"

Jackson did not answer. He placed his hands on the rail of the witness box, leaned forward and burst out sobbing.

"Didn't you frame Wes Beattie on the theft charge to keep him from finding that forged letter in the securities file?" Sidney said. "You thought Wes had been sent to the branch to spy on you. You thought Ralph Paget suspected you and sent Wes to spy on you. You framed him. You thought he'd be charged and remanded—and then the bank would suspend him. But he was convicted. You were safe for a while. Then Edgar started looking for your accomplice, Mrs. Leduc. You were afraid he would find her, and you knew she would break down and talk. Gadwell phoned her and begged her to join him. Where is she? Did Gadwell murder her, too? Edgar had found out too much. You murdered him and framed Wes again..."

"One moment please, Mr. Grant," the judge said.

Jackson looked up. His nerve had broken, and tears were streaming down his face.

"Ladies and gentlemen of the jury," the judge said, "a matter has arisen which I wish to discuss with counsel in your absence. Will you please withdraw, and you will be recalled in a few minutes."

The jury stood up and commenced to file out. Sidney turned and walked to the dock. Wes leaned forward to hear what he had to say.

"Wes," Sidney said, "listen carefully. More people get into trouble by not knowing that they're important than the other way. People love you. Betty Martin, your sister. That makes you important. Don't treat yourself as a nothing. Keep your dignity. When the end comes, no handclapping and shouts of 'Goody.' Act like a grown-up man. Now you're going to have to face life and truth. Remember that you're important—too important to make a childish fool of yourself. And if you remember that everybody else is important too, then you won't swing to the other extreme and become arrogant. Now, boy, sit up straight and start being dignified, and never stop."

The jury had departed. The judge leaned forward and spoke to the Crown Attorney.

"Mr. Massingham," he said, "have you any reason why this case should now continue?"

"None whatever, my Lord," Massingham said.

"Then you will see that this witness is taken into custody, and you will take any other steps which you deem necessary. Recall the jury, please."

Jackson, broken and quivering, looked up at the judge and then stepped out of the witness box. Massingham motioned to a police official, and Jackson, white and shaken, was led away. The jury filed back to their jury box.

"Ladies and gentlemen of the jury," the judge said, "I now direct you, as a matter of law, to find the accused Not Guilty. You may retire and discuss it, if you wish, or you may discuss it without leaving the box."

The jurors leaned in like a football huddle listening to the quarterback. They conferred for perhaps thirty seconds, then looked up, all grinning. There followed a brief ritual, in which they returned their verdict in formal style. It was, not surprisingly, Not Guilty.

Until that moment the spectators had sat frozen, listening to the drama as it unfolded. Suddenly a babble broke out in the court, and the judge was forced to call for silence.

"Wesley M. Beattie," he said, when order was restored, "stand up."

Wes, pale, but under firm control, stood rigidly to attention and faced the judge.

"Wesley Beattie," the judge said, "you have been found Not Guilty of the charge of murder. For this verdict, you have to thank the brilliant work of your counsel, who has performed a great service to justice during this trial. We have heard evidence which suggests that you have been previously the victim of a gross miscarriage of justice. I shall call the attention of the authorities to the circumstances of that conviction so that action may be taken to clear your name of that previous charge. Before I discharge you, I feel obliged to say that, in a certain degree, and in spite of the criminal conspiracy of which you have been a victim, you have been the author of your own troubles. I admonish you in future to rely on the truth, and you will find that it will always stand you in good stead. You are now discharged, and you leave this court without a stain on your character."

"Thank you, m'lud," Wes said, standing very straight and demonstrating by the "m'lud" that he was a reader of English crime novels.

A policeman opened the gate of the dock, and Wes stepped down, to be embraced by June, and Betty Martin, and Claudia.

The judge quickly withdrew, and the court became a pandemonium. Sidney Grant slipped away and escaped to one of the less salubrious beverage rooms on Jarvis Street, where he drank a great many glasses of draft beer, all alone in a corner.

Even Snake Rivers couldn't draw him into his social orbit.

Eighteen

AT THE INSTANCE OF Mrs. Charles Beattie, a special service of thanksgiving was held on the following Sunday, and on the Wednesday of that week there was a dinner party for family and close friends at the Rosedale house. Wes had tried to insist that Betty be a guest at dinner, but nothing could induce her to sit at Mrs. Beattie's table. She knew her place.

However, she consented to sit in the drawing room after dinner, when many other guests joined the intimate circle for liqueurs and coffee. Dr. Heber, Phelan, the hockey star, the Ledleys, the Whitneys, James Bellwood and Baldwin Ogilvy were there.

215

When all had been supplied with coffee, Mrs. Beattie spoke in her usual well-modulated voice.

"After all these tragic events, life must go forward," she said. "We shall never forget the tragedy, but we are very happy that my grandson has been completely cleared. And we have another cause for happiness. A *mésalliance* has been arranged. Mr. Grant, who has already done so much for our family, is going to marry my granddaughter June."

There was laughter and applause.

"But now," the old lady said, "we all of us are curious as to what actually took place. Although we have heard so much, it is difficult to sort it out, and Mr. Grant has kindly consented to tell us just how this conspiracy came about and how it was defeated. Mr. Grant."

When he rose, Sidney discovered that he was slightly more nervous than when he first appeared in the assize court.

"Well," he said, "I think we should start at the beginning. Both conspirators have made full confessions. They talked, each trying to blame the other, until the full facts came out. And here they are:

"Gadwell and Jackson got into a conspiracy. Jackson advanced Gadwell more credit than he should have, and Gadwell let Jackson play the market through his firm— really with bank funds. They were trying to get rich quick, but things went badly until all of a sudden they got worse. The one enterprise which provided Gadwell with a steady income was his blue cinema venture. Suddenly it vanished. The FBI cleaned out the U.S. end of the business. So we find Gadwell facing bankruptcy and Jackson facing something worse. He was probably in deep enough that he would have gone to prison.

"Then there came a Friday when Gadwell arrived in Jackson's office at four P.M., hot and angry, because he had missed the tip-off on Minerva Mines. The rumor was out that Minerva had drilled and found rich ore. The stock had climbed from about fifteen cents to over a dollar in the last hour of trading. The official announcement, expected on Saturday morning, would send the stock sky high.

"Jackson listened with keen interest. Then he told Gadwell that he was holding a sizable block of Minerva as security for a relatively small overdraft. He was in a position to sell the stock and simply deposit the money in the account. Mr. Beattie, whose stock it was, was paralyzed and unlikely to recover. His minor gamblings in the mining market were kept very private. It was more than possible that no one in his family knew that he owned any Minerva.

"So Gadwell then and there gave him a check, and the sale was back-dated a few days. The account was actually closed out during the late-opening hours of that Friday.

"Mr. Beattie died, and there was no further trouble. A bank officer questioned the authority of the manager to sell and liquidate the account, and the manager constructed a letter—forged—which satisfied him, and all was well. Gadwell and Jackson made a fortune. They bailed themselves out, and their other enterprises began to prosper.

"And then, one day, a callow junior in Jackson's branch walked in with a stale-dated check drawn by his grandfather before his death. Jackson said, 'Leave it with me.' He meant to pay the check himself and put a stop to all further questions. But this callow youth turned out to be the grandson of Charles Beattie, and he had come to the branch *after* his grandfather's death, without revealing to Jackson who he was.

"Jackson was terrified. He saw Wes as a spy who had wormed his way into the branch to do a little investigating for the family. But he kept his head. He took the boy out, flattered him, buttered him up and concluded that Wes was completely innocent and unsuspecting. He also discovered that he was— sorry Wes—a congenital liar, and therefore unusually gullible. Jackson made up a sentimental story that wouldn't impose on an idiot in normal circumstances. But Wes believed it. So far, so good. However, Jackson later found Wes prying into the closed-out account, and he couldn't get rid of his fears that Wes would, one day, betray the existence of that closed-out account. His fear forced him to act. He wanted to get Wes out of that branch, fast, without appearing to want to.

"A few days later he was with Gadwell at the mining convention. Gadwell had a girlfriend who would do anything for him. So Jackson told him flatly that they were in the thing together, that Gadwell had to help. Jackson was the Brain. He knew the motel very well—he had had some little intrigues there. Gadwell had never been near it. So Jackson worked out a scheme whereby Wes was lured to the motel. He was driven there by a young Buffalo woman, who immediately afterward left for Buffalo and never returned. He was left standing in the car park holding a woman's handbag, and his explanation of how he got it was extremely incredible. Wes cared more for credibility than truth. He tried to lie. He told several lies, which made the truth that much more incredible when he got round to telling it.

"Now all that Jackson hoped for was this: that Wes would be hauled up in police court and remanded. Then the bank would automatically suspend him. In due course the case would be dismissed for lack of evidence, and Wes would go free. But his reputation would have been irreparably damaged. The bank would probably ask him to resign. In any case, he would be out of the way for a while and would have more things to think about than his grandfather's account.

"Well, it worked. It appeared to work better than Jackson's highest hopes. The case was so hopelessly bungled that Wes went to jail, and all appeared to be well. Jackson was able to keep track of events by cultivating the friendship of Edgar Beattie and by pretending sympathy for Wes.

"It came, therefore, as a nasty shock to learn that Edgar was quietly investigating that theft charge. First of all, Edgar traced the stolen driver's permit used by Mrs. Leduc. This led to a blind alley. Next he traced a repair bill which was in the possession of the car rental agency where Mrs. Leduc-Wicklow had rented a car. The trail led Edgar Beattie to a man called Mayhew, an old school friend of Gadwell's. Briefly, our friend Rick Phelan here saw Gadwell and Mayhew in conversation while the car was in his garage awaiting repair, and he told Edgar that Mayhew knew the man he was seeking. Mayhew denied it when Edgar asked him, but phoned to warn Gadwell that a Mr. Edgar Beattie was seeking him. The news unnerved Gadwell, but it terrified Jackson. Edgar, you see, had let him believe that he considered the case closed.

"The first and worst danger was Mrs. Wicklow, the female conspirator. She was madly in love with Gadwell. She was threatening to come and join him. If Edgar were to discover her, she was almost certain to talk, and the game was up. And so, Murder Number One was planned. It was simple and easy.

"Gadwell called Mrs. Wicklow and begged her to run away with him. She was to come to Toronto via Ottawa, and he would meet her at the airport. He did, and he drove her straight off, at night, to his little love-nest hideaway in Muskoka. Her body, expertly weighted, was in three hundred feet of cold water before morning. Her disappearance caused no concern to anyone, except her creditors.

"At about the same time, Jackson told Gadwell to call Edgar and try to palm him off with the marital intrigue story. But Edgar was adamant. He insisted on meeting both Gadwell and the missing woman witness face to face before he stopped searching. He was getting warm—and Mayhew was undependable. Jackson was rich and expecting promotion in the bank. Gadwell was rich. They had already committed one murder. Another was necessary for security. Killing Mayhew would have been stupid. It had to be Edgar, but it was necessary to conceal the motive; the motive would have been a dead giveaway. And so there was born in Jackson's mind the plan of killing Edgar and framing Wes for the second time. It seemed psychologically sound that Wes should kill his uncle, but it was necessary to act fast. The first thing was to find a place where Wes could be kept out of circulation on the chosen evening. When Mrs. Whitney went to Jackson, her banker, and told him about her forthcoming holiday in England, he saw his chance. He knew the place, and realized it was perfect. So he had Gadwell pose as an English businessman and rent the Whitney apartment. Gadwell does an excellent imitation of an English accent. The rest of the plot developed very naturally from this beginning. A girl was needed to lure Wes. Gadwell's old film-making connection proved useful. A girl was imported from Buffalo—a girl whom no one would miss. And Gadwell then called Edgar to make a date. He promised to go to Edgar's apartment on that Friday, taking with him the woman—Mrs. Wicklow, alias Leduc. In turn he made Edgar promise to be alone. Edgar was the type of honorable sporting gent who would keep such a promise without fear or suspicion. Jackson *knew* that, and on the day when he is hanged, that is something to remember, in case you are feeling overly sympathetic.

"Well, one thing remained: to plant some evidence at the scene of the crime which would incriminate Wes. Planting ashtrays or whisky glasses bearing the desired fingerprints is too easy. Such things can be carried in by the murderer. Jackson wanted something that seemed fixed and immovable. He knew Edgar's apartment. He had noted the old-fashioned telephone. Now he made a visit and studied it carefully. It was perfect for the purpose. Gadwell had a fine collection of old phones. One of them was selected and flecked with paint to counterfeit the real telephone in Edgar's apartment.

"There remained the problem of entry. Again Jackson's facile brain provided an answer. He knew Edgar's habits. Edgar kept all his keys in one container—car keys and all. Jackson invited Edgar to lunch, just before Edgar's last business trip, at a club on St. Clair Avenue, where there is a members' parking lot. He got Edgar to drive him up in Edgar's car, and told him to leave the keys in the car in case the attendant wanted to move it. Gadwell drove in after them, parked in the adjoining space and removed the keys—except for the ignition key. He took them to a hardware store and had duplicates made, then replaced the originals in the car, long before Edgar and Jackson had finished their lunch. On his next visit—that same evening— Jackson was able to ascertain which of Edgar's keys was the apartment key, and a duplicate was made to be planted on Wes by the decoy girl.

"Now came the telephone flimflam, which can be called Jackson's masterpiece. On the Friday morning, the morning of the day when Edgar was to be murdered, the decoy girl from Buffalo was stationed in the Whitney apartment. She called Edgar's number. The housekeeper answered. The girl told her she had won free dancing lessons—a common come-on on the telephone. She kept on talking until the old lady hung up. But the girl did *not* hang up. Therefore, Edgar's telephone was dead. Within minutes, Gadwell appeared, posing as a telephone repairman. He said that someone had reported the telephone out of order. The housekeeper was puzzled, but tested the line and found that it was dead. So Gadwell, pretending to repair it, removed it and replaced it with a carefully doctored replica.

"He departed, taking the genuine telephone with him, and he installed it in the hall of the Whitney apartment, having carefully equipped it with a false number plate. Its real number plate had been inserted in the front of the substitute telephone at the Beattie apartment.

"All was now in readiness. The decoy girl had met Wes and had made a date with him. Never mind how. Her approach was not subtle, but what woman ever needs to be subtle in laying snares for a man?"

There were cries of "Shame!" but Sidney grinned and disregarded them.

"Anyway," he continued, "it went like clockwork, to coin a phrase. The girl fetched Wes home, without letting him know where he was. She got him to dial a number— he thought it was the number of a drugstore—to get his fingerprints on the telephone. She took him to another room in the apartment and engaged him in intellectual conversation while the technically competent Gadwell switched phones, then walked quickly to Edgar's apartment, carefully carrying Edgar's phone in a Gladstone bag. He entered the front door—using the key—without meeting anyone. He walked upstairs, and let himself in without a sound.

He had oiled the hinge and the lock that very morning while posing as a telephone repairman. He was armed with a revolver equipped with a silencer, ready to shoot Edgar. But Jackson had told him about the blackthorn stick in the vestibule, and Gadwell had seen it that morning. It was much better for the purpose.

"The housekeeper was in bed, as she usually was at that hour. Edgar, who never knew what it was to be frightened, was sitting with his back to the door. Gadwell seized the stick, took two quick strides and finished him. Then, with a speed born of practice, he changed the telephones.

"The housekeeper had heard the blow, but wondered if it were not a sound effect in an adult Western. She lay listening, until she heard Gadwell dialing—calling the Whitney apartment to tell the decoy girl to get rid of Wes. The decoy girl, of course, had only to tell Wes that she had been warned that her husband was in town. When she heard the dial, the old lady called out 'Edgar!' There was no reply. So she slowly, painfully, shuffled to the living room and found the body. By that time Gadwell was nearly back to the Whitney apartment. If she had arrived on the scene too soon, she would certainly have been struck down without compunction by the good Mr. Gadwell.

"Now all that remained was to meet the decoy girl and invite her for a fabulous weekend in Muskoka as a reward for her good work. She knew too much. So she joined Mrs. Wicklow in the depths of Lake Muskoka. Unfortunate girls of her type are the easiest murder victims. Nobody misses them. Blackmailers are also easy victims, if they are incautious enough to meet their victims in a private place. The revolver with the silencer had been saved for another victim—the parking lot attendant who tried to shake down High Grade Howie Gadwell.

"Once again Wes cooperated. He saw that his story was thin, and he tried to improve it, not realizing that the truth, however improbable, will stand every test, whereas lies can be broken down. In his highly upset state, he told his stories in such extravagant language that he convinced even trained psychiatrists that he was mentally deranged instead of just stupid. Again, my apologies, Wes, old boy, but you said you wanted me to give it straight.

"Now then, you no doubt want to hear the modest recital of my own spectacular achievement. How can I resist your entreaties? Well, I heard about the case at a discussion group where some earnest souls were trying to improve the social aspects of the treatment of young offenders. I was struck by one thing: the fact that twice Wes had told stories which were incredible, then had floundered into other lies and had finally ended up with something utterly fantastic. I really had the answer then and there, but I was too stupid to believe it without proof. The answer was that Wes had retreated from reasonably facile lies, in each case, to the incredible truth and that his enemies—or rather his enemy, Jackson—knowing his weakness, had put him in a position—twice—where the truth was almost unbelievable, confident that Wes would make it completely unbelievable by trying to edit and tailor it.

"And yet I was struck by something else. Weird as Wes's stories were, they were so wispy that they were difficult to disprove in a positive way. The only solid thing I could see was this: he claimed that the woman witness, who had testified that Wes had stolen her purse, had disappeared. Find her, prove her *bona fides,* and the whole structure would collapse. So I set out to find her. I followed the trail Edgar had followed. But I was luckier. I found Mrs. Ledley and was able to eliminate her once and for all. I found Phelan. I found Mayhew. But then—not having been murdered—I found Gadwell. Mayhew had told our friend Phelan that Gadwell was an old high school hockey teammate, more or less. Through a high school yearbook I traced Gadwell. Further research gave me the name of his female accomplice—Mrs. Wicklow.

"I brought this information to this very room. But Wes's own family were so convinced that he had killed his uncle that they were loath to make use of it. I went away beaten. Then there arose a heroine. Betty Martin is not the boldest person on earth, but love conquers all. Betty had heard my story—don't ask how. She felt sure it would help her Mr. Wes, to whom she had told bedtime stories in his childhood. In spite of her painful shyness, she followed me to my lair, but she was so startled when she caught me that she ran away home. No dishonor to her. She knew a bold, brazen hussy who would face anyone, so she called her and asked her to tackle me. So, after some ethical convolutions, I became Wes's counsel, with the kind blessings of the very distinguished counsel who, up till that moment, had been representing the lad.

"We had the bare bones of a defense, and we went to the assize court with it. But the evidence of Wes's fingerprints on that telephone appeared to be utterly damning— until a happy chance revealed that the telephone had been tampered with just before the murder. Then, in the nick, so to speak, of time, I stopped to consider: Could Wes have been telling the literal truth? Had he been lured to an apartment? He had described the apartment in minute detail in a taped interview under drugs to Dr. Heber. I listened to the tape. From it, I got the telephone number of the drugstore he claimed to have called from the apartment. His unconscious mind had preserved it intact. I traced the number. It was the number of the Whitney apartment. If you want to be sure of getting a busy line, call your own number. I visited the Whitneys. Their apartment exactly fitted Wes's description of the decoy apartment. At first I drew an incorrect conclusion—but then, when I discovered that the Whitneys had rented their apartment through Jackson, and that Jackson had been Wes's old boss, I thought again, and very little research turned up the whole vicious story.

"So that was it. Wes has been shaken to the roots. He is now painfully practicing telling the literal truth all the time. He dare not allow himself even the modest ration of social lies which all of us employ. So don't ask him how he likes your new hairdo. He might tell you. He is now passing rich, but he is working off some high school subjects and hopes to go to university on the coast next fall. My bet is that he will make out okay. He has authorized me to publish here and now his confession that during his black period he had borrowed all the savings of his beloved Betty, and that, if he hadn't cleaned her out, she would have lent him the money he needed at the time of that first unhappy frame-up. I hardly need to say that restoration has been made in full. But I should at this time state that Mrs. Beattie has granted to Betty Martin a retirement allowance which, if I had it, would keep me away from anything looking like work from now on. Wes, for his part, has given Betty an all-expense tour of England and the continent to celebrate her retirement and has arranged for her friend Nelly, who has worked a few doors from here for fifty years, to accompany her. Wes is aware that this is in no way a generous arrangement. He knows that it is simple justice.

"You wish to know more? Betty says she cannot face a life of idleness. Knowing that Miss June is no great shakes as a housekeeper, she has asked to be allowed to live with her after her forthcoming marriage and attempt to keep the place tidy."

"Oh, Mr. Sidney, you know very well I never said any such thing," Betty interjected. "I'm sure Miss June will be a splendid manager once she knows the ropes, as they say, but I should feel awfully lost to be cut adrift like in my old age."

"But you will never be cut adrift, Betty," Sidney said. "You've won your spurs. We all love you. And I believe that is the complete story."

Sidney sat down in a profound silence, which was presently broken by Mrs. Beattie.

"I have one thing to add, Mr. Grant," she said. "I owe you a personal debt which I should like to acknowledge here and now, publicly, damaging as it is to my pride. But then I know that my pride has been a factor in all that has gone wrong and to humble it is beneficial. After my dear husband's death, I had a secret sorrow, which I might have carried to my grave. When Charles was near death, he recovered his speech for a few moments when I was alone with him. He turned and looked at me, and said, fairly clearly: 'Minerva.' I was shocked. I said 'What is that dear?' He said 'Minerva? What is Minerva doing?' I could think of nothing to say. I was deeply hurt. He closed his eyes and never opened them. Those were the last words that he spoke.

"I know that when the late King Edward VII, to whom I was presented at Court, lay dying, Queen Alexandra led one of his mistresses to his bedside to say her farewell. I know that I, myself, am incapable of such 'civilized' behavior. I was wounded to think that, in his dying moments, my Charles was thinking of an old flame—or even of—but no, I won't say it. You, Mr. Grant, among the other things you have done, have lifted this burden from my heart."

Sidney was appalled to see her daubing her eyes with a lace-edged handkerchief.

"Very glad I was able to," he mumbled.

But June, who left the room hurriedly at about that point, didn't recover her composure nearly as quickly as the old lady recovered hers. Even after she and Sidney left the house she was still in stitches.

"Oh, Gargoyle, darling," she said, sitting down on an old hitching block at the edge of the Rosedale pavement, "isn't it too gorgeous? Toronto is the only town on earth where a man could be unfaithful to his wife with a mining stock!"

"But remember," Sidney said, "most of the mining stocks are priced to suit the little man's purse."

June sat on the hitching block and laughed and laughed and laughed.